T0208212

The
Holy Ghost
Stories

DAVID E. WEAVER

WESTBOW
PRESS®
A DIVISION OF THOMAS NELSON
& ZONDERVAN

WestBow Press books may be ordered through booksellers or by contacting:

WestBow Press
A Division of Thomas Nelson & Zondervan
1663 Liberty Drive
Bloomington, IN 47403
www.westbowpress.com
1 (866) 928-1240

Scripture quotations marked AMPC are taken from the Amplified® Bible, Copyright © 1954, 1958, 1962, 1964, 1965, 1987 by The Lockman Foundation. Used by permission.

Scripture quotations marked NIV are taken from The Holy Bible, New International Version®, NIV® Copyright © 1973, 1978, 1984, 2011 by Biblica, Inc.® Used by permission. All rights reserved worldwide.

ISBN: 978-1-9736-5877-1 (sc)
ISBN: 978-1-9736-5879-5 (hc)
ISBN: 978-1-9736-5878-8 (e)

Library of Congress Control Number: 2019904057

Print information available on the last page.

WestBow Press rev. date: 06/07/2019

A : God works with us, and not for us.

(Phil. 2:12–18; 2 Chron. 30:12; Heb. 13:20–21 [NIV]).

I was walking the streets of my neighborhood in Boerne, Texas. Currently there are four streets with about sixty-one homes, if I remember correctly. All the homes are on one to three acres with trees, grass, deer, squirrels, rabbits, cats, mosquitoes, and dogs, Noah's whole menagerie almost anywhere you looked. I was heading north toward highway FM 46 and thinking about when I would be home in heaven, sitting with God the Father and going through my life in His book about my time on Planet Earth. It would be my version of Father-son time.

Our Father was showing me good and bad decisions that I'd made while on terra firma. In my musings, I brought up the time, which never happened in reality, I went into H-E-B and witnessed to ten individuals.

He had not brought that subject up yet. He frowned slightly and asked, "Do you really want to bring that one up?"

Now the frown most assuredly should have given it away. But in my enthusiasm, I could not resist the urge to brag to my Father about something good that I thought I had done. The expression "Leave well enough alone" has a tendency not to want to come and take up residency at my front door.

So, 'of course,' I replied, "Because Lord, I witnessed to ten individuals that day!"

The Lord asked if I remembered being prompted by Himself via His Spirit to do just that and to go into H-E-B and tell the first individual that I saw about Jesus and His crucifixion for us, namely to save our souls from eternal separation from the everlasting God, who is life and the only source of it.

To me, that is what the grave is. The words of Jesus are true: there will be fire, and there will be weeping and gnashing of teeth. But to live forever without the presence of God, now that is the most horrible thing one can imagine. He, the holy He, is the cure and answer to that predicament.

Just a side note: Those who have never known the Father through His Son, Jesus, are like, "So who cares? Life without God ain't so bad. Eternity either. All you long hairs up in heaven with your harps, hanging out on clouds, singing 'Holy, holy, holy' all day long has got to be totally boring."

But I do know Him. I mean I know Him deep within my heart, far better than anything and anyone in this entire world, me, myself included. I also know that there is no joy, no satisfaction, and no anything without Him. And hell does exist, but without Him, life does not exist—although you most assuredly will. I lived this life twenty-one years without Him, and having been transferred from not knowing Him into His presence by now knowing Him, I found that He is life. He, Almighty God, is for really real.

So let us just say that the myth concerning the grave is true—that all those bad boys and fine girls are just going to party every day forever, as has been suggested in popular media. But without joy, there can be no satisfaction in anything. If I were in hell and could take all the dope ever imagined, numbing my mind, who cares? There is no joy and no satisfaction. My mind would not be subject to any meds or drugs; nothing could be numbed or changed.

If that place away from God, hell, were somehow infested with buxom, beautiful women all desiring yours truly, so what? Without life, joy, or satisfaction, who would even be in the mood for such close encounters? They, the women, would certainly not be. And for me, without a physical body, where is all that testosterone supposed to come from?

The thing about salvation is that I do know Him and know Him well enough to know how very creative He is. And there is never just going to be sitting around on a cloud playing a harp, but I will be singing, "Holy, holy, holy is the Lord God Almighty" because that is just who He is. I desire to praise Him. So bless You, Lord, for saving my soul from separation from You. Back to the story. Sorry, I got carried away.

"Now when you went into H-E-B, you saw that young woman, who you thought attractive, and you then said in your heart, 'She might think I'm a nut or at the very least strange to come up to her out of the blue and to tell her about Your Son, Jesus.' But I sent you for that specific reason. That was her day and your blessing to deliver the gospel, and you did not do it because you did not want to be embarrassed. Do you remember that day now? If you want to review it, it is right here." The Lord pressed His finger a few pages forward and popped the book open to the one He wanted. "It's right here on page 231."

I did not need to see it, and I now remembered vividly how reluctant I was to approach the young woman.

"You see, David, if you had acted in obedience to what I had said, then all of the individuals you spoke to would have been blessed because of that same love and obedience that naturally draws you and I closer. You could have acted in faith and trust in Me. But you, by an active choice of will, removed My sovereign hand from you at that moment by doing what you thought to be best, not by doing what I knew to be best for everyone I brought you there in My will to do. If you had told that young woman, My daughter, due to the obedience of one of your brothers, each of the ten individuals who you then did find the nerve to be courageous with would have—each and every one of them—said yes to your invitation, because I would be there with you.

"Instead you planted a seed, but the actual fruit belongs to someone else instead of you. So you see how that day is not one that you, David, used to show the true character of My Son, your Lord and King. I would also like to insist on the fact that is the challenge to each human being. But for those of you who know My Son, Jesus, it is to proclaim His character and My kingdom so that everyone will envy you for the life you have received and you, having been instilled with My grace, the ability to do My will. But instead you showed your own, which was not anything to get really excited about anyway."

I said, "Dad, you're tough."

"No. I am truthful and your Father. My expectation is your best. I put that opportunity in your path to prove to you what I saw as your potential and not the limitation that you saw in yourself.

(1 Samuel 15:23-25, N.I.V), 'For rebellion is like the sin of divination, and arrogance like the evil of idolatry. Because you have rejected the Word of The Lord, He has rejected you as king. Then Saul said to Samuel, 'I have sinned. I violated The Lord's command and your instructions. I was afraid of the men and so I gave in to them. Now I beg you, forgive my sin and come back with me, so that I may worship The Lord.;

"But I don't understand, Lord, why things work that way. I did do something by just going into that H-E-B, and yes, I found it difficult to speak to that one young woman. But I at least made the attempt."

"Listen, David, we are talking about eternal matters. Someone, an individual, was making a decision concerning a real relationship with Me. The obedience of what I desire is for everyone's good. Salvation is never going to be trivial; it is the manifestation of love being restored to you and to everyone."

The Lord God formed a circle with His two hands, obviously meaning everything, all of heaven and all the earth. "And to Me, as your Father and, I want to add, as your God, you, My children, always have the responsibility of being my ambassadors for reconciliation. You get to represent Me to someone who does not know Me. That is My gift to you. It is a high calling to speak wholeness, healing, and salvation into someone's life. On earth, the word *agape* is used quite a bit for a specific type of love. But what *agape* love actually looks like is the total giving of oneself in grace for the betterment of another.

"I placed *agape* in your human father, Adam, when he met Eve. He loved her more than himself, and that is all he knew about love. Sin brought in lust and the desire to please oneself first, and it is that human desire that cannot be satisfied, no matter how much you feed it. That very thing, *agape*, was present but now broken, and it is the item that every human being wants more than anything else yet cannot obtain because people seek themselves first and any others' needs last."

"Yes, Father, I think I get that ... now. But You are still doing all the work. The Holy Spirit comes and knocks at the door or the heart of the individual—me—who listens. Or what I've seen and done is to take only part of what is done. If you are sovereign, then why does the partial Christian or I receive the Word, Your Son, into my heart and then just let it go? Why did I lose sight of the cross in my walk with You? I was saved, I served, and then at a point in time, I turned away. And to top that off, I did not want to look back. It breaks my own heart to know that I was that unconcerned with the blood of Jesus. But I was. And if You did not go out of Your way to wake me up, You know, Dad, that I would most likely be separated from You forever. Your grace, Father, is so much more than amazing."

"David, you know and have heard countless stories about how I did not create robots, unaware creatures that just do what they are programmed to do. I created individuals to be like Me, who can choose and yet still able to not choose, commonly referred to as free will. But there is nothing free about it. There is always a cost in exercising will.

"Since I am life, then when we agree, My Son, Jesus, gets added into it, whatever the it is. In this case you are being obedient, therefore exercising faith. Faith is My life being added to your life since it is an action, which you are doing according to My will. The more life, the more freedom from sin. So if you are obedient, then life is added to it, whatever it is, **(Romans 6:1-23)**. Likewise, when we are not in agreement and you are acting in self, going about life without My personal guidance, then you, like your first parents, are right back at the Tree of Knowledge, and you already know that if you eat the fruit of the Tree of Knowledge, you will certainly die. And that is just what happens no matter how good the plan may sound in your own heart internally **(Prov. 16:2, 15:11)**.

"Your pre-salvation father, Adam, had the most complete will because he did not have to deal with a broken relationship with Me until that particular day arrived. Writers on earth seem to think that Adam and Eve were not just products of fiction; some think of it as science fiction. If they did exist, they were proto-humans, and somehow sin or rebelling against what I had said made them complete, now having a wider range of choices. Those children believing, they had a better or a fuller array of choices. It is as if an individual needed death to be fully cognizant of the fact that he or she is a participant in life within My creation.

"That does not make sense, even from a human's perspective. Is it not better to say to oneself, 'I am fully alive because the Lord, my God, is in me? Therefore to live or to be filled with life, do I need God?' This is the logical conclusion for you, David, since this is how you process information, but it is not as if you say to yourself, 'I am lost and need to be found.' Rather the sons of Adam have abandoned Me and have by an active choice of will find themselves without direction; now they are lost and innately desire to find Me. And the only way to actually know Me is through My Son, Jesus. The path to My Son is pure, plain, and full of light and truth. It's so obvious that no one can miss it, yet still denied by many."

I suddenly had a thought pop into my head, *But it is as if anyone who had been diagnosed with a life-threatening disease is now able to say about himself that he is walking in complete wholeness because he knows he is passing away, just like everyone. So now he sees that his health is no longer the issue.*

"Adam was the predecessor of the full potential of man like My Son, who was able to seek My will within My government on the Planet Earth and who could also choose love and respect. I am not only your Father, but I am God. My plans always have fullness, life, truth, and love, which is Me, along with respect, which is to deal with individuals on an unbiased foundation, which is My character. So as the primary components in a relationship—and believe this word that humans are always in a relationship—those same moving parts are to be a blessing. Death does not bless anyone. More so humanity's fear of death is their instinctive knowledge that if there is an end in our relationship without the means to correct it, then the actual death is an eternal future without Me and the provided cure, which is a divorce, because the love from one side has ceased to be given.

"One side does not want the reconciliation. For everyone, the cure is Jesus, and He has been made evident to everyone. All human beings have the breath of God in them so their natural inclination is to draw closer to their source of life. Adam in turn received my Spirit/breath from Me, and since I am life, then they all have life eternal. They will not cease to exist after the physical body dies. They will all live on, just as you are doing now, My son."

"I have a question then, Lord."

"You always do."

"But if we were created to be like You, then what went wrong? I know how I messed up in my life, but for Adam and Eve, they should have adhered to You without ceasing. They knew You personally. I was born with sin's rebellion. I lived in it daily, was conceived in it, and learned it from the world around me, again daily. When I think about it, I could not miss being a sinner from the moment some doc pinched my bottom so I would take my first breath. I inhaled sin."

"You are partially correct, but you inhaled life, and so you live. Every life starts with Me. You are also correct about sin. My Word states, 'For all have sinned, and come short of the glory of God,' which at its most basic is to be out of relationship with Me. This is hard to explain, and before you say anything, it is not because it is complicated. It's because of your limited understanding of being an active participant in a rebellious or a dependent relationship. Your view of Me is that I am whole and complete. So yes, I have always been that way. I have never second-guessed Myself, even when dealing with sin.

"If during the time when Israel was heading up to the Promised Land, Canaan, and they rebelled against Me and I told Moses that I would destroy them and begin again with him, then My Word that I gave to Abraham, Isaac, and Jacob would still have been true and fulfilled. As you know, Moses was from the tribe of Levi. Your parents always had a choice—and not a predestination to have to eat of the Tree of Knowledge. The serpent suggested but did not force anyone to do anything. A seed of self-desire led to that first bite. I knew it was going to happen, but you had the choice as to what happened. All that your parents had to do was look to Me, and I would have been there to assist them. That serpent would have received its fate because it too had a choice, but it is just as easy to say no as it is to say yes whether they knew the consequences or not.

"People like to think that they would have never put the Tree of Knowledge within My garden, and then no one would have sinned and rebelled. And so nothing would have ever gone wrong with humanity. They like to think that they are wiser than God or that I am cruel because My beloved, completely obedient, and innocent Son would one day give His holy life in exchange for those who are only capable of being in rebellion.

"That was only one thing out of thousands, just one piece of fruit that I said no to. Thousands of yeses and only one no. It is easier to be obedient than it is to be rebellious. Adam and Eve already had complete knowledge because they knew Me. You see, David, it becomes complicated only when you make it so. There was nothing made better for neither Adam or Eve nor their progeny by not having faith in Me. Today the same issues come up. Will you believe Me? You say yes and then do no."

"Lord God, doesn't that frustrate You? It would drive me nuts."

"It could, but I do not live in the moment. I see the entire picture and the consequences of each individual life. I know your potential. Now if you believe Me and walk with Me, then more and more you will see through My eyes and think with My heart. And you will see the real potential in each being in the spirit and on earth. But you must walk with Me daily. It is not a casual relationship but rather a parent to child or husband to wife, the two becoming one, and so not just when you desire My presence. I am your Father; you are each and every one My child. There is no reason to exist outside of My will. That is a choice on your part, and you always receive the consequences of the choice you have made until you make a better choice and turn back to Me and without turning back once again to rebellion. And then you are to walk in harmony with Me. I will never bless rebellion, but since I love My children, I will always most assuredly bless obedience."

B: Planting Seed.

I was walking and thinking about how seeds are planted within the human being and whether it is going to be sin or the righteousness of God in Christ Jesus that will cause that seed to bear fruit *(Gen. 1:11–13, 24–31)* and for righteousness *(Deut. 6:25)*.

Just a note: People sometimes say that when God finished creating man, He said it was very good, as if He had done something very exceptional, which He did with creating man, but not really in anything else on that week of creating. I also know that I am not speaking of everyone else in the world except me. God's actions of creating on the first week are mind-blowing, and many Christians are in wonder over it. But I have also heard Christians at different times speaking the following Scripture verses, as if mankind were God's only and entire point of endeavor. And so the rest of creation was placed there for man to rule over in the Lord's stead. And finally man and God were coexisting or dwelling together in innocent harmony.

I would also like to say that everything everywhere begins and ends in and through Him. Man was created to have a guiltless yet at the same time mature relationship with God and be surrendered to the sovereign authority of the Almighty as being far superior to man, even though the original model was perfect, as any child is to his parent, in this case, the only living God. Yet the Lord God does not say that about Adam and Eve, "I've created man, and he is very good."

Rather, once the sixth day was done, God looked over everything He had really spoken and made, and I refer to His living Word from **Genesis 1 (NIV)**. *"And God saw <u>everything that He had made</u>, and, behold, [it was] very good. And the evening and the morning were the sixth day."*

Another on that same subject that I've heard is that the first six days of creation were God days of approximately a thousand years apiece or vast extents of time. Although the only two places I have found in Scripture where it talks about this subject is in **Psalm 90:1–4** and **2 Peter 3:3–9**, it is not to be found in the first five books of Scripture.

This gets to me because it is not exactly what Scripture states but is more a philosophy from the flesh in trying to explain things that are either scriptural or scientific and somehow finding a common ground for both too exist. So I am then trying my best to comprehend or figure out life and why it is, but without the help of the Holy Spirit.

So in essence, worldly items, like evolution and the first six days of creation, become an inexperienced event that we as Christians can explain to the non-Christian how our Lord works, using untrue input. The non-Christian cannot understand the things of the Spirit, but the non-Christian is still no dummy and will apply reason to what you are saying. The things that don't add up will make the living—and unchanging—God untrue in his or her eyes by the examples we use while trying to explain creation. Any person of science will tell you in a heartbeat that the evolutionary process took far longer than six thousand years, or twelve for that matter.

Each and every day of creation has the statement: it was evening and the morning. To me, it sounds like one twenty-four-hour solar day, but still it was not until the fourth day that the sun, moon, and stars were created. So I ask myself: what comprised an evening and morning?

I would also like to say for the Christian because I have not had a revelation from the Holy Spirit on the thousand years being one God day that they are wrong and I am right. For me, the Holy Spirit has not taught me that, but for another brother or sister, perhaps the Holy Spirit has taught on this subject. But—and this is a big but—if my pastor or a different pastor or teacher has taught it and I am just taking his word on it that what he is stating is true because he is by far a better student at Scripture than I am, then I am a sluggard and a fool, no matter what he says or who he is. If I am a Christian, then the same Holy Spirit is in us both, and I can study God's Word to prove to myself that He is true. He, Jesus, is the truth and the light, so I trust Him with a revelation. I am no one's answer. Jesus is …

The simplest thing I can see from my own life is that I am in a continuous state of change. Sometimes the change is for the better, being closer to God and His desires through me. At other times, I am being willful and in my flesh, and I should not be telling anyone this is what God says because I am just not listening to Him anyway or the words that flow from my lips.

That is the point concerning the Word of God. It is always true. It is always supernatural. It is always for the benefit of the Christian first, to build us up to be stronger and to make us more mature in our relationship with God and our fellow human beings. But since the Word of God is supernatural, then it can also affect the non-Christian since it speaks to the center or, better, the mind and spirit of the human being. That is also why, for me, the Word of God should never be distorted or lessened with fleshly stuff that brings God's vision for man down to an earthly level instead of it bringing us up and into His holy presence.

Now the reason for these statements is to show that holy and fleshly things are being planted within me as seeds, and since this is my very own piece of real estate, then I can and should have an active part in taking care of what belongs to God Almighty.

Sow back to the seed. But what I was thinking about was that Adam was made out of the earth. God formed the man. Now thinking just about that, the world itself is mostly water. So why didn't the Lord just create man out of aqua or, better yet, *ague de Dios* (water of God). And then I thought, *Well, what about creating man out of air since that surrounds the entire globe?* When I think about it, no matter how man could have been created, man would have been complete in God's perfect eyesight. So that again goes back to planting seeds into soil because even seaweed needs a foundation, earth, to grow out of.

So a seed, no matter what type—grass, flower, fruit, or tree—all bear a fruit or offspring after its initial type. A grass seed is not going to grow a walnut tree; a banana tree is not going to grow cactus. Or else a monkey would have a rough time getting itself a banana. Sorry, that is just how my mind works. Mankind can manipulate types, but we do not create types. We modify currently existing forms. **John 15:5** reads, *"I Am the vine, and you are the branches. Whoever remains in Me, and I in him, will bear much fruit; for you can do nothing without Me."*

Luke 8:4–15 refers to the parable of the seed. **John 1:1–5** and **Revelation 19:13** state that Jesus is the Word. So I see that Jesus is not only the seed that has been planted within the Christian, but He is the bringer of life from His Father, whom He, Jesus, fully represents, *(Hebrews 1:1-4)*.

If you are not a Christian, then you cannot consistently produce the fruit of God, the Father, which are—and I quote—*"But the Spirit produces love, joy, peace, patience, kindness, goodness, faithfulness, humility, and self-control" (Gal. 5:22–23 NIV)*. And that is what God the Father is looking for as fruit that shows to the world His character through Jesus, who Himself is the fruit of God. And in every reality show to those who may be observing, the apple does not fall far from the tree or its source.

And so I was thinking about how sin and righteousness both get planted within me, and it is by my body, which was made from soil, but which is also not alive until the wind or breath and, better still, the Spirit of God gets blown into its nostrils. Without the Lord, I am just a pile of dirt.

So God is the first seed that is planted in this soil. Then by choice, I start to choose what is going to be placed inside of me. I am in a very small sense to be like God and a sovereign being over this particular piece of real estate called David. When sin comes to me and requests an area in my life to grow, a plot of ground, as T. D. Jakes said, "a territory," it is my own but in reality belongs to God because He purchased it with His blood when I asked for salvation. Then He asked me to be in charge of it, just as He asked Adam to be in charge of the earth and more particularly His garden spot, Eden.

I see that is why the enemy does not go and ask God, "Can I do this or that to him or her?" The answer would be no! The enemy will come to me and find that I am either in a close relationship with God and therefore speaking the Lord's truth, which in this case would cause me to tell the enemy no, just like my Father. Or I can be on my own or in disobedience and say "Aahhh, sure! What can it hurt?" Now I do not even have the vision of God and can only see from my own human perspective and current desire(s).

At this time, I do not think of sin as an individual. Rather sin is a choice, presented to us by myself or individuals of the flesh and the enemy with its league of spirits. Jesus said quite plainly in *1 John 3:7–10 (NIV)*, specifically verse 10, *"This is how we know who the Children of God are and who the children of the devil are: Those who do not do what is right are not God's children, nor are those who do not love their Brothers and Sisters."* You can see from Scripture that it is not just one or the other. It is both, and these determine where we stand in connection or in communion to Him.

So when I think about sin, I also see that a request is made of me. Some items have a long drawn-out process, which in turn wraps my imagination around it. And now I am in fellowship with sin to give it a fertile soil in which to grow such as, "Man, that girl is fine!" So I see that I can tell me that whoever that girl is, she is not a replacement for my wife, the actual woman I love. Or my imagination can start to toy with that idea of sinning and then try to rap to her or hide my wedding ring in my pocket, stuff that is sin since I am a participant and in rebellion to what I have already promised to God on my wedding day, basically in rebellion to what is right or His righteousness.

I would also like to say that about coveting. For me, the Lord has shown me that coveting does not only desire what another individual may have: his wife, his home, his car, his money, or his lifestyle, all his stuff basically. Rather it is wanting his stuff without the responsibility. I want his money, but I do not want his headaches or his eighty-hour workweek. His wife is fine, but I do not want to raise her children. His car is fast, but if it gets banged up, I won't worry about the large dent in the front fender. Coveting wants but does not want to be responsible. My neighbor may have a great lawn that I would like, but he is out there twice a week with his lawn mower doing the work. Although his yard sure looks great, and I wish it was mine!

What I have also seen in me is that some things are short and shot into me, like anger.

"Hey, boy [my son], don't speak to your mom that way!"

"Why are you flipping me off? You're the one who doesn't know how to drive, use a blinker!"

But if I am in the Lord, I would not be speaking to my son, also a son of God, or a stranger that way in anger. What is good for the goose/ Jesus is just as good for the gander/me.

What I have also seen is that the Lord never uses fear to get what He wants done. He uses truth; He also uses love and that quiet, still voice, which by the way demands faith on my part. But He, the Holy Him, does not use fear tactics. But because I do love my Father and the Holy Spirit, then I do fear Him, in the fact that my actions can and do disappoint Him. Consequently I affect those who may or may not know Him.

My very life is making God visible to the world in which I live and showing folks what God is like on this earth and in heaven. This, to me, is what sin is, and I fear that because He is and has been so gracious and kind to me, my family, and the family of man, Adam's offspring, that when I dishonor Him, I am back with Israel and Moses is talking to Aaron about when a false god, the golden calf, was created when there is no equal for the real Lord God. *Exodus 32:25 (NIV)* says, *"Moses saw that the people were running wild and that Aaron had let them get out of control and so become a laughing-stock to their enemies."* My actions should never make God a laughing-stock to anyone.

Now if all my choices were just that easy—pick one and refuse the other—life would be a breeze because I know that sin or stepping off the straight path or, as it is, rebelling against the Lord Jesus and that rebellion is listening to satan, myself, or anything and anyone else who might be asking, "Did God really say?"

This leads me astray or, more to the truth, to death, and I've also seen quite clearly in my life that when I seek the Lord and His divine will for my life that the Lord just happens to bless it. Or to put it more plainly, Jesus brings life into it, and in the fuller sense, it bears fruit after its initial kind, namely Jesus.

There are a ton of scriptures that I could add here, but perhaps at the end, in *John 14:6 (NIV)*, our Lord Jesus tells Thomas that He is the Way, the Truth, and the Life. Our Lord actually says, "I Am."

Or as a spiritual truth, the Lord is stating, "I am Yahweh, and if you and the other disciples are going north, then I am the way before you even begin. And if south, east, or west, look to Me alone even when you won't see Me, for I am the Way and will never steer you wrong because I am the Truth, and, best of all for you, the Life." The Holy He states He is actually in the Father.

In *John 15*, Jesus states a truth about His Father: that He, the Father, is the owner of the field, but He is also at work in His field and gets rid of the dead wood. But He prunes or makes clean the branch that is producing fruit. So God the Father, Son, and Holy Spirit are continuously at work on me and are working with me. And so I say "Hallelujah" because in the fullest sense, God is at work on humanity. Fruit gets born after its initial type when we accept Him. Now if we reject Him, then fruit is born after its initial types, rebellion death, and satan.

So the seed of God that is in us is Jesus or the fruit of the Spirit, which is God's very own Spirit that produces God's life, which was confirmed earlier. And His life according to Galatians is love, which is God's character. Joy is also His character, along with peace or in harmony with existence and patience in every circumstance. It is kind even when working with an enemy, good in every situation, faithful, gentle, and full of self-control. I would want someone to say of my life, just as I said earlier about Jesus, is that the apple doesn't fall far from the tree. Like Father, like son.

Also in *1 Corinthians 13:*, it looks to me like love is the manure or, better yet, the Miracle-Gro of God that makes the fruit of the Spirit active. Love is really life because love is not in any way self-serving, but it is serving all others before myself, me. The more I personally surrender myself, my life, to Jesus, the more stimulated the growth process is.

I also think that at this time in the world system that God is going to increase the growing process in His children, who have willingly prepared the soil for His holy presence. So that has a cost to you and me. If I just want to be blessed without cost, then first I am only a child because I want Santa Claus to be my old man. But every parent knows the time and money involved, whether we are rich or poor, that it takes to bring Christmas morning to pass. But sometimes the child is gratified with the box and totally ignores the fourteen hours it took to put the dollhouse together. God blesses faith, and faith is our putting into action what God has said.

If you are only thinking about the blessing and being motivated by what I get or desire, even if I am putting God's name to it, then I am not adult enough to take on the tasks that the living God has for this world since I am only a child at heart, no matter how old in years I may be. Although this is a bit off the subject, I have often heard individuals speaking about how our Father is just going to bless.

"Everyone who reads this is going to receive a healing."

"You are the head, and you will be blessed in the city, in the country, and so on."

But when I read **Deuteronomy 28:1-2 (NIV)**, it starts off with, *"If you fully obey the Lord your God and carefully follow all His commands I give you today, The Lord your God will set you high above all the nations on earth. All these blessings will come on you and accompany you if you obey The Lord your God."* My point is that I seem to have a great many points, so please forgive me.

If any plant does not mature, then it is not going to bear fruit. Pretty simple, huh?

I also see from Scripture that a seed must first die to self and then to the world before it can in reality begin to grow. You and me must be patient because it is also a slow maturation process (**John 12:23–25, 1 Cor. 15:35–38**, and as a progressive note, **Luke 9:23–26 [NIV]**).

It takes time to see the actual plant start to emerge out of the soil, and it takes a long minute before it becomes mature enough to bear fruit.

But as I stated above, the Holy Spirit gives us real love, and when we work, work is a big thing because it displays faith. But once the love and respect for and to our Father God is shown in our actions without our having seen Him, we incessantly believe Him and act on His instructions for my life and other lives that we come into contact with. Then that particular seed, which is Jesus, will grow within.

Since Jesus is life, just as the Father is life, then when we are obedient to our Father via the Holy Spirit. We are adding life to the method of growth. But without the Lord, the living Word, then no life is being added to us. Although we are alive and breathing, speaking, and going about our daily activities, we are in effect dead because He who is life is not in agreement or in contact with this soil due to the fact that we—or me—are not in agreement or in communion with Him.

So let us think that if I am not in partnership with fellow believers, not in prayer for His desires and concerns, and not in His Word or even concerned about those items, can I also state that these statements aren't absolute in that I am 100 percent of the time in fellowship, 100 percent of the time reading my Word, or in my local church working? Or the 100 percent for me gets dropped down to maybe 10 percent.

The result of that is that my heart is beating and I am breathing and eating, but I am still dead because I am not participating or in agreement with Him. Anyone who has ever owned a plant knows that it needs water, nutrients, and care. Basically it needs more than just the soil, you and I in which His seed has been sown into, for His growth to transpire.

If I wanted to grow at an accelerated rate, then the way to do that would be through the life that was provided to me when I gave my life over to the Lord Jesus and He and my Father gave me His Holy

Spirit. So for me to grow faster and to bear good fruit, then I must die to self, take up my cross, my destiny, and follow Him.

The words do not mean anything, even if I do believe them, but they are set in motion within me by my obedience to Him. And the superior thing or greater thing is that He is life, truth, and light. If I am a plant, then I need those things to grow. Hey, I need Him, Jesus, to grow, and He in love made that completely possible!

I also had the thought that Christians are God the Father's very own children, offspring after their initial type, Jesus. I also know how often someone has spoken about that as a subject, but what I was thinking was that my Lord Jesus was obedient to His Father because He, Jesus, was so totally in love with His Father. It was not just that Jesus was obedient because He was told, "You, Jesus, need to do this or that when You get to earth." But because of God's relationship with our Lord and Holy Spirit, God thoroughly equipped Jesus through love and His reverent relationship to His Father's will, although the only Son; scripture shows us in **Isaiah 11:2–3 (NIV)**, *"The Spirit of the Lord will rest on Him—The Spirit of wisdom and of understanding, the Spirit of counsel and of might, the Spirit of the knowledge <u>and fear of the LORD</u>—and <u>He will delight in the fear of the LORD</u>. He will not judge by what He sees with His eyes or decide by what He hears with His ears."*

So as an ingredient to accelerated growth, the Father has planted our communion with the Holy Spirit within me so I can show His glory to a lost and dying world because the world purposely does not choose life, a not growing/knowing world. This is where envy is a good thing. The more I surrender my will, just as Jesus did for His Father and mine as an example, then the growth moves along more freely. I see that our Lord was not coerced. He did not have appeals made to Him by His righteous Father for kingdoms or to have a throne set up right next to His, power, or amusements. Jesus is the Son in loving relationship with His Father and God, and it delighted His own heart to do what His Father saw as important for mankind.

Even though I know that the entire world would be going to that 'lake of fire' without Jesus and His substitutionary life was given for those very same sins against His very own Father and God, whom He, Jesus, loves, what I see as the motivation was not just that I, by an active choice of my will, deserved God's wrath. But Jesus saw His own Father's desire to dwell with His creation in Their united, power, and glory.

And because Jesus knew that all of God's desires are just and right or righteous, then He, Jesus, walked or worked that out. Now that is relationship. To see another's desires (our own as well as Father God) as more important than your own, that sounds just like *agape*. But since I see Them, the Father, Son, and Holy Spirit, as being one in heart and mind, then whatever the cost, He, Jesus, was going to do it, despite death and His own death on the cross.

Now that is saying a lot about who our Savior is, but the point is that I too am a child of God, and if Jesus loved His very own Father that much, to give His all for His desires to be fulfilled, then I as a son have the very same responsibility, to fulfill my Father's virtuous and just desires. Now if it were only as easy to do as it is to write, and it is difficult to write.

A non-Christian who may read this is going to say to himself, "This boy is a religious fanatic." Some of the Christians who read this will say the same, and others will just read it and think about correcting all the grammatical errors and avoid the spiritual (hopefully without the errors). But I must give all of myself, just as my Lord Jesus did, for any and all of my Father's commands to be done; which gives us more than enough to do for an entire life-time.

Can I say for me that the doing of that is completely against my very nature? I love Him, and at the same time, I am all about me. Earlier I used **Luke 9:23**, but Jesus knew what He was talking about, although **Matthew** and **Mark** have that same bit of scripture. **Luke** states, *"Then He said to them all: "whoever wants to be My disciple must deny themselves and take <u>up their cross daily and follow Me.</u>"*

So it is not that I surrendered myself to the Lord five years ago and I'm good to go. But I am daily changing and allowing the seed of Jesus by denying myself, taking up my cross or destiny, and following Him. I have two last scriptures for you to read, **John 15:16–17** and **Psalm 1.** Jesus has been planted. So go grow.

A parable or one more thought: In my imagination, I saw myself and the Lord Jesus as two bulls, being yoked together to plow a field, which belonged to me or was me. So the Lord God was giving me assistance on upgrading this piece of property called David. Now the area of ground covered about two flat acres, with no trees or boulders hanging out and needing to be removed. It was still a pretty good plot of ground to cover and make those straight furrows in me to plant seed and to ultimately reap the produce.

I was on the left; the Lord was obviously on my right. We started off in a straight line moving forward, but I suddenly began to feel a bit tired because of the amount of effort being put in by me. I thought, *I have God with me, so He can certainly do the job.* So I just folded my feet beneath myself and took a nap. After all, God was on my right side. What did I have to be concerned with when the Great I Am, the All-Powerful One, is working with me?

After a short while, since I was sleeping, I didn't know how much time essentially passed, but I did hear a "harrumph" as if the Lord were trying to get my attention. I popped back up and onto all fours and looked at my field. I saw that about a quarter of the field was done but also the furrows were all misaligned. Not a one was true and straight.

I said to Jesus, "Wow, Lord, that is some bad plowing."

"That is the results of working alone. I was supporting you and yet did the work by Myself on your field."

"Lord and my God, everything You put Your hand to should be perfect. What do You really need me for?"

"We, you and I, are to work together on your field. That is the request I received from you, David."

"I am sorry, Lord. Can we please continue and plow up the rest of the real estate mutually?"

"Of course. Let us get to it."

So I examined the next quarter of the field for length and thought, *Once done with this quarter, the Lord and I will take a break, like going over to get some hay and water, and maybe nibble on that salt-lick for a few minutes.* So we began in step to separate the earth, and although the work was hard, I sincerely did regret not helping the Lord with the first part. We talked and worked in concert. I looked up and saw that half of the field was now complete, but it troubled me that the first quarter was not as succinct as the second portion.

As we started the third quarter, we both began once again in unison, but after the initial couple of steps, the Lord folded His legs under Himself and went to sleep. I quickly realized that although I was a bull and quite strong, I was still dragging someone of girth around, and it was affecting my plowing. I could not be angry with the Lord because I had done exactly the same to Him.

I would look down at the sound-asleep Lord and then over my right shoulder, and I could plainly see that the furrows resembled lighting strikes from a 1940s cartoon instead of the straight lines I desired, zigzagging from the previous section. Finally I grew frustrated and harrumphed the Lord myself.

Jesus popped His brown eyes open. "Ahhh, so you now know what it feels like to work by yourself, just as I did."

"Yes, Lord, but You're God and well able to do it Your own self. Me, I'm a man."

"No, you are not. You, David, have been born again from the dead. You are now mine. We are to live, work, and enjoy this life as well as the new life in unity. We are husband and wife and to do everything as one individual. But just like a husband and wife, we are to do all things as if we are one being, one complete and cohesive unit."

"Lord, look at my field. It looks like a Pollock painting. Trying to harvest fruit from that field is going to be work."

"You, David, cannot do anything about the past. The future awaits you. Where you are in me and how we work together is what changes the present and future. So has the lesson been learned?"

"Yes, Lord, lesson learned. I guess my garden can only grow at its optimum with me and You together, as is true of everyone."

C: An Unusual Maturation Procedure

(2 Cor. 6:16 [NIV])

I was walking on the morning of April 20, 2012, when I began thinking about the Lord and a boxing match between myself and an overwhelming challenger. Me, I'm currently fifty-seven years old, but in my mind's eye, my opponent was seven-foot-two and three hundred and seventy pounds of pure muscle who had the fighting skills of Bruce Lee along with Mohammed Ali at their physical peaks. So he's not someone whom you could shake a stick at and he would then flee in terror.

In this large analogy, the Lord God was teaching me that this Christian life isn't as hard as I make it appear or think it is at times. I was also thinking completely outside of this analogy that although my wife is walking out her relationship with the Lord with fibromyalgia and still loves Him, she is one of the happiest individuals I know, yet she is at the same time in daily pain. But even in the fact that she is my wife and I relentlessly love her, I still do not fully comprehend the strength it takes for her to walk out her path each day because I'm busy treading my own passage.

That is not indifference on my part, of course. I am extremely well aware of her walk because I do love her and see the price tag that fibromyalgia has on her physically. One of the things that my wife, Gisele, is fond of saying is that the body counts for nothing. It is really the spirit of an individual that is being formed into the image of Christ. That is not a literal quote, but since we are married, I can use her stuff. For me, it is the whole being: body, soul, and spirit. I can give you a whole teaching on how the Lord and the enemy uses seed to have things grow within us because we are made of dirt and full of manure, but this is an analogy, so perhaps on a different writing.

In my imagination, I was sitting in a boxing ring, checking out who I was gonna be humbuggin' it up within a few seconds and thinking quite honestly to myself that I was not going to survive the contest. God our Father was at ringside, the Holy Him being my fight manager, coach, and doctor because I knew I was gonna need one. And I was fully ready to throw in the towel and call this a done day. Our Holy Father was the individual who was going to have to zip me up in a body bag and take me home after the first round. The Lord was currently asking me why I seemed so nervous.

I laughed through my mouthpiece. "Take a look, Father. Even You'd be nervous jumping into the ring with that monster, and You're God!"

The Lord asked, "Wasn't it you who asked Me for a challenge so you could mature and grow in our relationship, so here is step one, which actually is pretty straightforward."

"So You, Lord, are going to give me the strength of, say, Samson or one of David's mighty men so I can overcome this foe?"

The Lord laughed. "No, that was for them. This challenge is for you. After all, David, I am already God. I don't need to grow, but you are the one asking Me to evolve. How do you think it is supposed to happen, by Me passing a magic wand over you?"

"Well, in reality, since I can't lie to You, Lord, yeah! Or something like that. Maybe not a magic wand, but something a bit safer than me getting beaten to a pulp by Godzilla's offspring after cardinal knowledge with King Kong and, voilà, him."

The Lord, blessed me with a slight grin, raising His eyebrows at my remark. "It is not even round one, and already you want to throw in the towel?"

"Did you hear me think that about the towel, Father?"

"Of course I did. I live in your heart. Believe the words you say. Come on, David. Do you want to serve Me? If you want to serve yourself, you are going to face much bigger problems than your opponent, you yourself, for one? Listen to Me, David. You have not even put your hand to the plow yet, and you want to run off to another field. Take care of this first. I have a natural talent for knowing what I am doing. Even if you do not agree with Me, then at the very least believe that I Am God."

"Lord, I'm afraid! Look at that guy. He's gonna kill me, slowly, painfully, and surely!"

"So you're afraid. Come on. Have some faith. I would not send you into something just to get you messed up and then have a good laugh over it. Just believe Me when I say that I love you."

"Faith is an easy word to say, but my eyes are telling my body that it is in for some booty whoppin'. So should my faith be in You or my medical insurance, which I am going to definitely need before the next three minutes pass."

"You will put your faith where you want. Listen, David, here is what real faith looks like. I sent My only beloved Son into a rebellious civilization for every single one of you. Now I had to have faith in humanity, in every one of you sons of Adam. Top that!"

Well, to be quite honest, I couldn't.

"So listen to Me, my son. You have the wrong idea about fear. I placed caution in humans to cause them to pause and think. The correct concern is to stop and consider that it is a very long distance down from the top of a cliff to the bottom and not to just step off into empty space. It is to respect a thing, but humans …" He pointed at me. "Have taken fear to a different level that I never intended. And now fear is no longer respect, but it now stops you from doing what I've asked of you, which by the way only brings you into agreement with life. The sluggard states that there is a lion outside, and so does not. The wise man states there is a lion outside, and I need to remove it. You can plainly see that there is a big difference. Fear should never conquer you, but you are always able to conquer your fear. So get off your seat and get to it, David."

On the Lord's last word, the bell binged for the start of round one. I reluctantly got off my stool and headed into the center of the ring. I was thinking to myself that it was so much easier to believe God when there is no work to be done. My opponent practically ran across the ring to get the action going. He threw a quick right jab to my jaw, without even tapping gloves first, and I ducked under it and got popped hard on my right temple with an overhand left jab. I saw myself in slow motion falling backward as lights exploded around me.

"Ouch, man. Oh man. What did two seconds just pass?" I already felt my knees going weak. "Come on, boy. Clear your head. See what self-prophesy does!"

I shook my head and pressed my right glove to my eyes to focus. I knew I wouldn't be able to hit him seeing double because now he was twice as scary. My foe was moving quickly from my right to left, and I could not help but notice that he was seven-foot-two. I'm about five-foot-nine. So to me, he was a super heavyweight, and I'm lucky if I am even a lightweight or a featherweight, chicken feathers, that is.

In the back of my mind, I knew that no boxer got into the ring thinking he was already the loser, maybe at the end of the fight, like when Roberto Duran said *"no mas"* to Sugar Ray, but I needed the confidence of Ali when he roped a dope in Zaire. I don't think many at that time thought Ali would win that fight after the way Forman beat the stuffing out of Joe Frazier in the first two rounds of their fight in Jamaica. Now that is what I was lacking. I had to change my mind-set and agree with God that He was right, no matter what my current circumstances looked and felt like.

I shook my head again quickly to clear the cobwebs. To my mind's eye, I probably looked like I was saying no. I thought, *Please don't punch me again.* I took a deep breath and stepped into my opponent, faked a left jab to his noggin, and, with feet planted, hit him in the breadbasket, solar plexus, gut, or stomach, whichever you prefer. And if I could have hoped for the best, about eight inches lower would have made my day, and the fight would have been over on a technicality. A TKO instead of me getting my own eggs scrambled.

My punch was a good hard shot to the stomach, and he just blew a bit of air out of the side of his mouth, as if he had added a little too much chorizo to a burrito. Belch and like, "Oh, excuse me!" I wanted to hit him again just for not taking a good shot seriously, but hey, I sure did not want to get to close to any of his power punches, and I hadn't even seen one yet.

But speak of the devil, it will come a running to answer your call. He let loose with a flurry of punches all over my body. I had my arms up high protecting my head and then ducking down low, looking up over the top of my gloves to make sure I was not zagging left when he was throwing a hard-right cross. So far, it seemed like everything he threw was hard.

Suddenly I heard a "Bing!"

And praise the Lord and a righteous "Hallelujah!" Round one was complete and in the books, and I was still breathing and had not kissed the mat once. Thank you, Lord Jesus. Praise God. I live!

I felt good and tried to trot back to my stool but tripped over my own feet and almost ran into the ref, who scowled at me. "Ahhh, just think. Another eleven rounds to go with Paul Bunyan crossed with the Incredible Hulk, but hey, it's all good."

Father God was calling me over, wagging His index finger at me, like, "Come over here and sit down and stop embarrassing Me."

Oohh, man, how long was this night going to last?

I said, "Ok, Father, so I've completed my test, right?!"

"You just went one round. Nothing in life is that easy, except salvation."

"Salvation is not as easy as everyone seems to make it sound, Father. It is more work than I ever thought anything else could be."

"Ha, it is the same from My perspective concerning you, but perhaps you would prefer separation from Me for eternity?"

"Well no, but trust me, Lord. I'm gonna get hurt, and I'd be crazy not to take that into consideration!"

"You should trust Me and stop speaking defeat into your life. My Son's very Word states, 'And we know that in all things God, that is who I Am, works for the good of those who love Me, My Son, and the Holy Spirit, and who have been called according to My purpose.' I called you for this time of growth, just as I called everyone that I chose. There are no exceptions. The salvation you currently enjoy and the life I currently provide is given to you by the sacrifice of Me, your God, because I love every one of you. You all have been called, and just like each of you, it is on you to respond to Me and My request. There are no exceptions. The individual calls look different because of the uniqueness of you the individual, but all have been called, or else one of your own favorite Scripture verses would then be invalid. 'For I so loved the world that I gave my own beloved Son.' I believe you remember the rest."

Human logic was intact. I said, "Listen, Lord, my eyes are telling me that my opponent is younger, stronger, and quicker and has a ton more experience at this. So I would be lying if I started boasting about how easy it is going to be to wop 'em."

"Yes, but if you, My son, spoke the Words of My Son, no matter what, then that truth that never changes would stand. I say that His Word does not fail, and that is why it is incumbent for humans to read it. You cannot lie when speaking My Word; you can only lie when you start to interpret the Word without coming to Me through the Holy Spirit for guidance. My Son's Word covers every situation you could ever encounter or imagine. Speak it and not what your own limited vision and imagination tells you that you are seeing and how it is going to affect you."

Bing! Round two! Man, that was quick. Time sure flies when you're having fun and getting a lecture from the omniscient God of all creation.

I popped up off my stool and headed into the center of the ring, thinking like the Cowardly Lion in the *Wizard of Oz*, "I do believe in spooks," but instead I was thinking, *I do believe in Jesus. I do. I do. I do. I do believe in Jesus.*

Well, my confidence was catching up to my proclamations, and I thought, *Hey, what I speak touches the physical and spiritual worlds. Wow!* Thank you, Lord, and I was now up on the balls of my feet, thinking and looking for an opening to pop this big galoot in the noggin, to let him know that I did not come to just keep a distance from him but to win. The galoot was looking at me with a puzzled expression on his mug. I probably looked a bit more certain. I thought to myself, *Be strong. Be courageous. The Holy Spirit is within you.*

I ducked under an awkward left jab, hit him twice on the jaw with a couple of my own jabs, and backed up. I tried a body shot; he blocked it with his arms, I then hit him in his forearms to diminish his punching power. It felt like I was throwing punches at a wet bag of cement that had been left in the Sahara for a couple of weeks, basically big bricks. But I kept throwing, and things were landing more frequently.

He blocked another of my jabs with his left and leaned into a right uppercut and hit me with a solid punch that would make the Man of Steel crumple, and his fist connected with my own stomach. I heard all the air in my body migrate out into the atmosphere with a loud emmppphh, like I vomited air, as if all of the oxygen entirely exited my lungs and blood stream. My vision blackened, and it felt like I had no more strength in my legs, but that body shot only made me mad regardless of what my body was telling me. I thought, *Who you trying to kill, boy? I'm gonna wop you ten-foot-tall Goliath behind!*

At that exact same time, I was trying to suck some air back into my empty chest cavity. I spit my mouthpiece out since it was blocking my access to the oxygen I desperately desired. I thought, *Punk, you better back up*, but of course he didn't. He just coolly shook off my volley of punches, as if a slight chill had just come up out of nowhere to cause a minor irritation.

But there ain't no stoppin' me now. I kept pushing forward despite the agony of defeat and potential butt whoppin'. My adrenalin always started to flow when a fight with death presented itself. Now I was not only elated but angry and ready to make someone—him—pay. I could smell the leather gloves. I could smell me sweating and hoped he was enjoying my funk too.

But he smelled like a daisy. He hadn't even broken a sweat yet. I was gonna have to break his jaw or something. He was taking it far too casual, and that was my own fault. He threw a shot straight at my nose as I leaned to the right to avoid a broken septum and hooked a right cross into his own jaw, almost losing my balance to the right. I was hoping beyond hope that his jaw was made of glass, but once again, it wasn't. It felt more like taking a punch at a cinder block. But at least now he knew that he was in for a fight and to stop playing around because I now knew that I sure wasn't.

Punches were traded back and forth. I probably took too many of them to the head to remember them all. Plus why would I even want too? Bing! End of round two and ten to go.

I started to head back to my corner and noticed that the mountain was walking alongside me.

"What's up?"

The galoot looked down at me with a kind expression, Like. 'you, poor old man; lost again?' He pointed over his enormous shoulder with a smile on his face; "That's your corner back over there, Gramps," as he encouraged me to look behind myself.

"Shoot or one of those S words."

The Lord was patiently waiting for me with a water bottle in His hand and an expression on His face, like "We only have ninety seconds between rounds. Get on the good foot, and have a seat."

I took the seat gratefully. "Well, Lord, how am I doing on points because I am not going to knock him out?"

"You know, David, this is why you do not have the gift of prophecy. You are busy analyzing and not believing Me. He is ahead of you on points, but you knew that if you used your intelligence instead of your anger, you could score a bit better. Round three is coming."

I laughed and found that even that hurt, my toes as well as my jaw. "You want me to use my intelligence. If I had done that, I would not be in this ring, getting the sin beat out of me."

The Lord God turned away from me, and I saw His shoulders shaking. I thought, *Whoa, what's up with God?* But then realized He, the Holy Him, was laughing. Just as suddenly, everyone in the audience was also laughing, along with the referee. I was laughing too. I was just filled with joy when I realized that God does laugh. It was like that perfect spring morning when everything in the entire world was going to be ok. Joy somewhat unspeakable was just with us. I now knew real happiness, God happy.

I said, "Lord, I never thought you had a sense of humor. Well, sorry, Lord, but it is hard for me to think that you ever laugh, dealing with us all."

"Exactly why you are here, My son, to know Me better. Sometimes you just say stuff that will make Me laugh. Your life is an example that I'll use." He pointed at me. "When you get back together with family that you haven't seen in a long while, as soon as you see your children, brother, sister, mom, or dad, you are just happy. It is not because of the meal you might prepare. It is not even the stories you are going to tell about past experiences. You are just happy because you are back together with family that you love and who know and accept you for who you are. That is what salvation is, at its most basic. Relationship restored; family restored. You become My children, and I love every one of you. So on that great day when all is said and done, we are going to party and be a family like nothing that can ever be imagined. Our joy—yours and Mine—will be completely full. You in Me and I in you will be in complete unity with Me, your Father; my Son, Jesus; and the Holy Spirit. The work will be over, and the actual rest or Shalom and companionship will be settled forever. Remember **Revelation 21:1–7 (NIV)** what I said to the church and you,

Then I saw a new heaven and a new earth, for the first heaven and the first earth had passed away, and there was no longer any sea. I saw the Holy City, the new Jerusalem, coming down out of heaven from God, prepared as a bride beautifully dressed for her husband. And I heard a loud voice from the throne saying, "Look! God's dwelling place is now among the people, and He will dwell with them. They will be His people, and God Himself will be with them and be their God. 'He will wipe every tear from their eyes. There will be no more death' or mourning or crying or pain, for the old order of things has passed away." He who was seated on the throne said, "I am making everything new!" Then He said, "Write this down, for these words are trustworthy and true." He said to me: "It is done. I am the Alpha and the Omega, the Beginning and the End. To the thirsty I will give water without cost from the spring of the water of life. Those who are victorious will inherit all this, and I will be their God and they will be my children."

I heard the Father say, "Amen."

I said, "Yes and Amen, Lord!"

The Lord answered, "You need to get over your anger. You're fighting an embedded insecurity from your childhood, and you need to see your opponent differently."

"Huh? What? You mean that same guy who punched me in the head a few hundred times? Him!"

The Lord said, "My Son already paid the price for others' transgressions. Your anger is not beneficial to you."

"Lord, you are taking away all my advantages."

The Lord told me, "Anger is never advantageous."

"Well, You get angry about things like sin, wickedness, rebellion …"

"Yes, I do because they hurt you. They never help anyone; they always hurt you and whomever you come into contact with. Any sin is never kept within the individual; it is always passed along to another, usually those who are closest to you. I want to also point out that I Am actually the closest individual to you. I live in your heart. I passionately hate sin and will be sure. Take My Word for it. That sin will be erased from My presence eternally."

Mental note to self: Don't get God angry by bringing up stupid subject matters.

Man, now I was happy as is possible that I had salvation. Father God hates sin. I was ready to tie a blindfold around my own eyes and ask my opponent to hit me with his best shot for every minute I've spent on the Planet Earth. Whew, thank God for salvation. No wonder Jesus was praying in the garden of Gethsemane. Father, take this cup from Me. It is a terrible thing to fall into the hands of the living God. God hates sin, and Jesus became sin on our behalf and then suffered the wrath of God in my stead. There is no one like Almighty God and His mercy. No, not one.

Bing! Wow! Round three. I slowly got up off my stool. Now I was looking back over my shoulder at the Lord and thinking that I might get a lightning bolt shot up my behind. My opponent had become small potatoes compared to what God could do. I thought, *I now want to be obedient.* So hit my adversary more accurately. Don't use any anger, and don't get popped myself. After all this was a boxing match. I could only be beaten to death, so those items should be easy to accomplish. I was happy though that I had Father God in my corner instead of any other human being I could possibly imagine.

The best I could currently come up with was to run because it had to be safer for me than walking. The ring looked much smaller as I started to back up and keep out of his long reach. The ref came over and asked if I were enjoying the rest. He told me to get back to the fight before I picked up a penalty for nonengagement.

"Come on, this is worse than Pandora's box. If I don't do anything, it may be good for me. If I engage the galoot, I'm sure to take a pounding and let destruction out of the box. What to do?"

My opponent knew and threw a right uppercut, another of those oxygen-depriving gut shots, but I caught his glove and wrist under my left shoulder and would not let it go. My opponent tried to flick me off like an uninvited germ that got attached to his glove. I was holding on tight. Maybe we could waltz together for a few minutes.

The ref came over and asked if I thought that I was on *Dancing with the Stars*. I wanted to tell the ref, "Why don't you try going a few rounds with Godzilla's offspring and see how quickly you would be in the mood to do the Drunk-Man Frankenstein. You know I'm old."

The ref tapped me on my shoulder and pointed out that I belonged to the IBF and not the WWE, so I could release my arm lock on my versions of Haystack Calhoun or Bobo Brazil. I thought to myself that I was going to have to leave the ref in my will so he didn't have anything to look forward to after my opponent killed me, which was going to be what transpired immediately after I released him.

My challenger was leaning on top of me with all of his weight, and it was having an effect. He popped me a few times in the back of my head, reminding me of when I was in grammar school and Mr. Powell, our English teacher, used to pop us, his students, for not getting planted into our memories the English subjects he thought he had thoroughly sowed within our recollections and that he found so effortless to remember himself.

"David, do you know what a predicate is, and can you also use a predicate in a sentence?"

As he drummed his fingers on his desk, while the seconds slowly passed, Mr. Powell, having reached equilibrium, then reached into his top drawer to pull out his ruler to make you regret not having studied your homework.

But it was a bad idea to back me into a corner. "I think a predicate has something to do with a verb, which shows you something about the subject. 'David went to the bathroom because he had to go.'"

"Are you trying to be funny, Mr. Egan?"

"Like how high is up or why the sky is blue?"

Mr. Powell was drumming his fingers with determination; I was steeling myself not to cry in front of my classmates, getting my hand whacked by Mr. Powell. But that was then; this was now.

I released my opponent's right arm from my left underarm, faked a step back, and popped him in the jaw with an uppercut. I hit him once again in the stomach, and he countered with a perfect right cross to my jaw. I heard it snap and felt it more. He then punched me hard in the chest, a definite power punch, and that hurt twice as much as the shot to the jaw.

I was seeing a universe of dark spots cloud up my vision and was also finding it hard to breathe. I heard my own voice moaning as if some goofy ventriloquist had taken control of my vocal cords. I did not want those groans to be coming from me, but I could not help it. It was like being a hundred years old and still crying out for your mama the moment after your car left the highway and started that slow-motion flip. You just knew it was going to hurt and hurt bad once you hit the blacktop!

My jaw was clenched, and once again in anger, I tried to pop him, but throwing a left hurt like crazy. I did not want to tie him up again because I was scared of trying to hold his weight on my shoulders.

"Where in the world is that bell? Help me, Lord! Please!"

When you get desperate, you get honest. In my estimate, only two and a half minutes had passed, and the next thirty seconds were going to take an eternity. My opponent saw my weakened condition, and like any good boxer, he came in to finish the fight. He threw a wild punch toward my left jaw once again. I ducked under it and got hit hard on my left shoulder, which launched me across the ring. And if it had not been for the ropes, which prudently popped me back up on my feet, probably more luck than anything else, I looked across the ring at the Lord and remembered that I should not actually believe in luck.

But if not for those ropes, I would have found myself somewhere in the third row. Serious things on my body hurt, but my chest and jaw were getting the primary attention and affection from my brain. I was looking at Father God, like "Toss the towel, Lord. Toss the fight. Toss something, anything, because I am gonna toss my cookies! Help me!"

Bing! End of round three, and there were nine more stinking rounds to go. Man, this was the longest day of my life! I stumbled with knees shaking back to my corner and had an indeterminately hard time just trying to sit, kneel, fall, and collapse onto my stool.

I said, "I hurt. Help me." My teeth were clenched together so I was kinda smiling up at God with tears in my eyes.

The Lord asked, "What do you want Me to do?"

I was staring at the Lord, as if He were speaking a language that I had never heard before. "Well, if You remember, Lord, by Your Son's stripes I am healed. Heal."

"Yes, yes, everyone quotes that. I hear it more often than the disciples' prayer. But why do you quote it when you don't actually believe it?"

"I believe it. Now more than ever! You're here. I'm here. Heal me. Or at the very least take away all this pain, Father. Please, with sugar on top if you like!"

"Have faith and believe Me and the things I told you to believe. Instead you believe what your senses are telling you instead of the truth, which is currently with you, given to you, and learned, but at the same time not believed. Believe Me!"

"I ... I do believe You, Lord. Your Word is always true, but I'm a hurting and hurtin' singularly bad this very moment. I cannot go another round and get something else broken. My deceased grandmother would be able to kick my behind. I can barely think."

"Faith, My son, is to believe Me, but you do not believe Me. You believe everything else. An example." The Father smiled at me, as if we were having a pleasant conversation while fishing at a lakeside under a spreading Chestnut tree. "If you went to a doctor and he told you that you had a cold, a simple virus ..."

I nodded, which in turn caused a sharp electric jolt to erupt from my jaw, with my eyes adding a few more tears to those drying.

"And in seven to ten days, you would recover, and then when that week passed and you felt better, you, David, would say that the doctor was correct."

I started to nod again, but I was no fool.

My Father resumed His instruction. "But I designed the body and put those antibodies within every individual. So the healing is there. Broken bones, cancer, AIDS, diabetes, you can name it. But you currently want a miracle because you need it now and do not want to wait however long it takes your body to catch up to what has already been provided for. When you gave your heart to Me on your day of salvation, our relationship was healed, and you do not question that miracle because you are sure of My Word. And the proof is your life, heart where I live, and Spirit where we commune. So believe Me for the miracle, the mending of your jaw, and broken ribs, the exact same way you did for salvation. You just believed without any sugar on top."

"Lord, thanks, but I already asked for the healing. Am I going to have to wait a couple of months for it to take place?"

"You can change your mind, David. You do it all the time. Change your request and your prayer, and ask Me for the thing you need at this time. I prefer honesty. If you are wrong in a petition, then get it right, but most of all, believe Me when I say that I once again love you. I do!"

"Lord, no scriptures come immediately to mind concerning a miracle and me. What's the difference? If both are from You, aren't they both miracles, and why should I even ask if You already know and are going to take care of it? Me, I'm always stumbling around and guessing, but You … know!"

"You ask so that your faith in Me will grow. I Am already faithful. I have never sinned or doubted Myself. I am faithful to who I Am, but that just is not true of you children of Adam. A healing takes time. It is Me and the body working together. A miracle is just Me moving in a sovereign manner. You get what you ask for, whether you know it or not. Believe Me when I say that I am honest and just. You should be honest with Me. You do know scriptures concerning miracles. They just do not come readily to mind. But I know you do know them."

Round four. Bing!

I said, "Wait, wait, and wait! I am in no condition to box that monster!"

The Lord answered, "You better hurry. That ref won't wait very long."

As I stood up from the stool and tried to push upwards with my thighs, my weight on my rib cage sent messages to my brain that I had better stop my upward push. I fought through it, thinking, *When was the last time I had this much pain just standing up straight?*

With that thought, the ref came over, grabbed my gloves in his hands, and looked intently into my eyes. "Can you continue?"

I wanted to say, "No!" but heard my own voice speaking, "Yeah."

"Ok, look at me. Now where are you?"

My brow furrowed, and my eyes were asking a silent question that perhaps my opponent popped the ref a few times in the noggin because he was becoming bored with this fight or my having conversations with Almighty God.

So I responded to the ref, "Well, it feels like I've died and am currently in exceeding torment and being punished for everything I've ever done wrong in my life either against God or my fellow man. But just so you know, I am here in this boxing ring getting pummeled by that monster over there, who is anxious to go another hundred rounds with me as his living body bag."

"Ok, just as long as you know where you're at," the ref replied.

A song just popped into my head. "What's love got to do with it, got to do with it. What's love but a secondhand emotion?"

I wanna say "Thanks" to the ref, but my jaw was not exactly working. So I continued into the ring. "Shoot or one of those S words." Why didn't I just say "I can't continue, man"?

I was thinking that I had better stay away from any of my opponent's lightning-fast punches because I was in no shape to duck, weave, or outmaneuver him. Suddenly it began to dawn on me that my opponent was far larger, weightier, and younger and, as a natural consequence, not legally sanctioned to box me. Maybe in a street fight no one would care, but my Father God set this up.

And I just became conscious of the fact that He, praise His name, is never unfair. The test at times may be hard, but He does not break the law to teach me or anyone a lesson. The lesson and what I was currently going through was to teach and not destroy, so something was up because this was strictly unfair. If I were in the audience watching, I would not think it kosher.

"So why?"

I still had thrice minutes to go, and my opponent didn't look to be tiring after all the punches he had thrown and I'd been privy to receive. Now I was praying. It would be just as easy for me to shout over to my corner and tell the Lord what had just come to mind, but the Lord had also provided this means of communion between us through His beloved Son.

"Lord, I do know that You are never unfair or unfaithful to those You love. So I stand in that. I believe in Your holy character and do not doubt Your tremendous love for the whole wide world, Lord, plus and especially those You've redeemed."

My opponent came in quickly, flexing his enormous muscles, and I thought, *Who really cares? So you've got big muscles. Here am I and my left jab, and let us see if that'll bring you down to size, punk.*

Sometimes our mind-set must change, and what I was realizing currently was that God is true. It was just His nature. Because of that belief, I now knew that I know that everything He has ever stated in

His Word is also true and without flaw. My opponent was just that, an enemy someone who could conquer me if I gave him the right or someone I could overcome if I denied that right and stood on the firm foundation, Jesus, and God's supernatural Word.

I did not know my opponent's position, but I did know why I was here, to know the Lord betta and betta. So this boy was going down. I was thinking that if Moses by himself had to carve out those two new stone tablets by himself and carry them all the way back up Mount Sinai again by himself, then I could do what had been requested of me, no matter what it was or looked like.

"I trust You, Lord, and all things do work together for my good, even humbugging it up with Godzilla's little baby boy. Lord, my God, I ask You for forgiveness, for thinking that You at any time have a plan for my destruction. You are life, my life, and truth, and I actually can do all things through Jesus and Your very right provision. I repent and turn myself away from my own unbelief about the things concerning You. You Yourself are right, and my opponent is not greater, stronger, or more than You, Almighty God. Thank You, Holy Spirit, for that truth. Amen. I do agree with You, Lord."

Quite unexpectedly I saw my opponent differently. The somewhat ruggedly handsome gargantuan who seemed unstoppable, especially from my own perspective, what my physical eyes had been seeing, was growing smaller and uglier as I watched. There was a weary meanness to his eyes and an angry sneer at the corners of his mouth, and the more I watched, the more he started to become an it.

Because what I was seeing was not human, it reminded me of the old movie, *The Picture of Dorian Gray*, where Dorian finally saw the portrait of himself after all his years of evil and sin. Dorian then pierced the portrait with a knife and then got paid back in spades, the full measure of the life he'd lived.

And my opponent now made Dorian at the end of his life look like the handsome young man at the beginning of that story. I did not even want to hit it with my boxing gloves. The severe anger and sheer unadulterated and undiluted cruelty was palpable. I was afraid to hit him and find that some of that hate might rub off on me.

Through my mouthpiece, I spoke to it, "Peek-a-boo, boy. I see you."

Its eyes lit right up and stared at me hard, like "What happened?"

And the Lord and I were now ready for the real fight to begin because He was my strength and I was a gunning for bear. "You gonna feel me now gruesome." I popped my own self in the jaw with my glove and winked at it. "Nothing is broken now, boy, and I am no longer just a man, but a warrior of my Lord's Son and my King, Jesus. You are going to be wishin' on all of the stars that are going to be placed on your horizon that you never entered this fight."

I stepped into it and hit it hard with a quick left, followed by a right cross, and saw that both tagged it good. Now that I was agreeing with Father God, I could see that my opponent was not even human, but a demon, "a used to be," "a once was."

But now the corruption it had decided on, and it was obvious that it was never going to repent. You could see that truth in its eyes. I did not know how long this jomoke had been about its tasks, but it had spent millennium being out of the will of Father God, and that just destroyed, corrupted, and made one a companion of death in every manner possible.

Man! I began this boxing match in fear for my own physical well-being, not even considering how perfect and true my Father and my God was to me because of His very own bond of love to His Son, my Lord Jesus. Now I was angry, but for the very shame of being in my flesh and own mind about how the Lord my God works. I only saw my own pain and no vantage point.

But I'd been saved, born again by His life. What in the universe did I have to be afraid of? Jesus had me. At this moment, if I put all my imagination into it, I could not think of one single thing greater than Almighty God. I was ashamed of myself on His behalf. I let that demon punch a child of God and believed that it hurt. What power did it have that was more than His? What a fool!

Man! I was mad. This should never be! God, who is in me, was never ever again going to take a beating on my behalf. "Demon, you are about to get hurt." I popped my gloves together and all but ran across that ring to get into a for-real humbug.

This 2012 David was going against a real demon/Goliath on behalf of the Lord, so it was by His might and power pressed into me that I threw a haymaker from way down low, basically from my knees to its head, wanting to send it back to wherever it came from.

In a boxing match, I would never throw such a punch because that punch would leave you wide open to an opponent's counter punches, but in my mind's eye, I wanted it to be pinging off all the ropes in the ring, like a pinball on speed.

That haymaker connected with a loud smack on my enemy's right forehead and sent it flying backwards, off its feet and sliding across the ring. A blues song from one of my favorites, Buddy Guy, came to mind, but I thought it appropriate on behalf of my opponent. "You're right I got the blues," and for a good reason.

I could see it more clearly now and loathed the sight. With all the hate and despair in its eyes, I now saw some fear blossoming there. None of it was pretty to see. It picked itself back up and tried to once again cloud my mind with the image of the previous opponent that I had been humbugging it up with and losing too. But I now knew who I was fighting with, and since the Lord had opened my eyeballs to it,

I had no plans on falling back into the same snare that I had trapped myself in from the previous rounds.

It came up to me and threw a hard-right cross, which I ducked under easily. I began to speak the first thing that came into my mind, right after the right cross with a left hook to both sides of its jaw.

"The Lord is my Shepherd-King. I shall not want. He alone maketh me to lie down in green pastures. He leads me beside the still waters because He alone restores my soul. He leads me in the paths of His righteousness for His name's sake. Yea, though I walk through the valley of the shadow of death, I shall fear no evil. Especially you, for Thou art with me Lord. Thy rod and Thy staff, they comfort me. Thou preparest a table before me in the presence of my enemies. Thou anointest my head and my heart with oil, Your very own Spirit. Therefore my cup continuously overflows. Surely goodness and mercy shall follow me all the days of my life because of You, Lord, and I will dwell in the house of the Lord forever and forever.

"I'm gonna drop you by the good and faithful grace of the Lord, like a useless addiction. Father, You and my Lord Jesus are my wonderful Shepherd and King. You alone!"

Bing!

Whew, that was fun! I did not think that would ever be possible in this particular boxing ring and on this particular day.

The Lord said, "So, My son, a change of heart. You look happy!"

"It's You, Lord. It is funny, but when I am on the same page with You, everything just works. The clarity alone in knowing who my enemy is and who You are is more than sufficient, but everything just lines up with You. You are God, and I am a man!"

The Lord replied, "So, David, we are done with this lesson then."

"Well, not quite, because I really do not understand why You had me getting into a boxing match with Lucifer. I mean, that is really more than I should try to handle."

The Lord said, "That was your enemy, an inheritance from your family, not from Me. And it was not Lucifer. You fought an enemy, a thing that has plagued you for years. It was deceiving you to keep your mind on yourself and not honestly believe Me. Your opponent needed to be defeated by you being in Me, My son. The enemy Lucifer is a created being and follows the same laws as every created being. He is not omnipresent."

"You are, and I love it when You call me son, Dad."

The Lord concluded, "I love it when you call Me Dad, My son."

D: Walking Away

On April 29, 2014, I was walking and started to think about this one, but the actual writing of it is much harder than you may think because it deals with what takes place after death. From these short Holy Ghost stories, it may seem like all I do is to take liberties with Scripture, but that is a hard thing. I love the Word, and taking liberties with the Word of God is identical to my taking the freedom I've been given by God's very own blood as if it were my own and treating the Lord's Word as if there were no results or penalty forthcoming, with me therefore making the Word of God worldly.

In my heart, I do not want the Lord God to be misrepresented, and I most assuredly do not want to lead my fellow brothers and sisters down a path that is useless. The subject matters in these shorts go all over creation. When I speak about our Lord, then I try to keep it scriptural. I want to share what He has been speaking to me, which is mostly by parables and short stories because that is how I see my life. Occurrences and this everyday journey are the fodder for these stories.

So again, I do not really like to take liberties with the Lord and His trust. Although it may seem that way, the Holy Spirit initially gave me the following as a seed. There are some very serious eternal ramifications in these words, so after this seed had taken root and my imagination had the beginnings of a plot, I began to write.

I was walking up our street and started to imagine that there was a plastic bag blowing around, which happens in our neighborhood when individuals put their recycling out. But I picked up that plastic bag, and since I was so far from my own house, I was going to chuck it into one of my neighbor's garbage cans that happened to be out for Thursday trash pickups.

As I popped open the lid and tossed in the bag, the owner came out and asked me what I thought I was doing. I told him the truth that a piece of garbage was blowing around on his lawn and I was putting it in the trash to go to the dumps.

In my mind, it was just a small plastic bag and not a car tire. My neighbor did not take kindly to this act of altruism, so I said, "Fine, I'll just take it out and bring it to my own garbage can." He agreed that I needed to do just that and that if I thought throwing garbage into his can was a good idea, the next time he saw me doing that, then he was going to shoot me "deader than a doornail."

I have no idea what that actually means since dead is dead and a doornail has never been alive, but I am also quite sure it was not an "I love you and have an extremely exhilarating day." Now I let my flesh rise up and to become offended because of many insecurities that I had yet to yield to the cross where my flesh actually belongs. I allowed my neighbor to just tick me off.

Since I was not taking garbage from my own house or lawn and tossing it into his trash collection but was going out of my way to clean up his lawn and being dogged for the effort, I told my neighbor that he could be sure that I would leave any and all garbage on his lawn alone from this time onward. But he should not be making any threats that he was unable to fulfill, especially where someone's life, my own, was concerned.

The neighbor barked a short crotchety laugh and reached behind his back.

Suddenly every criminal act pictured on the evening news, including 9/11, came flooding into my heart. I totally forgot that I had a Savior by the name of Jesus, and I became completely concerned with keeping myself alive and far from harm. Basically it was me, and everyone else in the world, except my wife and kids, could just be sent directly to the domain below, oh yeah!

I figured he was reaching for a gun to be able to back up his threat, so I punched him in the throat, kneed him in the crotch, and punched him in the temple. I thought to myself, *You just do not play with a city boy even if you are some distant relative of Calamity Jane and a for-real sharpshooter.*

My neighbor hit his driveway hard, with hands clasping his throat, and was having trouble breathing. And since there was no mercy coming from me, I grabbed him by his shirt collar and belt and lugged his heavy behind across the street and out of the peering eyes of our other neighbors. I tossed him into the small batch of woods on Dresden Wood Drive. I was going for broke now and took off his belt. I tied his hands behind his back, removed his sneaker laces from his white low-top Pumas, and tied his feet behind his back to his hands, then I flipped him back over to stare into the sun. I slapped him in the head and asked him how he was currently feeling about his desire to shoot me because of a single, used, plastic bag.

The look in his eyes told me that he had graduated from a handgun to an atomic weapon, all of which were to be centered on me. *Well, so very happy for you,* I thought. I knelt and punched him in the stomach, and when his mouth popped open, losing a lungful of air, which smelt as if he had just eaten a salami and turkey sandwich, I pulled off a sock and stuck it in his mouth. After all silence is golden, and my neighbor did not need to be calling for help.

I waited for him to recover and told him that I was going to leave him in the woods for three days, and then I would be back to release him and to critically contemplate the lesson. He was now receiving on how to better treat his neighbors and to seriously reconsider his obsession on garbage.

Now the Holy Spirit of the living God will come and talk to you when you, the individual Christian, are taking His temple into the slums and trashing it up with my own personal garbage, with the majority of it being emotional. I ignored Him and fixated on continuing my daily walks. I also knew in my spirit that I was on a straight path and was walking away from the Lord under my own power instead of His righteousness. I was determining in my heart to purposely not seek Him. I did peek in each day to make sure he was still kicking and breathing and basically suffering.

The Lord's story of the Good Samaritan would pop into my imagination, but in my version, he could stay there lying on the side of the road until he learned not to be rude to his fellow neighbors. On that third day, I did just what I said I would and came to release him.

I saw that he was bug-bitten and had been fasting, and like anyone who fasts, he had been thinking about only one thing. Probably the first was to get his smelly sock out of his mouth, the second, well that could clearly be seen in his eyes. But I was obligated to do just as I said, and I untied his legs and hands, told him that I hoped he learned not to be so foolish with his lips, and turned my back on him. I headed out of the woods and was immediately shot in the back at a very close range by the gun he actually carried.

I felt as if a mule had kicked me hard in the chest, as my breath was flung out into the wild blue yonder, along with the immediate bright light of pain for about three hot seconds.

I fell over dead—or as dead as any doornail ever was—and I was flung headlong from this planet and straight as an arrow into a vast galaxy. And by the grace of God, I was taken to heaven and was standing before the Lord my God, who did not look to happy to see me.

He asked, "David, what have you done?"

I knew the Lord already knew, so I did not say anything other than "You know." Which He did. But when you are the individual looking into the eyes of Him who is always true, who is the truth, then it is difficult to come up with a valid response, even if you want to give one. After all, He is God!

I was still upset and wondered how I could be standing in front of the living God and feel that way. I had always thought that once I was home and with Him, then all my earthly stuff would just disappear since a bunch of it was sinful and I was now in His holy presence and domain.

The Lord asked, "David, how many times over the last couple of days did I try to turn you aside from this endeavor? You have entirely erased all of the effort put in by you and I for your life by this one act. Why?"

When the Lord asks you why, it is not because He does not know. He is looking to see whether you know and understand your very own actions.

I could easily think of about fifty different excuses, but when you are the individual looking into His eyes, every act looked from my perspective to be the acts of an immature and spoiled child. My actual justifications that I had been storing up in my mind while on earth currently numbered zero and were heading into the negative. Plus, when the living God tells you that you've undone all the work and effort that you've put in while on terra firma, that will give you reason to pause.

You know that your heavenly Father does not lie, so I was now thinking, *How do I undo what I last did while on the earth?* I had heard of individuals like William Booth who had momentarily passed from this life into the next and were sent back. For William, his life was saved to start the Salvation Army, and just like us, there were many things to just mature and grow. So the question is: why not me?

I asked, "Lord, can I go back and ask my neighbor for forgiveness?"

At that moment I sure wanted to. The sadness in God's eyes is more than enough to make you desire repentance, so much more than life. I had always dreamt of the day when I would be home and in the presence of God. Now that great day had arrived, and He was sad to see me because of my very own actions. "What could be worse, oh thou fool?"

Then the Lord said these words from **1 Samuel 2:25**, *"If one-man sins against another, I will judge him; But if a man sins against The Lord, who will intercede for him?"*

You remember Israel when turning back from taking Canaan as I commanded them: **Deuteronomy 1:39–42 (NIV)** states,

> *And the little ones that you said would be taken captive in Canaan, the children who do not yet know good from bad—they will enter the land. I will give it to them and they will take possession of it. But as for you, Israel, turn around and set out toward the desert along the route to the Red Sea. Then they replied, "We have sinned against the Lord. We will go up and fight, as the Lord our God commanded us." So, every one of them put on their weapons, thinking it easy to go up into the hill country. But The Lord said, "Tell them, 'Do not go up and fight, because I will not be with you. You will be defeated by your enemies.'"*

The Lord continued, "In the same way, David, you were defeated by your enemy, and just like Israel, you cannot undo what you did."

I yelled, "Lord, I need to fix this!"

The Lord said, "You cannot. Be thankful and indebted that you did not lose salvation. But all the work that you have put in has attached itself to your sin. Your sin cannot exist here with Me. Again, be thankful that My salvation can and does."

"Father, please."

"These are the consequences of your very own actions. When you are outside of My will and you intentionally act outside of My heart's desire for you, the result is death. I love you, My son. That has never changed, but all your treasures that you put your hand to have been erased."

For me, I did not know the how since I was physically deceased, but there were many tears flowing from my eyes when standing before the Lord God, wanting to counteract what I had done as the individual or I, the deceived, in this instance, yet my heart's desire was to offer Him something that He considered valuable. And because of my choices, I had nothing. Zip. So much for anger and me exercising my supposed free will. They are worthless and did not profit me one tiny bit.

I provided an excuse. "Father, I did not shoot anyone. He sinned against me."

"You belong to Me. Your actions should have been My actions. Instead they were completely based on your emotions since they are your own and are out of My will. You, David, are responsible for your death by your actions. The individual needed to know Me, and you were to be a blessing by doing the inviting. Instead you acted from inherent fears. You heard Me speaking to your heart, but the more you ignored Me, the less you heard Me. And you were determined to not listen. Now you have what you earned. Your neighbor blessed you because if you stayed on the path you set your feet upon, then you would have lost your very salvation. Your neighbor was good to you."

Ezekiel 18:23–25 (NIV) reads,

> *"Do I have any pleasure in the death of the wicked," declares The Lord GOD, "rather than that he should turn from his ways and live? But when a righteous man turns away from his righteousness, commits iniquity and does according to all the abominations that a wicked man does, will he live? All his righteous deeds which he has done will not be remembered for his treachery which he has committed and his sin which he has committed; for them he will die. Yet you say, 'The way of the Lord is not right.' Hear now, O house of Israel, David! Is My way not right? Is it not your ways that are not right?"*

Proverbs 18:12 (NIV) says, *"Before a downfall the heart is haughty, but humility comes before honor."*

So let us go through this same piece of fiction once again, but this time, when the Holy Spirit speaks, I will have more of a tendency to listen since this is our story. So part two …

I was walking in my neighborhood, about a mile from home. It was three days earlier when this whole business began. Since it never happened, no results have yet to occur. I again saw a plastic bag blowing across one of my neighbor's lawn. I walked over and picked it up to throw it into the garbage can parked on the roadside because it was garbage day.

As I closed the lid on the nearly full can, I heard a voice behind me. "Who do you think you are throwing your garbage into my can, man?!"

"Excuse me?"

"You, what do you think you're doing tossing your garbage into my can? Put your nasty throw-aways into your own can. You just can't come to my house and toss your junk into this can. Who do you think you are?"

Well, I am certainly not your child, so don't speak to me as if I were, I thought. I could easily see how angry this guy was. His cheeks were flushed, and his eyes squinted to being almost shut. He kept pointing at me. I felt as if I were back in grammar school and getting a lecture from the principal on why it was not a good idea to get into fights with fellow students, even if they were related to me. I figured that I had an inalienable right to do them damage. After all that's what family is for, without salvation, that is.

I could feel my flesh rising up, and I was thinking about pulling my neighbor's finger off and poking him in the eye with it. "Can you see better now?"

The Holy Spirit spoke to my heart. "Be holy because I am holy."

"Well, Lord, I don't feel very holy at this moment, so that is going to have to wait a bit."

"Treat your neighbor just as you want to be treated."

"Well, Lord, how about I treat him just as he is treating me?"

Finally since I was listening, the Holy Spirit hit me with the biggie. He brought to complete remembrance a portion of Scripture that I'd studied earlier and found such a challenge from **Luke chapter 6 : 27– 38** because it is so easy to tell other Christians that they should walk this out, without ever putting my own feet onto the road for myself.

> *But to you who are willing to listen, I say, love your enemies! Do good to those who hate you. Bless those who curse you. Pray for those who mistreat you. If someone slaps you on one cheek, offer the other cheek also. If someone demands*

your coat, offer your shirt also. Give to anyone who asks; and when things are taken away from you, don't try to get them back. Do to others as you would like them to do to you. If you love only those who love you, why should you get credit for that? Even sinners love those who love them! And if you do good only to those who do good to you, why should you get credit? Even sinners do that much! And if you lend money only to those who can repay you, why should you get credit? Even sinners will lend to other sinners for a full return. Love your enemies! Do good to them. Lend to them without expecting to be repaid. Then your reward from heaven will be very great, and you will truly be acting as children of the Most, High, for He is kind to those who are unthankful and wicked. You must be compassionate, just as Your Father is compassionate. Do not judge others, and you will not be judged. Do not condemn others, or it will all come back against you. Forgive others, and you will be forgiven. Give, and you will receive. Your gift will return to you in full measure—pressed down, shaken together to make room for more, running over and poured into your lap. By the method you give will then determine the method that you get back.

Man, when the Lord speaks all of that to you, then you must pause a second to be prudent and to think about what He just said. I was looking my wild-eyed neighbor in the eye but praying in my heart, "Lord, guide my lips and my tongue. Help me to speak You and not me. In You, in Your very heart, I pray, Lord. Let this prayer be so."

I was thinking, *Why is this guy so unyielding and angry about his garbage? It is going to the dumps, hopefully never to return.* I could sense that there was more going on. I'm deep that way. I mean, *Really, a plastic bag?*

I would hope that none of us head out of our house to get in the face of our neighbors for a plastic shopping bag. Just as quickly as that thought appeared, my neighbor reached behind his back, like an old detective movie, and now I was staring down the barrel of a handgun. I was no expert on guns, so I could not tell you if it were a .25 automatic, a .38, or a Glock, but I did know a gun when I saw one. And this one, which looked like a cannon, was about three feet from my mug.

A scripture came to mind concerning my neighbor. *2 Corinthians 4:4 (NIV)* reads, *"Satan the god of this age has blinded the minds of those who do not have faith, so they couldn't see the light of the gospel that reveals Christ's glory, Jesus Christ is the image of God."*

My neighbor's hand was shaking, and he was getting ready to pull that trigger, whether he wanted to or not, and end my life. Hot dog! I was off to the races!

"Ok, hold up a minute, Quicksdraw, before you do anything you cannot back out of. Are you sure you want to do this, to end a life, mine, over a used plastic bag? Look around you. There are other neighbors probably looking at us at this very moment. Perchance a couple are dialing 9-1-1 since you've got a gun in your hand. Me, I have no qualms about going to meet our Maker. You can shoot me dead, but then what are you going to do? How do you explain your actions? And although I don't think you are concerned about it, your actions have eternal reactions. I belong to someone, the Lord God, and my Savior and love, Jesus Christ. How are you going to explain to Them, to anyone, what you are about to do?"

I hit a nerve because he just got angrier, so much so that I thought he was going to have a stroke, a for-real conniption fit, as my mom use to say.

My neighbor's voice was guttural, spoken between locked teeth. I could barely understand what he was stating, "Don't tell me about God! What has He ever done for me?"

"Well, quite a bit for you. You have your gun trained on the right person. I, whether you believe me or not, can tell you what He has done for you and me," I said with a smile.

Right now, the prospect of going home to be with the Lord was just making my entire day. "First, let's just clear up what is happening." I waved my right hand in the air casually; "You want to shoot me well and good. I want you to shoot me. I've been on this planet for a lengthy period. I'll be more than happy to say, 'So long and thanks for all the fish.' But you don't have those options. The things your emotions are telling you are just lies, which in the end, affect your entire eternity."

Now it was me pointing at him. "I know you don't know me, and in your own heart, you don't want to hear a word from my mouth. But please, please, don't think that you can do this. When you pull that trigger, that you can then pop yourself, and there is just never-ending silence waiting for you. You'll pull the dirt up over your head and rest in peace forever."

"Hey, you're not in a position to tell me anything!"

"In fact I am. You may not see it, but before you ever pulled that gun, we were peers, equals, but once you pulled that gun, you threw away all your power and gave it to me. If you kill me, then I am going home, and as said earlier, I can't wait to go. Now you have the weapon, but I have the power. You will have all of the consequences, and I'll be home, waiting to see my wife again.

"What do you have just in this world, a murder rap and possible prison time, if you're lucky? If the police are coming, then you might also be full of lead before you get the chance to explain why you shot me because of a plastic bag. I couldn't explain that, and I have a pretty good imagination." I laughed. "You're in the worst shape of your life. Please let me help you. I'm being as honest as you've ever seen a man. Let me please pray for you. Let God help you! Please!" I was putting my entire heart into the request, hoping that he could feel me.

Then he said, "Ok," like a tiny whisper, "Ok …"

Man, I wanted to leap into his arms and kiss him, but he still had a gun trained between my eyes. "OK, ok" they were the sweetest words spoken by the human tongue. "Ok, ahhh, ok then."

"First things first, Lord, in the power of Your name, Jesus. Demon, get yourself out of here now! In the name of Jesus, I command you to leave this man."

I could see my neighbor stand up a little straighter. It was apparent that a physical weight had just been lifted from his shoulders. I had been there myself, but it was unusual to see it taking place with another individual.

Since all of this began, he smiled. "Ok [my new favorite word]."

"But don't you want to put that gun away? Isn't it getting rather heavy?"

"Yeah, but I don't trust religion. I hate religion."

"Listen, brother, I hate it also, probably more than you, but we are not turning to religion. We, you and I, are turning to the Lord. He has nothing to do with religion; religion just wants to use His holy name in vain. Do you trust me?"

My neighbor nodded his head in the affirmative. Ah, what a neighbor! I just loved him!

"Ok."

There's that word again. Ok, David, just calm down. You're getting too excited. Calm down.

"Ok, I don't know what you know, but before you said that you hate religion. I know that Jesus, the Son of God, died for you and me and, for that matter, everyone everywhere. So if you want to know Him, then just repeat these words with me. Are you in agreement?"

He nodded his head once again, but I asked him to say that he agreed. He then said yes.

"So repeat these words. Jesus, I give you my heart, my life, my all because I now believe that You gave me Your Life, Your Heart, Your all. In Jesus's name, I pray. Amen. Let it be so."

He did the repeating and then said, "That's it?"

"Yup, that's it!"

"I don't need to do more?"

"Nope, nothing more. I would suggest that you now find a church to attend, but you can ask the Lord which one He wants you to go to."

"Well, I want to go to the one you go to, if that's ok."

"Well, it is, but the church I attend is all the way in San Antonio, but if that's the one the Lord is directing you to, then you can sure come with my wife and I. What's your name anyway? Mine's David."

"Oh, Harold. It's Harold."

I laughed. "Harold. It's a great name."

I just started to cry with joy, and Harold started to cry. We were both standing in the middle of his yard, two old men, and I saw God was crying with joy. I thought, *Lord, you must have done these a thousand, million times.*

Then I heard the Spirit say, "Life is worth giving your all for."

And I don't think I'll ever stop crying for as long as I live. Praise You, Lord!

E : Throwing Stones

I was thinking about how in **Exodus 33 (NIV)** the Lord is speaking to Moses and is saying, "I will not go with you [plural], Israel, or My presence will not go with you because you've created for yourself a make-believe god, the golden calf, but My promise to Israel will now be completed by an angel that will do the dirty work, guiding, protecting you as a Father would, in My name. Because if I do go with you, I might destroy you on the way since you are such a stiff-necked people." I'm ad-libbing here.

But I started to think about my son, Isaac, when he was much younger. He is currently thirty-seven years old, so the analogy would not apply. But let us say that Isaac totally disobeyed me on a specific issue when he was a child that I had firmly spoken to him about.

In this story, he was told, "Don't throw rocks from our driveway at the picture window in our living room to see how many of them it will take to shatter it."

This is a serious subject, not only counting the cost since my wife had a preschool and daycare. The things he could get away with, other children might think about doing the exact same thing. And before you knew it, I would be replacing every pane of glass on the entire block. But even after being told not to, my son continued along the same path regardless of what I had spoken to him about.

So the warning progressed to the next level; now a consequence to the actions had been added for both of our benefits. "If you do that again, Bug, you are going to receive your lesson in Braille."

Still speaking to him, I said, "So if you do not understand my point, then your next instruction will be hands-on." I showed Isaac the palm of my right hand. I believed from the large intake of breath that he got my drift.

Then my son in arrogance the very next day went right ahead and did the exact thing, winding up and throwing rocks from the driveway at our living room window, so totally disregarding my words spoken to him in patience.

So I gave him yet another chance because I love him and did not want to damage him later when he became an adult and then tell a psychoanalyst how horrible it was to grow up with me as his father. So I told him of the consequences without any humor and stated clearly that I will be spanking his hiney if he did it again. And then once again, he disregarded my "turn from your wicked ways" entreaty.

I would like to add something here before going on with the story. In our Christian communities almost, every parent or adult who does not yet have children will quote Scripture to you. For disciplining your own child, you will most likely hear a modern proverb, "Spare the rod, spoil the child."

That proverb basically came from **Proverbs 13:24**. I was spanked a lot as a child. Those spankings did not teach me respect, good manners, or how to better treat my fellow man. God taught me those things; spankings taught me fear. And if I in this particular case wanted—rather desired—to avoid a butt warming, I then found it would be better for me to be a good liar. I did not want pain to be inflicted on me physically; guess I'm human that way.

When I look at my youth, it was for the most part trying to avoid punishment for something that I had done wrong. I was also aware as an adult that I was emulating my parent or parents (single mom for me most of my life). Spankings, punishment, and general discipline for me only taught me to rebel.

Since telling a story is a natural part of my nature and since I had five other brothers, then blaming them for something I had done was good for me. I am telling a story here, but back to "spare the rod, spoil the child." Christians take that word and are literal concerning it. I am also not condoning just letting your children run amok. The story below indicates that when words fail and you, my child, cannot for your very own benefit listen to what I am telling you, then you will receive just rewards. But as a Christian, my heavenly Father has never taken me across His lap to teach me not to sin against Him.

Rather He, my Father God, speaks to my heart. He allows me to run headlong in my sin because I refuse to listen to His Spirit and I will suffer worse consequences than a good butt whopping for not walking in and with Him. But He is always teaching me to be more like Him. Like Isaac in this story, it is easier for the both of us to listen to Him. My point in this brief interlude is that many of us take that one Word of God as a standard to live or raise our children by and yet neglect many that are far more important.

Exodus 34:11 reads, "Obey what I command you today." How about *John 14:15* when Jesus speaks, *"If you love Me, keep My commands"*? There are plenty of others, but the final one for this teaching is *John 14:16–24 (NIV)*.

> *And I will ask The Father, and He will give you another advocate to help you and be with you forever—The Spirit of truth. The world cannot accept Him, because it neither sees Him nor knows Him. But you know Him, for He lives with you and will be in you. I will not leave you as orphans; I will come to you. Before long, the world will not see Me anymore,*

but you will see Me. Because I live, you also will live. On that day you will realize that I am in My Father, and you are in me, and I am in you. <u>Whoever has My commands and keeps them is the one who loves Me</u>. Anyone who loves Me will be loved by My Father, and I too will love them and show myself to them.

Then Judas (not Judas Iscariot) said, "But, Lord, why do you intend to show Yourself to us and not to the world?"

Jesus replied, "Anyone who loves Me will obey my teaching. My Father will love them, and we will come to them and make Our home with them. Anyone who does not love Me will not obey My teaching. <u>These Words you hear are not My own; they belong to The Father who sent Me.</u>"

My point in all of that is not just to quote scriptures that I like, but to show that the easier thing is to do the thing Jesus said to do, and not to plop our own children over our individual laps and paddle their young fannies to try to keep them on the straight and narrow. But the very scriptures that work on me, the individual, are for someone else to carry out because they take a great deal of work. To change my character from being David-dominated to being Jesus Christ-dominated takes a great deal of willpower, and surrender to a superior model, namely Christ.

But in those few verses, if we are doing that, God the Father, His Son, Jesus, and Holy Spirit will not only love us but make His home in us. I know that when I gave my heart to Jesus on the day of my salvation, He in turn gave me His heart, or His Spirit. So God does live in me, but if I give the Holy Spirit a room in the basement where I never have to see Him or hear from Him because I really do not want to be God's child, then I will not do the necessary things to change that which I know better than anyone is broken and can only be fixed by Him and Him alone.

Ok, back to the story. So I told my wife about the impasse with our son and went and took my son by the hand to fire him up for not listening to me.

His mom also loves him. (Although this sequence of events has never happened in reality, Isaac is a good listener, but I say who is good but God and at the same time who listens more attentively.) My wife of course came to his rescue and stated that instead of spanking him, she would take his place. And if anyone were going to be punished, she would stand in for her very own son. Somehow my DNA part in his creation, much like our own heavenly Father's part in our creation, has been forgotten or relieved of duty by someone's opinion and spoken word.

Well, I've never struck my wife because I not only have to live with her and I love her, but she is my very own best friend. Plus, we are peers, and she too is a child of God. And if I were to speak to her even if she did not really agree with me, at the very least she would see the point and not try to upset the apple cart just to see how many apples gravity would make hit the ground.

Now I have a dilemma: what to do? My son was the only one who seemed happy because he was off the hook. And I thought, *Well, if he saw me spanking his own mother because of the crime he himself committed, then I would never have to tell him not to do said crime or any crime involving punishment again because I know that Isaac loves his mom.*

But do I lay my wife across my lap to tan her behind? I in no way wanted to spank her or him for that matter? But if my son were to know that there are real consequences and no tiny love taps were going to take place when you don't listen to my instructions, then the sterner stuff was what would be administered to him, to teach him that a parents' love entreaty was actually easier to hear. And so, he should listen attentively to his old man.

Man, I should let them both slide. It would be so much easier for me not to do anything. So my thoughts and prayers were in a jumble. I adore my wife and did not want to spank her. I love my son and needed to spank him because he just did not understand the urgency of this life lesson and there are impacts now for lessons that I was going to tell or teach him that have future benefits. And if he ignored them, then he would not ever become an actual mature adult because if you ignore the right things to do, then you will most certainly accept the incorrect things. So one seed or another was being planted within him.

So I saw—and I was saying to myself—that he would eventually learn all of these schoolings, but then I would be in agreement with a world system that was not involved in the lives of their children. The result was, as is the current state with many children, that our lives are lived in general chaos, without regard for others unless it fits nicely with our own values of what I think is right or wrong without evidence. My only concern was really just about me, which is basic immaturity.

So reluctantly, which by the way is far more than intellectual reluctance but is that my heart and soul are unwilling, I chose to spank my wife, knowing how much my son deeply cares for his mom. I figure that if any lesson is going to have import on him, then he will learn not to disregard the words of his very own father who loves him and desires his best, no matter the circumstances.

The day I've set aside for this event had arrived. I took my son and my wife. I explained to my son that his mom was going to be punished because of his very own rebellion against what I plainly told him not to do and that such actions always had a consequence. And for this act of not even wanting to listen, a spanking was now going to be administered.

Now Isaac was repentant. He most likely never believed that I would take this lesson to this extreme level. I have no doubt that he was relieved, but you can see that he was still not getting the fact that his own actions—from the first stone thrown to the last words spoken—had led to this and that no one wanted to walk it out.

My wife is not my enemy. Whenever we have issues, we discuss them and work them out, but as I said earlier, I have never whooped my wife's behind, as I was going to do so now and not to teach her but rather to school him. Because of my son, my heart's delight was incapable of taking on his own punishment. He was still in denial that what was taking place was nothing less than an overzealous and chastisement-loving father. And if he had only obeyed me in the first place, none of this had to have happened.

So now I spanked my wife, whom I love with my whole heart. I keep saying that, but I do. I did not really want to punish my son, but some things needed to be understood within oneself. When you, Bug, play with fire, you will get burned. So his mom was currently taking the heat in full.

Finally done was done, and now we were all crying, my wife for obvious reasons. She might thoroughly understand my actions, but understanding does not make it feel any better. My son was crying because his mom was crying and had suffered on his account. She was an innocent loved one who just took a whopping on his behalf, and I was convinced that I would never have to punish anything ever again. This was so hard to do that I do not want anyone anywhere to have to be punished at all, for not believing that every crime has a punishment. We were all three of us telling each other that we are sorry and that it will never, ever happen again. Amen!

Whew! I was as happy as can be that the lesson has been learned.

Then a short period of time passed, like a few weeks, and I was heading out of my front door for work one afternoon. I heard the ping of rocks hitting my front window. What!! I peeked outside through the curtains and saw my own son standing there with Tyson, one of the other kids from school, chucking rocks from the driveway at the very same window Isaac was earlier told not to throw stones at. He was now totally disregarding his own mother, who took his punishment for him.

Aahhh! was the very thought that rang loudly within my mind. I put my Star Wars lunch box down on the couch and popped open the front door to look my own flesh and blood in the eyes. So now his judgment and the consequences had arrived, and all of that led me to my version of ***John 3:16–21 (NIV)***.

> *For God so loved* [agapao, the verb of agape or to have charity without regard for one self] *the world that He gave His one and only Son, that whoever believes in Him would not perish but would have eternal life,* without punishment. *For God did not send His Son into the world to condemn* or punish the world, *but to save the world through Him. Whoever continuously believes, without stopping, in His atoning sacrifice for sins is not condemned or punished, but whoever does not believe stands condemned already because they have not believed in the name and actions of God's one and only Son. This is the verdict,* so there is judgement for actions taken: *Light [Jesus] has come into the world, but individuals loved* [Agapao once again, so loved to give themselves to] *darkness instead of light because their deeds were evil. All those who do evil hate the light [Jesus] and will not come into the light for fear that their deeds outside of the light will be exposed and shown for what their actions are. But those who live by the truth come readily into the light so that it may be plainly seen* [by everyone everywhere]. *That what they have done has been done in the sight of God.*

F: Creation or Evolution

The nature of Christ's existence is mysterious, I admit; but this mystery meets the wants of man. Reject it and the world is an inexplicable riddle; believe it, and the history of our race is satisfactorily explained.

—Napoleon Bonaparte

My son Isaac asked me one day, "What do you think about creation and evolution?"

I knew without being told that his reason for the question was due to the fact that he has a specific ministry with children and that subject would or has come up on occasion. I was just about to go into a long discussion concerning the subject matter when the Holy Spirit gave me the following.

I told Isaac, "Hey, I am sixty-one years old at the time of that conversation, and to be honest, within those sixty-one years, I cannot truthfully account for my own history, my own life. I interpret events through the filter of my own life experiences. If you were to ask me what I ate yesterday for dinner, I could tell you the highlights but would certainly not mention my picking at my teeth to remove an unwanted sliver of meat that got stuck in a molar. I was thinking about one of the caesars, Claudius, born 10 AD, who was a historian but had a couple of disabilities, one being clubfooted and the other a deviated septum, but he seldom went out to collect data for his histories, which was physically demanding. But the caesars were supposed to be related to the gods, so his physical appearance could cause some doubt on a lucrative enterprise called religion, in Rome. So Claudius instead had individuals collect his data for him. This caesar was curious about all the talk he had heard about Jesus, but instead of finding out on his own, he sent one of his soldiers or senators to find out and was given a disparaging report, which in turn affected both his natural and eternal life, no doubt."

I also thought as further proof about the above statement that one of my younger brothers had passed away. While attending his funeral, I told the story about something that had happened while my brother, our mutual friend, Timmy, and I were playing army outside when we were young children. There was the punch line about something my brother had said about how to make quicksand, so according to my brother Barry, all we needed to do was to take some mud, water, and quicksand and blend them together. And voilà, quicksand.

I told my son that if his Uncle Barry were currently present, he most likely would have a different interpretation of the event. Timmy would also because each of us sees the event happening only to us. I told Isaac that I can barely account for sixty-one years that I have lived on this planet. To me, there is no valid history before 1955, and never mind the history that others through their own experiences or reasoning are telling me how this world got to be where it is.

But there is always a *"but"*. God is always true. I do not think or hope that God is always true, but I know that He is true because salvation is true. Just ask anyone who has been saved. Jesus will not lie because He is completely full or whole. We usually lie to either cover something up about our own weakness or to build ourselves up, basically because of our own insecurities. Our Lord God did not have angry godparents who sent our Lord off to bed without His god-dinner; nor was He, the Holy One, ever given a whoppin' for something He had not done or done wrong. Even the cross was our own punishment. It was certainly not for anything that Jesus did or did not do, other than to obey His Father in everything put before Him. He is the "I Am," the "I Am Fully That I Am." God is basically stating that, 'I am fully and completely whole and true.'

With or without us, He is fully God alone. There are no others hanging out in the vast real estate of the universe or various dimensions. All those others that we humans want so desperately to believe in are created beings, whether in our imaginations or other individual myths. They had a beginning and will eventually have an end (out of the presence of the One True God).

In my own history, I wanted more than many to believe that the others essentially existed, but once I myself met the Lord through my own salvation, there is nothing that comes remotely close to Him. The bonus that I see is that God wants and desires to dwell in fellowship with me.

To say that God is good totally underscores the magnitude of His love and grace to me. I did not believe at all in our Lord Jesus. I had heard about God in church. To me He was a god, a universal consciousness that was just aware of either life in general or chuckling over the actual big bang theory science (and not sitcom).

So as I told my son, if the Word of God states that God instead created the world in six seconds rather than six days, then six seconds is exactly the time frame it would have been for God to command, to issue a royal decree, or to speak it all into existence. Genesis says that there was evening and there was morning. The first day, then the second, and so on. It does not say God days of a thousand years apiece, but there was evening and morning, a day.

One note though on these statements is that the Lord created the planets on the fourth day, so there were three other days without a rising or setting sun and moon. And if I just happen to be looking out of the window and see a T-Rex munching on a cow in the parking lot at our church, the cow having been taken from someone's ranch right in front of me, then I am still going to believe God. And I most assuredly was not there in Eden, but I do know that God is always and will always be and He is positively, absolutely true.

Now Scripture states in *1 Corinthians 2:14* that the person without the Spirit does not accept the things of the Spirit but rather considers them to be foolishness. But to me, Scripture even proves itself to be true from a scientific venue and not to be relied on by faith alone.

Please don't misunderstand me. Faith is essential to our walk with the Lord, but there is plenty of evidence for a completely scientific approach to creation. Basically I could debate with the worldly person what God has to say concerning His creation. Since I am a Christian and when I now think about evolution, that theory of evolution seems more like science fiction than probable reality. I also must hand it to Chuck Darwin for the steps he took to come up with the theory in the first place. So please bear with this one portion of an argument against evolution.

I am a single-celled organism, basically protoplasm that by its own will replicates and develops into higher organisms without the hand of God. So protoplasm motivates itself to a godlike state by seeing and heading toward a greater goal than the one it currently exists within. All of this is done not due to overcrowding or that everyone else living in that body of water is looking at me as a hors d'oeuvre.

Over long periods of time, the protoplasm gets bored with its existence and becomes different types of aquatic life. I know I am really simplifying the process, but it would take a book to write this all out. Since I cannot replicate myself in the exact same manner, there are mutations. So one day I am sitting in a body of water with my other mutations, and I happen to pop my viewing apparatus out of the murky depths and see a thing called land, which is not covered in water, and my natural inclination is to explore it. I drag myself up and onto the shore, and after struggling for about five minutes to check out this new environment, I die. As an aquatic being, I have mutated breathing equipment called gills to extract oxygen out of the water to live, eat, and breathe in.

Now one of my offspring, having the same explorer gene that I possess, sees my dried-up corpse on the beach and wonders if it will have better luck. It follows suit and so on and so on until this idiot offspring decides to go from gills to lungs, which only takes a few more million years of corpses on that or other beaches, and how do you figure out you need lungs when you don't have a model of a lung?

Now just to believe in that very simple cycle of events takes more belief than every Christian ever born who has said that Jesus Christ is the actual Son of the living God. Really?! And the above does not even bring DNA into the discussion and how only compatible beings can produce offspring after their preliminary types. Eagles are not going to mate with worms so it can sit on a riverbank dangling its talons in the water to catch a salmon. But all this wonder that we call life on this Planet Earth is amazing.

For me to depend on a cheap and unproven philosophy is science fiction. But at one time, well over forty years ago, if you had asked me about evolution, I would have said, "Sure, it's true. What's not to believe because better minds than my own have already figured it out?" I tend to be lazy like that.

But since we are Christians, we can rely solely on His perfect Word to guide us. *Psalms 33:4–9, 102:25–28, 104; Proverbs 3:19–20, 8:23;* and *Isaiah 40:21–22, 41:4, 26* all say that the Lord is setting up from the beginning.

Isaiah 42:1–7 speaks of Messiah and what He produces. *Isaiah 66:1–2* says that as creation began, due to sin is how it will end.

Jeremiah 4:23 and *Job 33:4 (NIV)* speaks, *"The Spirit of God has made me; the Breath of the Almighty gives me life."* **John 1:1–5, Isaiah 55:11, Revelation 19:12–13, Hebrew 4:12–13**, and **Genesis 1:1–8** all say that Jesus is the Word of God, our Father.

The Holy Spirit hovered or moved over the face of the deep. *Rachaph (rä·khaf')* means "to be moved, affected, especially with the feeling of tender love, hence to cherish." "Moved over the face of the deep" means to brood over young ones, to cherish young (as an eagle). **Deuteronomy 32:11** figuratively means "used of the Spirit of God," who brooded over the shapeless mass of the earth, cherishing and vivifying it (or bringing life to it or animating the earth). That description from Strong's Concordance is very powerful to me. It is equal to a parent who keeps a close loving watch over his or her newborn child.

Genesis 3:8–10 states that *God walked with Adam and Eve in the cool of the day.* In **John 1:35–42**, Jesus is walking in the cool of the day with man once again.

G: The Sacrifice

I began to ponder one day about those ancient days well before the Lord's birth, as well as my own, when the ancient Hebrews required offering an animal as a substitute for the individual's sins against God and man. I thought, *What if the animal could respond and was also cognizant as to what was about to take place?*

So in the short conversation below, I used a bull as the animal just because it fits a bit better as a character choice.

So the story is one man, pretty much me, and one sacrificial bull. The one man is standing before the tabernacle with his hands placed reluctantly on the head of the sacrificial bull. The Levite is standing behind the bull's right shoulder with his flint knife poised to hopefully put a quick end to this stand-in for this man's sins against God.

A man says, "Adonai God, please forgive me for the sins I've committed against You and against Your holy name."

A bull looks up at the man with its dark, sad cow eyes seemingly unaware. The Levite brings the knife close to the bull's jugular.

"Wait a minute. What's going on here?"

A man looks at the bull, astonished. "I'm … I'm repenting for my sins against God and offering you as a sacrifice; basically you are my stand-in, my substitute."

A bull replies, "Un-huh … And why am I standing in for you? What did you do that was so bad that you cannot take care of your own sins, and what did I do that was so good that I can stand in for you? Man."

A man says, "Me!? Well, I've sinned against God, and it is our law that without the shedding of blood, there can be no forgiveness of that debt to God, so …" He points at the bull. "You are paying the penalty of that offense."

"By jabbing me with a knife! Wait just wait a moment here. The other day while you had me plowing your field, I defecated on your wheat. So why don't you just throw yourself up here on my horns and let me gore you a few times, and we'll call the whole thing shalom for shalom."

"It doesn't work that way, bull."

The bull laughs. "I bet! Look, I see many animals being offered up, a couple of lambs, and you can't miss the sound of those kids caterwauling all over the place. What's up with that? Different sins require different species. What if you have a great big sin? Do you drag in one of those elephants or a whale?"

"Yes and no, bull. There are different types of offerings for different things, like sin is usually a spotless lamb or yourself. There are Thanksgiving, praise offerings, and free will offerings, but it is always the best of what I have, what I own, basically what is mine."

"Look, those lambs are pretty young, along with those kids. They're barely out of the womb. Why in the world should they be asked to take on your own sin against God? What did they ever do to the Creator?"

"That's just it. They did not do anything. I did, but if we humans were to be held responsible for our own sins, then we would all be dead because we have all sinned against God and so deserve the just punishment. After all God is holy."

"So what do you think? That this world would be worse off without you? Hey, let me inform you this whole planet would be better off without you. Ask any one of those animals that is standing in for you. Ask me! Those are babies over there, and I haven't been around too long myself!"

A man retorts, "Like I said, we offer our best. Those without blemish, please remember the shedding of blood is necessary."

"Well, how about we do this, man? Just take that knife and jab me in the hindquarters a couple of times and take about a pint of this precious blood you say you need. How would that suit you?"

"Sorry, bull, but no, it is death. That is the penalty of my sin."

"So then for you humans, all sin naturally leads to death, and as you just said, all men sin. So it is not the shedding of blood, but rather the shedding of a life for the forgiveness of sins and more so my life. It seems a little steep to me. You, man, sinned against the Creator. So you, man, should be the one to pay the penalty, wouldn't you say?"

"That sounds good but cannot work since each and every man can acknowledge that he sins. And yes, I'm afraid so, bull. It is a life that is required. You see, He ..." The man and Levite look heavenward. "Is a Holy God. What could I possibly offer that is equal to His truth and His holiness? So what I understand—but I am no expert—is that something personal and belonging to me is the requirement to pay for my actions against the Lord God, which happens today to be you."

"Well, for me I would change the rules, and I would start with your own life. Shoot, I didn't sin against the Creator." The bull then laughs. "And you have the nerve to say 'I'm afraid so.' Oohh, man, you guys are really messed up. So I do this, and it takes care of you for life. My life for your life?"

"Sorry but no. I will have to do this again next year."

The bull looks incredulous. "Next year, how old are you? Twenty-five? Thirty? How many more times do you think you'll be doing this?"

"Who knows, bull? Ten, thirty, maybe forty more times. It depends if we encounter those Philistines again. Drought, war, pestilence, or my wife."

The bull yells, "Are you crazy? If this thing you do catches on and your kind continues to multiply like you do and to sin like you do, then there won't be any animals left on the entire planet to stand in for you. Don't you think that it would be better if you took care of your own business instead of me and mine? After all you are man. You're supposed to oversee this world. Wasn't it your dad, Adam, and his wife, Eve, who named us? Listen, if I were you, I would just stop sinning. You would be happy; the Creator would be happy. And I'll tell you what. I too would be extremely happy! Just say no! Come on, man. Give me a break!"

"Bull, if I could stop, I would, but I've tried and can't."

The bull tells him, "Just stop! Hey, wait a minute. How come that man over there has a turtledove? I love those turtledoves. They are just some cute little birds. Ahhh, no. I didn't need to see that! Its neck was just broken. I mean, that was a turtledove. They're just so sweet, tiny, and precious!"

The man says, "We use pigeons also." He states this with a slight smile.

The bull answers, "Well, pigeons I can understand. As a matter of fact, you can let all of us go and only use pigeons. I hate those little vermin. They keep me awake at night cooing all over the place and messing up my stall, and they multiply like your race, nasty creatures." As the bull extends his neck trying to imitate a pigeon, he is perforated by the knife. "Owww! Whoa! Wait a minute there, padre. Let's not get carried away!"

"Bull, that was your own fault. You can't blame this Levite because you stuck your own neck out!"

"Perhaps you should try it, man! Why don't you offer up one of your own children? How about your favorite child? Your heir? I bet you'd stop sinning then!"

"That is not practical, bull. I am following the law. We only bring our best. For some, a pigeon is all that can be afforded. Others like me …" he says with some pride, "can bring more to the altar, the best we have."

"I'm the best you had. Man, that's not true. You have about five other bulls that are in much better shape than I am—younger, healthier, and not better looking. But what can I say?"

The man tries to hush the bull by quickly placing his hand into the bull's mouth, grabbing the bull's tongue. "Poor bull, it is so afraid he is having delusions. Of course you're the best that I have bull, none better."

"Mffuulffl muffluulll mammmmfllullmm. Patooy, man! Those are some nasty-tasting digits you got there! Don't you ever wash those things? They smell like cabbage."

The Levite looks over at a sundial, indicating with his eyes that they should get a move on. "Ok, bull, we haven't got all day. Let's get this sacrifice over with. I gotta get home. I have things to do. Gotta get some mud up on my roof."

"Yo, wait up, man. You got time. I'm actually the one that doesn't have any! You know that's half the problem with you human beings: you are always thinking about yourself, never looking ahead or back from whence you came and never in the present. How in the name of the Creator do you individuals manage to survive?"

"Remember last week in the stall when you were talking to the rabbi about the Messiah. Didn't the rabbi say that He, the Messiah, would rule your nation righteously?"

"Yes, bull, but what does that have to do with you? The Messiah will be the greatest king of Israel. All other nations will be subject to Him and to this land. I cannot wait for that great day to arrive." The man nods his head at the Levite with "what a good boy am I" expression on his mug.

A bull says, "Well, if this Messiah is so great, won't He do away with all of these sacrifices? Really?! If you are going to be set up as the people of the Creator, wouldn't sin against God be done away with? How else can you say you are a better people if you are still the same as everyone else and you're continuously running around and sinning against God? What good is a great Messiah, if you are still just a man?"

A man replies, "The rabbi was saying something like that, but it does not seem correct to me because if the Messiah sets up the new kingdom, then how do we get reconciled to God? The only way that can be is if the Messiah somehow finds an acceptable sacrifice once and for all or once and for all we stop sinning against God. The way I read it, the Messiah is going to reign for quite a while."

A bull retorts, "Well, what if this Messiah gives himself as the sacrifice instead of, let's say, me?"

A man says, "Yes, that sounds good in theory, but if He does, then how can he also reign as king over the nations? After all, dead is dead."

A bull answers, "Hey, listen. Adam died, and he really was a great man, along with Noah, Moses, and Enoch. Well, no one seems to know about Enoch and your progenitor, Abraham, and they all kicked. So I figure if your Messiah is expected to hang around for a while, then He can only die once. If God finds no fault with His Chosen One, then for sure He cannot die a second time. Now that is a great Messiah!"

A man states, "That is a pretty good stretch, to die and then be raised back up from the dead. How do you think that is supposed to actually happen?"

A bull replies, "Well, man, how often do you have a conversation with your livestock? If the Creator wants it and it does not dishonor Him, I'm quite sure He can bring His Messiah for your people back from the dead. After all, He is the God of all creation. Doesn't He bring life to everything?"

"It sounds like a good plan, but that is for tomorrow. Today I am still obligated to the law."

The bull speaks rather quickly. "If the Messiah fulfills the law, forbearing man's debt to the Creator, then the shedding of blood or a life will no longer be needed. From everything that I've heard tell, He should be the one to take care of all of that. And if that is true, then believing the Creator will send His Chosen One to fulfill the law or that the law at some point will be fulfilled with no more requirements, namely me, what is the need for a sacrifice today? Rather believe today in your Messiah, in the Creator's provision!"

The man stands there, tapping his index finger against his front teeth. The priest strokes his beard. Both are in deep thought.

"If the Messiah fulfills the law, what then?"

A bull answers, "Emmm, why don't you believe now? After all, He is the special anointed one."

The bull then peeks at the two contemplating individuals as it slowly and as silently as possible walks away wondering if he can make it out of the courtyard without anyone spotting him?

"Forty more feet and then I run like mad. Just thirty more feet and run!"

H : Why and Who Has Authority

Another thought is authority in the life of the believer and that the wonder of salvation brought by the very life of Almighty God. Our authority in Jesus Christ is vast since we not only represent Him individually as God's ambassadors *(2 Cor. 5:20, 14–21)* here in the physical realm, but more so because we the church have been transferred into Christ and basically raised from the dead to live for God.

The Father's purpose in our individual and daily lives *(Romans 6)* speaks to this for me. Man, I feel like Paul with a runaway sentence that never seems to stop. He—or better yet, They, the Father, His Son, Jesus, and the Holy Spirit—is showing forth who God for really is. With that, it should now be completely understandable what type of authority we have. *Philippians 4:13 (NIV)* says, *"I can do all things thru Jesus Christ who strengthens me."*

All things, whether in the spiritual or the physical world, have been placed under the feet of our Lord and King, Jesus Christ, and we should know this, not just in our intellects but in our hearts or more to the point through our experiences with Him. *Ephesians 1:22–23 (NIV)* reads, *"And God placed all things under His feet and appointed Him to be head over everything for the Church, which is His body, the fullness of Him who fills everything in every way."*

Each one of us has read it, heard it, and sung it, but have we walked that out? For a new Christian, those steps should be tentative only because you are growing. No parent who now has his mind working correctly would ask his or her two-year-old child to run the Boston Marathon. It would just be ridiculous.

On that same path, if you have been a Christian who has been in a constant state of growth and maturity in the purpose of God, through the revelation of Jesus Christ, then any race metaphorically should be right up your alley. And you, the individual, should be eagerly showing God's wonder to the world around you. I mean, really the only living God loves you and, as a bonus, has spiritually asked you to join Him, the living God, in His very worthy endeavor called life and more so your life!

When I was much younger in Christ, I used to daily put on the armor of God found in *Ephesians 6*: shield of faith, breastplate of righteousness, feet shod with the gospel of peace, the belt of Truth, and so on. I would put these on, mentally thinking about what each was.

But what the Holy Spirit had me realize is that the armor of God is the blood of Jesus Christ, which covers me entirely. There is no power or authority greater than the life blood of God for His redeemed. There is no greater truth anywhere than His life's blood. Now the onus has been placed on me once again because if I am in fellowship with the Lord, then I am also constantly aware of His love and life given on the cross for me.

So in effect, I am aware of His blood and what His protection means. It is not just to keep the enemy's fiery darts from wounding me, but it is for my mind and heart to be in harmony with Him. So in knowing that truth, I am fully equipped to take on any battle, be it physical or spiritual. Since His life is within His blood, then He also must be the one who is in control. If I am in control, then I am lost before I even begin.

You can see that is where the difference lies. If I think because I am putting on the armor of God, then I am equally equipped for the battle, but if I know that anyone who is saved knows that His life's blood was given for me to save me from death, then the truth is greater than the thought. Even if I physically get slaughtered in a war, I, even in that battle, can have full confidence in Him. I can rejoice because I know that scripture from **Romans 8:28 (NIV)** states, *"All things work together for good for those who love The Lord and are called according to His purpose."*

It's not my purpose, but according to the desires of His heart and His purpose, I then delight in His purpose because our relationship is growing. The more I know Him, the more goodness I see being poured into my life from His very own Spirit. So now I in faith walk out the absurd to my human senses because no matter what He has asked, I am able to do it. Since trust has been developed in our lives, relationship has joined together by heredity ties, namely His very own blood. But that whole statement is based on my knowing Him because if I do not know Him, then how in the world am I supposed to believe Him? Jesus may be the Truth, but if I have no faith in that statement, then no matter what He asks of me, I will invariably have doubt and therefore question Him on whose authority is better for my life. Logically it would be mine since I am the one occupying this body. But in my spirit, it is Him, and that is called faith. I trust Him far more than I trust myself.

Authority is not only to battle satan and his band of demons, but it is authority in every aspect of life. Authority is to be in your household and over your family; authority is in the student's life in any academic or social setting and any of his day-to-day activities with peers. There is also the authority you have in your job with coworkers and those who are in positions of authority over you.

Who has more authority over your life: Almighty God or the individual who hands you your paycheck? We are to submit to God's holy and perfect authority because we know Him to be right, but as His very children, we are to take full authority in and through Him, along with the Holy Spirit's guidance in Jesus Christ. One thing on this authority is that it should be poured forth in love and in me the individual with humbleness or humility.

When I read Scripture, I see no one anywhere who is as humble as God, but don't get freaked out with thinking God is a mouse or has no nerve. But because God is so completely whole and without flaw, He can be humble, even if He is all powerful, and not be concerned with being called on it. Basically God states, "I Am exactly as I Am, and I Am making no apologies."

Now we, as belonging to Jesus, can never get around that, being humble and working in *agape* love. I as well as you need authority over our family. That's well and good, but begin it all in the love that God has drenched your life in. Greater is He that is in me than he that is in the world. Another statement for authority that through these lessons has been quoted often, just a few paragraphs ago, is the truth from **Romans 8:28 (NIV)**, but to just drill it into you, *"And we know that in all things God works for the Good of those who Love Him, who have been Called according to His Purpose."*

Well then, what am I to do with that? The easiest thing is to believe what God, who will never lie, has said. It takes maturity to realize that I have been called to maturity and to listen to what the Holy Spirit is saying within me. I am hardly bragging about my own maturity. I have a long, long way to go, but the more adept we become at walking out that purpose, the more responsibility the Lord will give to us. Does this maturity mean that I am going to be another Billy Graham or world-renowned individual on Christian radio or television or have a million podcasts to my credit? I hope that whatever the Lord has called me—and you too—that we do it all in the will of the Father, seeking His guidance. In that respect, you cannot go wrong, and your purpose will be to see Him glorified, just as it was for Jesus, His Son.

In the New Testament, Paul is one of the few who was born again with a bang and just kept on going like the Energizer Bunny. But Paul was met where he was at. While still being Saul, he was steadfast in the persecution of the Christian church, which in turn are individuals who make up our Lord Jesus's physical body here on this earth. As His bride, we are showing humanity who our Husband is. But Saul saw the possibility that the very works of God Almighty were trying to be destroyed, with the establishment of this thing called Christianity.

Once Saul became Paul, he hit the ground running. The early Pauline epistles have Paul talking about the rapture occurring, but later toward the end of his life and ministry, all he says is that "I might know Christ better." Now that is maturity. We are also going to be met where we are at. If we do not strive to move forward in the Lord's intention for us, we will not be pushed forward by Him. If I love Him, then I will fear bringing the living God down to my level, as a man just made of earth. When I look at Jesus, I see that He came to earth to show us who God in all certainty is.

All of the Lord's actions showed me that He wanted us to know Him, not to know about Him, which for me is religion, but rather that I know Him as He is. If the Lord God just changed me into the completed process, then the fundamental law of free will, such as Adam and Eve who had a choice to obey God or not, is the same as it is today. We will be taught along the way, and if the lesson always seems to be the same, then we can be sure we are not getting that lesson.

Once an item for your betterment has been served up to you and you grow, then another is brought to the surface. This is to wear out the earthly individual, which is to be replaced by a more fruitful one, which is heavenly according to the pattern for the human being, and He is Jesus, God's one and only being replicated within us. You have the Holy Spirit living in you, hand in hand to accomplish the task that God assigns to those He trusts. **Galatians 5:16 (NIV)** says, *"So I say, live by the Spirit, and you will not gratify the desires of the sinful nature."*

Each one of us should make that our heart's cry, "to live by the Spirit." That is who you are. The Holy Spirit is the means that had you being born again: you by a trust in God that Jesus actually did die to save you and me from eternal separation from His Father and now the Holy He who has become our Father as well.

I said this in an earlier lesson that the Holy Spirit has unlimited access to God continuously. Therefore, maturity is trusting that which cannot be seen, but is known by having first trusted, believed, or apprehended whatever the word that resonates with you, but taking a hold of God through faith that He is always true and will not do anything that is against your development as His very own child. That is more than my just believing Him, but the reality is that I put into action in my life the words that God has spoken to me and His church. If Scripture aligns with what has been requested and since I have it, I can ask the Author to see within Scripture the example to what I must do. The Gospels give us ample evidence of how our Lord dealt with difficult situations, as do the entirety of Scripture.

John 8:3–11 is one that I like. You can read it, but basically the authorities on the law came to Jesus to condemn a woman caught in sexual activity and the male for not being her husband. It was a trap for Jesus. If He chose mercy, then He was denying the validity of the law. If He stood for the law and the woman was stoned to death, then He was okaying murder. I love these words of Jesus, *"Whoever is without sin, then let him throw the first stone."*

The Lord's Word totally diffused their intent. Jesus did not call the mob, sinners, in league with satan and say that they were going to receive exactly what they gave. Instead He spoke to their hearts and told them the truth, a truth that we are all aware of. Whoever is without sin, you be the one to cast the first stone. From the oldest to the youngest, they all walked away.

That is how maturity works. We are meant to be mature, acting in full authority in God's will, not just to be in a church hearing the Word delivered on Sunday and other days of the week, or to be in fellowship with brothers and sisters in the Lord. Those things are excellent, but that is still being a child if you are on the receiving end of everything gifted by God. Consider yourself still on the breast, not having yet been weaned.

The church has already been saved. It is God shown to the world and to those who have yet to be saved, which is the point. Our pastors speak often on this point that the church should be touching our community and your own neighborhood. Once you do, you will see that the outreach of God has a much further reach than you thought possible, being directed by the Holy Spirit, and that is a must.

What do you need for maturity? That last statement says it, so listening to the Spirit within you and knowing that it is not about you. It is about Jesus Christ. Start by taking those very small steps, making sure that the stones in the God lesson above with the woman caught in sin have been dropped or disposed of and begin to mature. We are then capable of taking the larger strides in God's perfect will. Of course, study, read, and get into your Bible, the road map to God's heart. And pray, and when praying, listen, be still, and wait on God for direction. If the Holy Spirit has unrestricted access to God and the Holy Spirit lives inside of you, then listening to Him is just a matter of common sense.

I have two completely different testimonies on taking authority, although there have been many times in my life where that has been necessary, and there have been many times where I did not take authority and allowed by noninvolvement another authority to have dominion. So maybe there are three testimonies, two positive and a negative.

The first was when I had just gotten married. I had no skills in marriage. I grew up in a household where my mother was the only parent, so I had no male role model. I also spent the majority of my youth existing on welfare, so I never saw my mom keep a checkbook. As a matter of fact, the only checking account we ever had was when as a child, we brought our nickels into school and they put them in an account for us, called Bank Book Day. But as I got older, I found that my mom had emptied those accounts of the few bucks that were saved up.

When I got married, Gisele was extremely capable of taking care of our household. She is great at keeping the books and almost anything that came up, and as newlyweds, since I did not have those financial skills, I let her do them. Gisele never complained and always took care of our business. I found though that I was resenting her, but when I questioned myself on why I was resenting her, I had absolutely no earthly reason to. I knew that I loved everything about her. She was just a master at keeping everything on track.

As an adult, the first time I went grocery shopping alone and had to sign a check, I and it were a blank. I stood in line staring at the checkbook, wondering how to fill out the boxes on the check correctly, which I eventually did with some embarrassment, having to ask the cashier for assistance. Since I was still having problems with resentment toward my wife without a verifiable reason, I determined to change myself, which is always the harder action. But I began to take authority in the household on decisions not in anger or power, the "I'm bigger and stronger than you," which is how I grew up. But I just started to share in the overall decision-making for our lives, and that unwanted resentment vanished.

Gisele still controls the books and is still making most of the decisions for the house, but we discuss those things at various times. What I resented without even knowing why was that I was not being the man, even though I had no model in the core of me on what a man should be like. But as I grow in relationship with Him, I also grow into the man that I see clearly in the Gospels.

So what that showed me was that it is not only a physical principle but also a spiritual one. I was aware that I wasn't aware. A few years after that, my mother in-law, Gloria, told me that when I did start to take authority in our household, she and Gisele were very happy because they both knew that needed to be done, but the decision had to be my own and not something that was told to me that I must do. Romans 8:28 once again.

I just want to say, "I thank You, Lord. It is Him alone that I need, Him alone I praise, and Him alone who is my all in all. It is You, Lord!" Thank You, Lord, my God.

The second is taking authority over a demonic principality, and the third would be associated with that. But I was driving to work one morning, somewhere back in time around 2004. I was driving on Texas Highway 32, heading for Austin and talking to the Lord early in the morning as I drove along and praying that He remove a principality that I knew was in the Bay Area where we used to live on the coast.

While we lived there, I was not sure about principalities because I was directly in it, and they like to keep you more concerned with the desires of day to day living than in my undoing of their affairs. Although there were many battles being fought, I do not need to list those since it is not relatable to this teaching because it will distract you from what the Lord is saying into events that have been used to teach me lessons.

Needless to say, my mind-set after moving to Texas became clear once I had been made more aware of the authority that I had been living under while going about my day to day in Half Moon Bay.

So I'm driving to work and asking the Lord to bust up that principality, and then I started to think about just how wonderful God in His love to me is. And instead of asking for this task to be accomplished though some means, like God slamming His fist down on Northern California, since it is 1,800 miles away, I just start praising God on His wonderful love and how He kept me and my family in His plan even while we were living in that negative spiritual influence.

I'm just driving along, praising God, singing Him hymns, and thanking our Lord for His patience with the likes of me around 6:00 a.m. The sun is not even up yet. As I'm turning onto Highway 12, the Holy Spirit tells me, "Now you break apart that principality."

And I did. I prayed for it to be demolished and broken apart. Authority is not only knowing who you are in God Almighty, but more so knowing who God is and what stands against His authority. God is completely able, to say the least, of taking down anything that stands against Him, but God is not the one attending school here on earth. We are.

A last note on this subject, but many of the items in these short stories are the result of the Lord teaching me how to live a life worthy of the call that the Holy Spirit has placed on me, which is according to Father God's will, which is true of every Christian. God fully knows what speaks to my heart since that is where He lives.

But we Christians, servants of Jesus Christ, must be active participants in His will. The more difficult the situations are for me, the better because the process shows me that God thinks I can do more or show Him better to a lost world or for a church that has settled for a mediocre life while awaiting eternity. It does not work that way. The life of Jesus on the cross is God's supreme example of what a Christian life should look like to every single being on this earth and all of the heavens combined.

So the life of Jesus is certainly not a worldly life because the world and its philosophies are under God's wrath. In *Jeremiah 4:22–26 (NIV)*, it reads,

"My people are fools; they do not know Me. They are senseless children; they have no understanding. They are skilled in doing evil; they know not how to do good." I looked at the earth, and it was formless and empty; and at the heavens, and their light was gone. (So this is the opposite of the creation or the creation being undone.) *I looked at the mountains and they were quaking; and the hills were swaying. I looked, and there were no people; every bird in the sky had flown away. I looked, and the fruitful land was a desert; all its towns lay in ruins before the Lord, before His fierce anger.*

So this world and its philosophies, intellectual thoughts, and plans for all our lives are not all they are cracked up to be. For me, if God is not involved in it, then what good can it be? But what I also see in Scripture is that God Himself so loved everyone and everything in this world that He gave us His very own Son, Jesus. So He is not all about revenge; rather He is all about us and knowing His heart. This fact shows me that no one is more vulnerable than God because He invites everyone to come into that heart relationship with Him, knowing at the same time that many will reject the offer of His extraordinary, stupefying, pure, and graciously good love.

I also know that the Holy Spirit of God is in each and every Christian's heart. The more He speaks to our hearts and the more we listen to His voice, the better able we are in hearing Him once He does speak. If we the Christian are listening, then the more like Jesus we become, and amazingly the more our very own personalities develop in God the Father's image and likeness. On the same note, the less we listen to the Holy Spirit, our paraclete who walks with us, an advocate who counsels me. Any lawyer on this planet may state that I am innocent, but I would personally have one who knows me and is able to tell me the right way to go and the wrong way to avoid.

In His counsel, I then have the relationship that began with our individual salvation, which the Lord God never wants to get tarnished since it is the temple He speaks to the world from. So if scriptures are read less, along with going to church and hearing and understanding the Word of God less, then more often than not, I will find all of it totally boring. I will then find fellowship, just another group of people to gossip about, basically making all of Jesus the Son of God's life worldly.

Sorry, but that is how the world works, self-absorbed and not God absorbed. Now is that every Christian except me? No, these are the very issues that I deal with, so I am not blaming but rather relating to what I see. God, because He loves us, shows us how to be free from slavery to sin. (**Romans 6** really addresses this.) Into the power of His Spirit placed within us for the purpose of revealing Jesus Christ as our Lord, King, and Savior.

Now the third is on not taking authority when you should. That same principality was initiated on the California coast by people, individuals whose goal it was to set up that demonic principality, individuals who think they can somehow make being on the losing side a success without the Lord being engaged in it.

We have a yearly event called the Pumpkin Festival in Half Moon Bay. Many artists come to sell their goods, music, clothes, art, and food. It takes place about the second week of October. One of the events is to have a Halloween parade for the kids. But at a point in time during the day coming down the center of Main Street would be about six or eight individuals, adults and children, in full skeleton body suits playing an American Indian melody on wooden instruments and dancing to those notes.

Now the hairs on the back of Gisele's and my own neck and arms would stand straight up. The Holy Spirit would get agitated, but I just would stand there and watch, thinking, *Who allows this?* Well, I was allowing it because in my logic I did not think that people would be doing something like this so brazenly right out in the open with thousands of people walking around.

But one of the things I have always known even before being saved was that almost all our actions here on the physical plane of existence have a spiritual result or reaction. We humans open spiritual doors every single day. Why do you think prayer is so important, along with having fellowship with the Holy Spirit and fellow believers? If everything were just on this physical plane, then what would be the point? If there were no spiritual point being made continuously, then God would just have us chasing fireflies, and the life of His beloved Son would have been foolish. All things tie together. We affect the worlds both physical, which we readily see, and the spiritual, which I have much difficulty in perceiving.

By the result of not doing anything, not going out onto Main Street, not marching around that group, and not praying in tongues or exalting the Lord and His all-powerful name like the walls of Jericho that Joshua was told by the Holy Spirit to march around, I allowed that principality to come into existence by acquiescence. I had far more authority than those dancing individuals.

I am a son of God, and the Lord had already used me before that time to take a demonic principality down that was in the Bay Area. So I knew what I could and should do. The only thing I can say on my own behalf was that I did not know until after I moved that is what was being done, but I did know at the time that it really upset the Holy Spirit.

I never once asked, "Lord, why is this bugging You, and what am I to do about it?"

That statement is really the point. "Lord, why is this bugging You, and what would You have me do about it with You?"

Now here is the central theme of what happens when we do not take authority in the purpose of God. My family and I started to drift from church fellowship. Bible reading just did not happen.

Not only my household but many were under the influence of those demonic authorities that same principality I let slide. Many—and I mean many—children and young adults lost their lives with suicide, car crashes, and the like from getting involved in drugs. Those same drugs were a very big problem in the small schools of those towns.

The general things of the world ruled, and they only lead to death. Now I know that there were other Christians living on the coast, but I also know that I could have done something then if only I had just asked. I take responsibility just because I was just a lump on a log instead of the offspring of Almighty God, which He Himself gave His life for me to be His. No action on this Christian's part allowed satan to act and to set up authorities, to support its stinking and lifeless kingdom.

Our maturity is acted upon in service to God; our authority is also acted upon in our service to God in and through Jesus Christ via the Holy Spirit. It is about you from God's perspective, and yet it should not be about you from your own perspective. It is really all about Jesus Christ. Everything we do should be moving away from ourselves to touch the world with the authority and the love of God that He placed within us to do His will.

The incentive program on serving God is far greater than anything we can possibly imagine. Within the scriptures, particularly **Solomon's Song of Songs 8:6 (NIV)**, it says, *"Place me like a seal over your heart, like a seal on your arm; for love is as strong as death, its jealousy unyielding as the grave. It burns like blazing fire, like a mighty flame."*

Also **John 15:15 (NIV)** reads, *"I no longer call you servants, because a servant does not know his master's business. Instead, I have called you friends, for everything that I learned from My Father I have made known to you."* Everything I learned came from my Father.

My last lengthy point on authority is from Genesis. The scriptures after this point have to do with taking authority and those who did take it or how we are instructed from Scripture on taking it. But from Genesis, the Lord God gave the man, Adam, and his wife, Eve, authority over creation. We, as His, are to submit ourselves to His will. So basically authority is over His creation by obedience.

Without obedience, then it is our will, like at the Tree of Knowledge, and that only leads to death. When I think that I have authority over everything, then I am veering far off course, and in truth I do not believe that. My own pets are a good example, but one of our dogs, Chulo, got into big trouble with my wife for going potty on her chair, which Chulo had done before and gotten into trouble for. Since the chair was new and had not been used for anything, I do not think it had even been sat in. But Chulo for some reason picked up the scent and made my wife's office chair a stopping point as his restroom.

I would also point out that about five feet away is the dogs' doggie door, which they can slip through into our backyard and go potty. I am also available to take Chulo and Lola out whenever they desire. Also since they are both small dogs, they have a puppy pad in our hallway just in case we are not at home to take them outside to go.

Now since Chulo belongs to us, my wife could have booted him in the crotch or picked him up and spanked his tail, and she was mad enough at him to do just those things. Instead she told him how disappointed in him she was, and she would not look at him, all of this being done in a high volume. I of course felt sorry for him. That was until the very next morning while reading my Bible on the couch in our living room that I saw Chulo prancing in from the den, happy-go-lucky. So I got up and went back to the den and saw that Chulo had once again sprinkled my wife's office chair.

I pointed at Chulo and told him to come here, which he did. I then told Chulo while he was looking into my eyes with his beautiful brown eyes that I was very disappointed in him and I was going to clean up his mess before his mom got out of bed. But I knew he was a dog, but I also knew that he understood me and if he ever again decided to put his mark on his mother's chair, he would be in big trouble with me.

Now all of that is to say this: God gave us authority over everything that has breath on this Planet Earth. That authority is for every person on this planet when I read Scripture. Yet because I am a human who has lived on this planet all my life, I do not believe that to be true. Now Chulo has not gone back to urinate on my wife's chair since I told him not to. So he heard me and accepts what I have declared. Now the reason is that Chulo and I have a relationship, and I believe I have in love authority over him.

But when I step outside my front door and see some birds flying around, I do not think of calling one of them over and asking it to sing me a song. I just do not believe it is possible. But by my own mind-set, I deny what the Lord has spoken over humanity. It is not God's will for me that I should disbelieve Him. If He said it, then it is true. But in my heart, do I believe that if one day that I am out walking in some deep woods and come across a momma bear with her cub and I tell her that I mean her nor her cub any harm in any way that she will prance away and not slash me to shreds because I am much to close too her cub, whether I mean any harm or not?

Well to be honest, I would turn away from her and get my tail on the move in the opposite direction. I believe that is just wise. So that is the point about belief. Did God say it? If the answer is yes for healing, driving out a demon, or a having a mind set free from intoxicants, which is what **Isaiah 53** is speaking about and which the apostles walked out, then that authority also is a part of the Christian's life … when I believe it.

I do not need to yell at a demon to get it out of an individual since Jesus already did that. He spoke, and they took a hike. I and you just need to believe Him, and the second part is to do what He has asked. One other point I would like to make is this: when anyone asked the Lord Jesus to be healed, He never said no. Even the woman who had an issue of blood in **Matthew 9:20–22** was healed, she did not dare to ask but was healed. He never said no.

Now Jesus had another agenda, to bring glory to His Father. Those healings were designed for that purpose. But whoever asked, whether they were present, a servant, daughter, or son with a demon who was being thrown into the fire, Jesus healed them all. And I believe that Jesus's Father sent Him to show us who we can be in relationship to Him. So everything He did, we can do.

These are those other scriptures from the NIV.

- **Esther 9:29** reads, *"So Queen Esther, daughter of Abihail, along with Mordecai the Jew, wrote with full authority to confirm this second letter concerning Purim."*

- **Matthew 7:29** says, *"Because He taught as one who had authority, and not as their teachers of the law."*

- **Matthew 8:9** states, *"For I myself am a man under authority, with soldiers under me. I tell this one, 'Go,' and he goes; and that one, 'Come,' and he comes. I say to my servant, 'Do this,' and he does it."*

- **Matthew 9:6, 8** asserts, *"But so that you may know that the Son of Man has authority on earth to forgive sins … Then He said to the paralytic, 'Get up, take your mat and go home.' When the crowd saw this, they were filled with awe; and they praised God, who had given such authority to men."*

- **Matthew 28:18** reads, *"Then Jesus came to them and said, 'All authority in heaven and on earth has been given to Me.'"*

- ***Luke 9:1*** says, *"When Jesus had called the Twelve together, He gave them power and authority to drive out all demons and to cure diseases."*

  Luke 10:19 states, *"I have given you authority to trample on snakes and scorpions and to overcome all the power of the enemy; nothing will harm you."*

  John 10:17–18 reads, *"The reason My Father loves Me is that I lay down my life—only to take it up again. No one takes it from Me, but I lay it down of My own accord. I have authority to lay it down and authority to take it up again. This command I received from My Father."*

  Romans 13:1–3 says, *"Everyone must submit himself to the governing authorities, for there is no authority except that which God has established. The authorities that exist have been established by God. Consequently, he who rebels against the authority is rebelling against what God has instituted, and those who do so will bring judgment on themselves. For rulers hold no terror for those who do right, but for those who do wrong. Do you want to be free from fear of the one in authority? Then do what is right and he will commend you."*

- ***2 Corinthians 10:8*** reads, *"For even if I boast somewhat freely about the authority the Lord gave us for building you up rather than pulling you down, I will not be ashamed of it."*

- ***Colossians 2:6–12*** states, *"So then, just as you received Christ Jesus as Lord, continue to live in Him, rooted and built up in Him, strengthened in the faith as you were taught, and overflowing with thankfulness. See to it that no one takes you captive through hollow and deceptive philosophy, which depends on human tradition and the basic principles of this world rather than on Christ. For in Christ all the fullness of*

The Deity lives in bodily form, and you have been given fullness in Christ, Who is the head over every power and authority. In Him you were also circumcised, in the putting off the sinful nature, not with a circumcision done by the hands of men but with the circumcision done by Christ, having been buried with Him in baptism [Romans 6] and raised with Him through your faith in the power of God, who raised Him from the dead."

- **Titus 2:11–15** reads, *"For the grace of God that brings salvation has appeared to all men. It teaches us to say 'no' to ungodliness and worldly passions, and to live self-controlled, upright and godly lives in this present age, while we wait for the blessed hope—the glorious appearing of the great God and Savior, Jesus Christ, who gave Himself for us to redeem us from all wickedness and to purify for Himself a people that are his very own, eager to do what is good. These, then, are the things you should teach. Encourage and rebuke with all authority. Do not let anyone despise you."*

So why do we have authority? It is to act, be, or fully emulate Jesus in a world that is thoroughly lost without Him. We have authority to do His will and fulfill His desires, His heart's desires, which is a privilege far beyond comprehension.

Who has authority? Well, that is everyone who has some type of authority, but for those of us who have been born again, we have a unique authority to produce a result on God the Father's behalf, if in faith I am acting or living my daily life according to His Word. It is not just that I am going to church or even just reading my Bible and praying daily. But it is an authority to be present enough to be a participant in the spiritual and physical revelation of God's kingdom, with Jesus Christ as our King and Lord, the one we have surrendered our own authority to. God is so good because once I do that surrendering, then He turns around and blesses me with His own authority. Man, what a job! Amen, family of God.

I : The Spirit and in Truth

First off, I would like to say that we, you, and I as Christians get into these mind games. As an example, we say commonly, "I [or we] worship in spirit and in truth," but if I were to ask, even if I were to ask myself, what that actually means, I would start with truth, knowing that it is not a lie. But to expand on that, the truth is Jesus and everything about God the Father and Holy Spirit. So God is the truth, but then we come to spirit and truth and about me acting in accord with Him.

Well, now I'm lost, but as I was talking to the Lord about this, He showed me that when I speak in tongues because I've had the baptism in the Holy Spirit, I surrender myself to the Holy Spirit and let Him do the talking. For those who have yet to experience that, I do not fall into a trance or have some type of epileptic seizure or a divine revelation. I just open my mouth and let Him speak. Nothing else is involved except I turn my lips and tongue over to the divine. I can but do not keep cutting Him off and saying out loud, "Well, what does that mean?" since per Scripture I know that speaking in tongues edifies the man, me myself. Praise God.

So now if I say I am worshiping in spirit and in truth, what I should be doing is to surrender myself to the worship of the Holy Spirit in the same way as I surrender when I speak in tongues. This is one other example since we are many, but salvation is the same. I had to completely surrender to God before I knew Him. In both of those, how could I come to Him if He at first did not call me, and how could I speak unless He had something to say? I have come to realize that there is no lie in Him, so now I see that the whole fits perfectly together and now spirit and truth have a definite meaning to me that this mind, body, and my spirit can comprehend.

I can give many examples of the body of Christ speaking Scripture and yet not believing a word of it or even attempting to understand it. First, please forgive me if anyone is offended. We are each of us different. If you say to yourself, "90 percent of the Scripture I've tried to read I just do not understand," another individual states that it is about half. Then obviously we—you and I—need help from the Author. I have no authority to condemn anybody other than myself. God wrote Scripture for our benefit, to know Him and ourselves and not to be anyone's divine Santa Claus.

For me I'll use *John 3:16 (NIV)* which Christians and nonbelievers state all the time. We see it at sporting events from the audience in the stands. *"For God so loved the world* [Not just this big hunk of water, dirt, and lava floating through space] *that He gave us His only begotten Son, that whoever believes in Him, would not perish, but would have ever lasting life."*

That little piece of scripture is stunning to think about. This is not your pastor speaking to you about today's message. But in moments when we are reading the very scriptures that God has spoken prophetically over His body, His wife, the church, and the many who are pursuing the Lord, it is so we ourselves don't forget what Almighty God has in store for each unique portion of His holy body that He loved so much that He gave His all for, that very Word of God. Scripture is an important part of our very nature in Him.

2 Samuel 5:17–20 (NIV) was spoken over a church that I used to attend in San Antonio, Texas, but I feel that each and every body of believers has a purpose and scripture to hang its own hat on. For my old church, it was **2 Samuel 5:17–20**. If I can ad-lib those verses, we see that David has just been appointed king over all of **Israel, 2 Samuel 5:1–5**.

The enemies of Israel, the Philistines, knew this to be trouble for themselves because David had been kicking everybody's bootie all over the place without working up a sweat. So the Philistines went up to basically kill David and take over all the land of Israel and its resources, much like most of the world wants to do today.

So now as a new king with the enemy on his doorstep, David should have just marched out and, like any other king in the lands about them, and either defeated the Philistines or got defeated himself and his army killed. These are not just nice stories, but they are histories or biographies of actual people who either turned to God for deliverance or turned away from God and then to themselves for deliverance.

On the statement above for us, whether we are saved by the Lord or not, I can see that **Genesis 2:16–17 (NIV)** states, *"And the Lord God commanded the man, 'You are free to eat from any tree in the garden; but you must not eat from the tree of the knowledge of good and evil, for when you eat of it you will certainly die.'"*

Here's my point: since God is life, not only just being alive but more so the actual essence and knowledge of what life is, then when I am in an active relationship with Him and am supported by His existence, even though at some point this individual is going to kick the bucket, I also see that if I am in Him, then He continually adds life, or His Spirit, which will never die. So I have real life because God is and has always been alive. But the opposite is just as true of breaking His command. Then I will surely die, so without Him, I purposely want and take a strong hold or a death grip on death. That is an important point on anyone of our locations in relationship with Him. Am I holding on to life, or for the reverse, will I not let go of death?

Like I said, David could have told his army to saddle up. He could have said, "We're going to go and kill us some Philistines!" What else do you do with a hunk of metal that has been sharpened so it easily cuts flesh and is very pointed so it pierces whatever it is pointed at? Don't we yell at our children to stop running through the house with a pair of scissors in their hands because we do not want them getting hurt? But David, as God's representative, takes a moment to go down to the stronghold and seek God's face. Or in our common vernacular, David prays.

David does not tell the Lord that he and Israel are outnumbered ten to one. How would he know? And so he would not be speaking in truth. David speaks to the Lord, "Shall I go and attack the Philistines? Will You deliver them into my hands?"

And so, should we, the church of Jesus Christ, know for whatever the enemy has in its playbook to foil our walk with Him? If it is a drug addiction from being unable to quit cigarettes to hard-core anything, they have a spirit that is not the Holy Spirit behind them or pornography from the obvious to internet chat rooms. Listen, anything that does not lend itself to uplifting your spiritual life in the Lord's purpose is sin, which by its very nature is death because it is not of God. It is eating from the thing that the Lord God said would hurt you in relationship to Him.

One of the things about that Tree of Knowledge was that it too must have died because it is never mentioned again in Scripture. The Tree of Life is referenced multiple times, but once Genesis 3 is done, so is the Tree of Knowledge. For me, it is pushing up daisies.

Along the same lines, we may say that you or I are worshiping your television, but now many Christians don't even own a TV, but they do own an iPad or iPhone where they spend a great deal of time chatting it up with someone I or you may never see face-to-face, whether he or she is married or single.

Don't forget whose child you are. You did not save yourself from sin. God did by being nailed to a cross so He could bear everything that was keeping you from His own Father's holy presence. If anything is taking up your time so you cannot spend it in His love, then that is sin. I don't really care how much makeup and gloss you put on it. Whatever it is, it is keeping you from God. In this scripture, David is showing by the Holy Spirit what we have had spoken by God over JPCF and not the building but the body. Whatever you take to God in prayer will be defended by God if we only act according to His will.

God said in the scriptures mentioned above, "Go up for I will surly deliver the Philistines into your hands." So David did just that. He did not wait for God to send an earthquake to devour the enemy, but David went up as directed, and he and his troops engaged the enemy and defeated them there. Now in our times, if we had defeated a great enemy, we would be bragging about it to no end.

"Man, we kicked those puppies' bahooties all over the place, didn't we? I'm the best king you're ever gonna get, and you are the best army any king ever had!"

David did not do any of those bragging things. He knew because he had asked his Lord for help against not only his own enemy but the people of God's enemy. That is also what spirit and truth mean. It is an action predicated on what God desires. David was the brand-new king. The previous king was Saul, and he and David's best friend had recently been killed by the same army that was waiting on the surrounding hills to do him in as well.

He most assuredly could have just taken a hike, but David's own heart was for the Lord and the Lord's people. First and foremost, David asks the Lord, "What should I do?" The Lord answered him, "Go for I will surly deliver the Philistines into your hands." So David went. The Lord spends much of the time waiting to see our response to His requests.

That is an entirely different subject than spirit and truth, but like the Word of God and our response to it, it has a great deal in common. When we as individuals surrender to the Holy Spirit, the more truth there is in our lives, and the more like Jesus we can then become. The effort is not just the desire for personal endeavor because I may want to be famous in heaven, but rather I think His light will be more of a draw for those who are lost, in the same way that His light was to me, from Himself.

I do not want to be the main anything for this world. I promise you. I know that I will fail you, but Jesus cannot fail. You must put more effort into rejecting Him, if you have been saved, than accepting Him. He is true and sure. I know that more than anything I can hope to name. Therefore, spirit and truth are not just a couple of items we say when in the company of other believers, but rather an intrinsic function of who a child of God is.

Basically when we as the church are led by the Spirit, we then walk in His truth so it can be seen plainly by our Father God that I want to be just like Jesus, who is the Way, the Truth, and the Life. Whew.

J : *Exodus 32–34:11 (NIV)*: A Commentary

Please read the scriptures posted. They add to what took place. For me, they are giving each of us a fuller picture of what the Lord is stating, Old Testament to New, all of them. Read **Deuteronomy 5:22–31; Exodus 20:18–21, 24:9–18; 19:3–6;** and **Psalm 127:1**.

Exodus 32:1, *When the people saw that Moses was so long in coming down from the mountain, they gathered around Aaron and said, "Come, make us a god who will go before us. As for this fellow Moses who brought us up out of Egypt, we don't know what has happened to him."*

When the men of Israel saw that Moses delayed in coming back down during the forty days, Israel took matters into its own hands, left the Lord God Yahweh totally out of it, and now cast their suspicion or lack of hope on Moses, a fallible human, and came to Aaron to ask for a god in the image they imagined Him to be.

In Strong's, it is Elohim, so the word *god* or *gods* is the standard translation, but I mean really in **Genesis 1:1**, it states, *"In the beginning, Elohim created the heavens and the earth."* So it can be said that the people and from what I see the men in particular asked for a god or gods since the word *Elohim* is plural, to walk before them.

Given that it was only one golden calf that Aaron pulled from the fire, no one objected to that, and it was their desire to bring God down to their level instead of them being the created and going up to His level, Moses, like Jesus, is a perfect example of relationship. The people wanted to create a divine being of their own design. For the rest of these verses, I am going to go with a singular god where Elohim is mentioned.

Exodus 32:2, *Aaron answered them* (the men, most likely the elders and leadership), *"Take off the gold earrings that your wives, your sons and your daughters are wearing* [so we know that women were not marrying women and they were not having offspring by themselves; today that statement would not be true, but back then it was something different] *and bring them to me."*

There may have been over two to three million individuals heading out of Egypt, so to me all of them did not come to Aaron to ask for a replacement for the Lord Yahweh, and they did not ask Moses, but rather the elders or, in a fuller sense, the parents of Israel. The gold that Israel had was God's payment to Israel from Egypt for their forced labor. Earlier in **Exodus 11:2–3**, it reads, *"Tell the people that men and women alike are to ask their neighbors for articles of silver and gold."*

The Lord made the Egyptians favorably disposed toward the people, and Moses himself was highly regarded in Egypt by Pharaoh's officials and the people. So it was God's gold in effect that was being used to create a false god. Aaron, the leader/parent for the people, did nothing to oppose them.

Exodus 32:3, *So all the people took off their earrings and brought them to Aaron.*

A scripture fits here for the comment. **James 1:13–15** reads, *"When tempted, no one should say, 'God is tempting me.'" For God cannot be tempted by evil; nor does He tempt anyone. But each of you is tempted when you are dragged away by your own evil desire and enticed. Then* *after desire has conceived, it gives birth to sin. And sin, when it is full-grown, gives birth to death.*

Exodus 32:4, *He took what they handed him and made it into an idol cast in the shape of a calf, fashioning it with a tool. Then they said, "This is your god, O Israel, who brought you up out of Egypt."*

All of these actions took a good amount of time gathering the gold. Since Israel was in the process of creating its own god, they had to be thinking of the consequences. Who was going out and collecting those pieces of jewelry? And then Aaron got it all together and put the pot on to boil, and once it got hot enough, the gold became a formless 24K soup. But that had to take most of a day, plenty of time to reconsider and to repent. Another point is that "Then they said," again the elders said to Israel.

Exodus 32:5, *When Aaron saw this, he built an altar in front of the calf and announced, "Tomorrow there will be a festival/feast to The Lord, Yahweh."*

My TNIV study Bible states that Aaron saw the wrong that they were doing and was trying to get the people back by reminding them that they belonged to Yahweh. I do not know about that and do not think so because the only festival Israel was celebrating at that time would have been Unleavened Bread and Passover.

In **Exodus 24:1–2, 4–11**, *Moses got up early in the morning and built an altar at the foot of the mountain. The people offered up burnt offerings and sacrificed young bulls as fellowship offerings to the Lord Yahweh, and they sprinkled blood as a sign of the Lord and their own covenant to Him.* So they understood at least in part of the magnitude of each of their actions. But it was them bringing God down, just as their slave masters did in Egypt.

When Moses returns to the camp, he does do the right thing and does it by himself. Back to Aaron, who announced, "Tomorrow there will be a festival to the Lord, Yahweh." Once again, all of them had time to think about what they were endeavoring and celebrating the Lord Yahweh by their own strength. It is the fellowship with the Lord that changes things.

Exodus 32:6, *So the next day, the people rose early and sacrificed burnt offerings and presented fellowship offerings. Afterward they sat down to eat and drink and got up to indulge in revelry (Hos. 7:3–5) to indulge.*

I like that statement, "The people rose early and sacrificed." It recalls getting my children when they actually were children instead of the adults they are currently, but getting them ready for church on Sunday morning was work. "Come on. Let's get ready to go to God's house to worship!"

"Do we have to?"

I was asking myself the same, "Do I have to?"

But Israel's eagerness and our own eagerness to indulge our flesh for me might be my imagination, but it looks to me like they were more than ready and eager to go. I would also like to say that in all of this, I do not believe every single individual was in agreement with what was going on; but the majority had reverted to the worldly system.

Exodus 32:7, *Then the Lord Yahweh said to Moses, "Go down, because your people, whom you brought up out of Egypt, have become corrupt."*

No human nor any angel had to tell God, who was busy with Moses, what the people were doing. It is one thing I like about Scripture: God is always in the know. He never needs to be informed about anything. And Moses is a type of our Lord Jesus and the appointed advocate between the people and Yahweh needs because of personal relationship, which as a side note is what our Father wanted with Israel in the first place.

The people have become corrupt, and the Lord God no longer sees them as belonging to Him. After all He Himself said that He is a jealous God in **Exodus 20:5**. I can also see that God was giving the people what they desired. Instead of God, it was now Moses who brought them out of slavery. God agrees with their desire and tells Moses the same thing. The covenant, relationship, has been broken, as shown a bit later when Moses casts the two stone tablets to the ground and they break, somewhat like when we allow sin to enter our lives. That is what sin does. It takes us the individual out of agreement with divinity, and likewise, we cast ourselves back onto the earth, ground, or dirt.

Exodus 3:10–11 and **19:3–6** asserts where the Lord states that they are My people, My priests.

Exodus 32:8, *They have been quick to turn away from what I commanded them and have made themselves an idol cast in the shape of a calf. They have bowed down to it and sacrificed to it and have said, "This is your god, O Israel, who brought you up out of Egypt."*

In **Genesis 2:16–17** and **Genesis 3:11**, for the first time the Lord God commanded, and it too was not obeyed.

I would like to also state that from the people's perspective, they may have still been seeking Elohim, but it is still from the limited view of humanity. God should know who He is, and we are learning through relationship that truth that does not actually change. But on the same note, if God is who I make Him out to be, then my God is certainly going to be different than your God and so on and so on, but the Lord God wants us to know Him as He is, without our filters and what best suits me. I know that He best suits we.

Exodus 32:9, *"I have seen these people,"* the Lord Yahweh said to Moses, *"and they are a stiff-necked people."*

They will not budge, whether for their own good or not.

Exodus 32:10, *"Now leave Me alone so that My anger may burn against them and that I may destroy them. Then I will make you into a great nation."*

Man, oh man, what an offer Moses is getting from the Lord God. The Father does not need to bribe. He is not making offers He does not intend to carry out, but He is in fact stating that He will destroy the work He has done called Israel and begin again with Moses.

What an honor. If God told me that, I would have a hard time telling the Almighty God, especially after He had just told me to leave Him. I'd think about leaving Him alone, and I really do not have a better idea than the Lord. God is changing His plan, His promise, made to Abraham, and I Am going to transfer that to you Moses. I'd be like, "Yes, sir, see you later after You've cooled off and they/those sinners are all gone."

Exodus 32:11, *But Moses sought the favor of the Lord Yahweh, his God. "O Yahweh," he said, "why should Your anger burn against Your people, whom You brought out of Egypt with great power and a mighty hand?"*

I greatly admire Moses. It would be simple to just agree with the Lord, but Moses knows the heart of God and is stating and reminding God of His own words. There are at least three major things here:

1. Your people, not mine.
2. You brought them out with a mighty hand.
3. For verse 13, the covenant promise is made to Abraham, Isaac, and Jacob.

Exodus 32:12, *"Why should the Egyptians say, 'It was with evil intent that He brought them out, to kill them in the mountains and to wipe them off the face of the earth?' Turn from Your fierce anger; relent and do not bring disaster on Your people."*

God can do what He wants, but at the same time, the Lord is also trying to save humanity from eternal separation from Him. Now it may not matter what the Egyptians think or say, but for me, the entire world is supposed to know who God is by His actions. So why should the world say it was with evil intent about God? Now God once again does not have to worry about our opinions, but He is concerned about how we relate to Him. To fear Him is correct, but to love and to fear damaging that love is so much more important to Him.

Exodus 32:13, *"Remember Your servants Abraham, Isaac and Israel, to whom You swore by Your Own Self: 'I will make your descendants as numerous as the stars in the sky and I will give your descendants all this land I promised them, and it will be their inheritance forever.'"*

I see that the Lord wanted the relationship that He had with Moses to be the exact same as that with the people of Israel. I would also like to say that is God the Father's intent for us with Jesus. The exact same relationship is being presented to me and, for that matter, the church. But the giant step up for the church is that the Son came to show us how to be in relationship with each other, as all the stipulations and commandments that the Lord gave. The relationship is also with God. You must admire—and I do—that relationship which God established with Moses, and he, Moses, lived it each day.

In ***Exodus 32–34***, Moses gets a lot of offers from our Lord God that personally I would have a hard time refusing. I don't think any of Moses' arguments could change the Lord's mind. I like ***Job 9:14–20***. *"Even if I were innocent, my mouth would condemn me; if I were blameless, it* [my mouth] *would pronounce me guilty."*

Exodus 32:14, *Then the Lord Yahweh relented* or repented *and did not bring on His people the disaster He had threatened* **(Gen. 6:6–7; Ex. 32:12; contrast Num. 23:19–20).**

Moses was speaking God's heart. Gotta love it.

Exodus 32:15-16, *Moses turned and went down the mountain with the two tablets of the testimony in his hands. They were inscribed on both sides, front and back. The tablets were the work of God; the writing was the writing of God, engraved on the tablets.*

Exodus 24:12 reads that everything about the covenant was from God, placed into the hands of man, which was given for the maturity of a people. This is also what Scripture is. It is from the hands of God, written by God for our maturity and growth in our relationship with Him and for the most part certainly not every Christian. But for many, it is never explored. If we had the physical Ten Commandments in our hands, people would be like, "Oh, look what God gave us."

The reality is that we minimize all the things He has spoken. We also rely on things from the Word that tickle our fancies, or we know it but don't in our daily lives prove to ourselves that His every Word is true. I am speaking to myself also. I can give a whole lecture on this subject, but for brevity's sake, I will move on.

Exodus 32:17-18, *When Joshua heard the noise of the people shouting, he said to Moses, "There is the sound of war in the camp." Moses replied, "It is not the sound of victory, it is not the sound of defeat; it is the sound of singing that I hear."*

I like Moses' reply. He does not say it is not a war, but you do not hear victory shouts. There is no mourning because of defeat, but a battle is taking place, and all I hear are the people singing. Sin makes the individual unaware that a problem, a war, is taking place and exists.

Exodus 32:19, *When Moses approached the camp and saw the calf and the dancing, his anger burned, and he threw the tablets out of his hands, breaking them to pieces at the foot of the mountain.*

So many things in these three chapters show how close the communion between God and Moses was. How much our Father shows us through Jesus of what His expectations for the human family are.

Back to Moses. He just got finished entreating God to keep the covenant that Moses currently held in his hands with Israel, but when he sees with his own eyes what is taking place, now Moses' anger burns, and he breaks the covenant commands that has established Israel as God's chosen people. Can I say of the church that exact same thing applies to us and that the weight of it is more since it is God's own Son and Spirit that the covenant is based upon?

Exodus 32:20, *And he took the calf they had made and burned it in the fire; then he ground it to powder, scattered it on the water and made the Israelites drink it.*

These actions were proving to Israel that the god they had made, even if you call him Elohim, has no power. What is also amazing to me is the fact that Moses just came down from the mountain that was ablaze with fire and Israel heard for themselves the thunder. They did not want to approach the mountain out of fear, and yet at the same time, they wanted to make for themselves a god who they can handle.

Whew! The people also did not object. Some were still too busy partying, but if I said that the thing you believed in, the thing I am going to burn in a fire and then throw the ashes on the water just to show you how worthless it is, you will have to digest it. And there is the fact that Israel's leadership, along with pastor Aaron are not much different than what we have here in the United States.

Exodus 32:21, *He said to Aaron, "What did these people do to you, that you led them into such great sin?"*

Aaron could have told Moses that the people wanted a god because of their 430 years of living in Egypt and learning their lifestyles. Even though they hated being treated as slaves, he could have said they forced him to do it strongly but also against his will. But the truth is in the question that Moses poses, that is, "What could they possibly do to make you join them against the perfect desires of God?" In my imagination, I see Aaron saying, "What desires?"

Exodus 32:22, *"Do not be angry, my lord," Aaron answered. "You know how prone these people are to evil."*

My lord, in the Hebrew, is *adown*, a short version of Adonai. For men to speak it is to say firmly that you are very superior to me. Aaron was speaking to his baby brother, even though they were both adults. Sin leaves our hearts knowing that we are going to be punished, saved, or unsaved. So Aaron, like Adam and Eve, both start to blame someone or everyone else. We humans may not know what the punishment is, but nonetheless we don't want it and are willing to let someone else stand in for us, which God did with His innocent Son, our Lord Jesus.

Exodus 32:23, *They said to me, "Make us a god who will go before us. As for this fellow Moses who brought us up out of Egypt, we don't know what has happened to him."*

I like how Aaron tells the exact truth when it implicates others.

Exodus 32:24, *So I told them, "Whoever has any gold jewelry, take it off." Then they gave me the gold, and I threw it into the fire, and out came this calf!*

Aaron said, "So whoever has any gold take it off, and they gave it to me. I was getting rid of it and threw it into the fire, but out leapt this golden calf. That had to be an act of God, right? Because it completely mystified me!"

Exodus 32:25, *Moses saw that the people were running wild and that Aaron had let them get out of control and so become a laughingstock to their enemies.*

This is such an important verse, but Moses saw the church/Israel from the Old Testament. They were running wild and had gotten out of control, and so they had become or made God become since we are His representatives here in the world and had become a laughingstock. For me, these three chapters hinge on how the Lord God is shown to ourselves, and then our relationship is shown to those who do not know Him. Moses is a perfect example of what a relationship with the Lord looks like. And when we take God and make Him into the image we perceive, then He is lessened. The result is that we naturally become worldlier *(Matt. 6:22–24)*.

Exodus 32:26-27, *So he stood at the entrance to the camp and said, "Whoever is for The Lord, Yahweh, come to me." And all the Levites rallied to him. Then he said to them, "This is what The Lord, Yahweh, the God of Israel, says, 'Each man strap a sword to his side. Go back and forth through the camp from one end to the other, each killing his brother and friend and neighbor.'"*

Matthew 10:37–39 and *Luke 9:23–26* reads, "Whoever is for The Lord." Every one of the millions who were present should have rallied to Moses, but they were distracted by their desires. The Levites, whom Moses and Aaron were members of, listened.

A thing that I see from Scripture is that at times an all-inclusive statement is made. Review *Genesis 6:5–8*, *1 Kings 19:9–18*, and *Numbers 16:28–35*, but the truth is that God is working out his purposes. And blessed are we is the fact that He has continued to include us in the desires of His heart. In *Exodus* in these three chapters, I did not hear the Lord make that statement about strapping on a sword, but I can see that Moses knew the Lord and God's heart and was acting in accordance with His divine will.

But that is a big deal to be asked to go through the entire camp of Israel and to take the life of your own fellows, those brothers/adults, to kill a brother, friend, and neighbor. I think it is also striking that the women were not included. My opinion, not the Word of God, is that the men and leadership had the responsibility and so received their fate of disobedience.

Exodus 32:28, *The Levites did as Moses commanded, and that day about three thousand of the people died.*

To show how the Lord God works, here in rebellion about three thousand die by the sword. But in **Acts 2:36–41**, on the day of Pentecost, about three thousand gave their lives to the Lord and were saved. It is amazing what difference there is between obedience to the Lord and disobedience to what He has said. Obviously one brings life; the other brings certain death and destruction, quickly and/or slowly.

Exodus 32:29-30, *Then Moses said, "You have been set apart to The Lord, Yahweh today, for you were against your own sons and brothers, and he has blessed you this day." The next day Moses said to the people, "You have committed a great sin. But now I will go up to The Lord, Yahweh; perhaps I can make atonement for your sin."*

1 Samuel 12:15–25 states, *"You have committed a great sin."* They have asked for a false god and to have asked for a king instead of the King to be over their lives.

Time is of the essence with sin. The very next day, even after three thousand have perished because of their desire for it, Moses tells the people what they have done, committed, or acted out in their lives a very great sin or action against the Lord. Now Moses will try to make amends on their behalf because, just like God, he too wants reconciliation. But in this situation, Moses does not believe there is a solution. Sin or rebellion against the Lord God keeps us from Him, "The sooner begun though, the sooner done." So Moses is heading back up the mountain to face the Lord.

Exodus 32:31-32, *So Moses went back to the Lord Yahweh and said, "Oh, what a great sin these people have committed! They have made themselves a god of gold." "But now, please forgive their sin—but if not, then blot me out of the book you have written."*

Moses is climbing up and down Sinai a bunch, but I believe that where Moses is concerned some things are better face-to-face. Moses tells God exactly what he told Israel. Please forgive their sin … but if not. Moses is in love with Yahweh, so this next statement is not one that anyone who is in love makes on another's behalf. "But if not, then blot me out of your book, or break it off with me forever."

Exodus 32:33, *The Lord Yahweh replied to Moses, "Whoever has sinned against me I will blot out of my book."*

The Lord God is fully in control, and whoever has sinned or rebelled does not care what I say to him, her, or me. Then I will blot them out of my book. That statement makes repentance such a wonderful item from the Lord, to be forgiven when I am wrong.

Exodus 32:34, *"Now go, lead the people to the place I spoke of, and My angel will go before you. However, when the time comes for Me to punish, I will punish them for their sin."*

So the Lord is not giving up on His Word to the people; instead He is sending an angel or messenger in His stead. But the result of this sin has a consequence. "And I will punish them for their sin." I would also like to comment that if I were a part of Israel back then and three thousand individuals had just been killed with the sword, I might have a complaint. "Hey, man! I thought that we were just punished!" The only thing I can say in this case is that God knows hearts and takes care of problems that might have been missed while people were carrying out their own demands.

Exodus 32:35, *And the Lord Yahweh struck the people with a plague because of what they did with the calf Aaron had made.* (Which the Lord did.)

Exodus 33:1–3 reads, *Then The Lord, Yahweh said to Moses, "Leave this place, you and the people you brought up out of Egypt and go up to the land I promised on oath to Abraham, Isaac and Jacob, saying, 'I will give it to your descendants.' I will send an angel before you and drive out the Canaanites, Amorites, Hittites, Perizzites, Hivites and Jebusites. Go up to the land flowing with milk and honey. But I will not go with you, because you are a stiff-necked people and I might destroy you on the way."*

Acts 7:51–53 refers to the stiff-necked.

The Lord's Word is good, but now Moses is having His own heart broken because God is stating that He will not accompany them. I like how the Lord set this up. Moses is the mediator between Israel and God and likewise between the Lord and Israel because Moses does not relent for the people's relationship with God. He, the Lord, had said in chapter 19 that He would dwell with them.

That is God's desire, and it is also Moses' desire. So now even when the Lord states that He will no longer go with Israel but that an angel will go in His stead, Moses wants what God wants, but He does not know how to bring that about. The people need to change, but how do you make that happen?

Exodus 33:4–5 reads, "When the people heard these distressing words, they began to mourn, and no one put on any ornaments. For The Lord, Yahweh had said to Moses, 'Tell the Israelites, 'You are a stiff-necked people. If I were to go with you even for a moment, I might destroy you. Now take off your ornaments and I will decide what to do with you.'"

That is a good way to start. They began to mourn, and I would if God told me I might destroy you. And for me, the deeper point is that I no longer desire relationship with you, Israel. At the very least, I would think that I had gone too far with my own sins. Taking off the ornaments reduced their pride in what they possessed, what made them look worldly.

Exodus 33:6–7 says, "So the Israelites stripped off their ornaments at Mount Horeb. Now Moses used to take a tent and pitch it outside the camp some distance away, calling it the 'Tent of Meeting.' Anyone inquiring of The Lord, Yahweh would go to the Tent of Meeting outside the camp."

Moses at times seems to stick things into what is taking place. The Tent of Meeting or Tabernacle of Meeting was not the tabernacle because that had not been created yet. It was set outside of the camp while the tabernacle was centralized, and each of the tribes of Israel had specific places to camp around the tabernacle. I also like that anyone inquiring of the Lord could go there. It does not speak about any of those individuals, but I would also say that I do not think that the entire Israelite nation except for Moses and Joshua totally avoided the Tent of Meeting. I also believe that the following conversation between the Lord Yahweh and Moses took place in that Tent of Meeting after this brief description of the Tent of Meeting **(2 Cor. 6:16–7; 1 Peter 2:4–6)**.

Exodus 33:8–10 reads, "And whenever Moses went out to the tent, all the people rose and stood at the entrances to their tents, watching

Moses until he entered the tent. As Moses went into the tent, the pillar of cloud would come down and stay at the entrance, while The LORD, Yahweh spoke with Moses. Whenever the people saw the pillar of cloud standing at the entrance to the tent, they all stood and worshiped, each at the entrance to his tent."

The people stood and worshipped each at their tent. For me, the tent often speaks about our individual lives. The Lord Yahweh has come to the tabernacle with me. The Lord also came to communicate with flesh and blood that was in relationship with Him. *Exodus 19:20–25* has the Lord telling Moses to warn the people so that no one forces his way onto Mount Sinai. But the Lord knows hearts, and some in the crowd must have been contemplating those actions because even the priests had to consecrate themselves.

Exodus 33:11 states, "The LORD, Yahweh would speak to Moses face to face, as a man speaks with his friend. Then Moses would return to the camp, but his young aide Joshua son of Nun did not leave the tent."

It is a strange statement for Joshua. For us in these times, it would be Yeshua, or Jesus, in our English. But I can say that Jesus does not leave the tent either. But Joshua, son of Nun, sure did at some point.

Exodus 33:12–13 says, "Moses said to The LORD, Yahweh, 'You have been telling me, 'Lead these people,' but You have not let me know whom You will send with me. You have said, 'I know you by name and you have found favor with Me.' If You are pleased with me, teach me Your ways so I may know You and continue to find favor with You. Remember that this nation is Your people."

Moses knows his Lord Yahweh and he does not want an angel but the presence of the one he loves. Moses reminds the Lord about what He has said, both to himself and for Israel. I love verse 13, "but if you are pleased with me, then teach me Your ways, to find favor with You."

This is my own prayer. Moses did not need or want anything else other than the Lord Himself, and Moses is willing to deny himself and take up his cross daily to follow Jesus.

Exodus 33:14 reads, *"The LORD, Yahweh replied, 'My Presence will go with you, and I will give you rest.'"*

The words *you* are singular; in the KJV, it states "will go with thee." If I'm in love and my wife states that she is only interested in me, then I should be contented, that is, until we have children. Moses could have taken what the living God had just said and been extremely happy with what He said and believed Him. But Moses' heart was for what the Lord his God desired as the next *verses 15–16* state.

Exodus 33:15-16, *"Then Moses said to Him, 'If Your Presence does not go with us, do not send us up from here. How will anyone know that You are pleased with me and with Your people unless You go with us? What else will distinguish me and Your people from all the other people on the face of the earth?"*

If we are the most handsome, the most intelligent, the most prosperous, or the greatest nation of warriors, none of these will distinguish us as a people, but only Your very presence with us is what is going to tell the world that we as a people are Your very own. The proof of that is You alone, Lord. Amen.

Exodus 33:17 states, *"And The LORD, Yahweh said to Moses, 'I will do the very thing you have asked, because I am pleased with you and I know you by name.'"*

After Moses makes that confession, the Lord Yahweh makes a tremendous statement to Moses and the church. I will do the very thing you have asked because I am pleased with you. How many of us want the Lord to speak those same words to me/us? Review *John*

14:11–14, **John** *15:16–17,* **John** *16:12–15, 23–28,* and **Matthew** *7:7–12*.

Exodus 33:18 *reads, "Then Moses said, 'Now show me Your glory'* [majesty, glory, splendor]."

There are a number of ways to read **Exodus 32–34**. Moses can be considered a hardheaded individual. God says this, and Moses says that. God is angry. Moses asks God to calm down. But what I see is that Moses wants God's heart. Moses burned with anger just as the Lord did once he himself sees Israel running around having an orgy and dishonoring the covenant just made between Israel and the Lord.

I mean, Moses grew up as a prince in Egypt where excess had to be happening all of the time. Moses desires that Israel and himself get to have the Lord God dwelling with them. Since the Lord just stated in the previous verse "I will do the very thing you have asked," Moses asks for the very thing he wants more than any other, God's very presence. Now I know that Scripture states that Moses and the Lord spoke face-to-face, but what I also see is that the Lord would show up in a dark cloud. And if at night, then the cloud had fire within it. But what Moses is asking for here, I believe, is to see the Lord as He really is. I am somewhat sure that in his heart Moses was expecting, "Sorry, Moses, but that is just not going to happen."

Exodus 33:19 *says, "And The LORD, Yahweh said, 'I will cause all My goodness to pass in front of you, and I will proclaim My name, Yahweh, in your presence. I will have mercy on whom I will have mercy, and I will have compassion on whom I will have compassion.'"*

Since God is also in a loving relationship, He gives one of His children exactly what has been requested. I will cause all of My goodness to pass in front of you. If I said that and was able to do that, then you would have nothing to be concerned about. But when the living God makes that statement "all My goodness" and "I will proclaim My Name in your presence," the Lord's name is who He is. It is not just a name. So the Lord is stating that He is going to reveal who He is to Moses and not just to recite His own name. So because of Moses' actions, God is taking Moses into a much deeper relationship, to know one another better and all of God's goodness. The universe cannot contain it all.

Exodus 33:20 reads, "'But,' He said, 'you cannot see My face, for no one may see Me and live.'"

The Lord is not telling Moses that there is a strict rule in place that if anyone sees My face, he, she, it, or they will die. When I read Scripture, Adam and Eve had the Lord come down in the cool of the day (Gen. 3:8–9) to fellowship with them. But from those same verses, God also always knows when there is a problem with His people. There is an inseparable rift between the Lord and sin, and since we are straight-up sinners, then there is a rift between God and man, even if that man is of the caliber of Moses. So I see that even though Moses has had very close encounters with the Lord, it would be to Moses' well-being, namely staying alive. So you must not see the face of the One he loves. But Jesus, the Lamb of God, cured that because Jesus can freely do that, to see the face of His Father God. I sure look forward to that.

*Exodus 33:21 states, "Then The Lord, Yahweh said, 'There is a place near Me where you may stand on a rock'" (**1 Cor. 10:3–4; Eph. 2:19–22** [also the Tent of Meeting]; **Deut. 32:3–4; Ps. 40:2**).*

Jesus is our firm foundation (***1 Tim. 3:15–16; 2 Tim. 2:19***).

Exodus 33:22 asserts, *"When My glory passes by, I will put you in a cleft in the rock and cover you with My hand until I have passed by."*

The verse reads "My glory," but Moses just asked to see the Lord's glory. God's hand reveals His strength and purpose *(Deut. 4:35–37; 1 Chron. 16:28–30, 29:10–13; Ex. 13:3; Ps. 20:6)*.

I also like the symbolism of Moses being put within the cleft of the Rock. When we give our hearts to the Lord, we are also put into or inside the Rock. And the Rock changes my heart to flesh. Now that's glory! Sorry for overdosing on exclamation points.

Exodus 33:23 reads, "Then I will remove My hand and you will see My back; but My face must not be seen."

Exodus 34:1 states, "The LORD, Yahweh said to Moses, "Chisel out two stone tablets like the first ones, and I will write on them the words that were on the first tablets, which you broke."

I love the Lord God, but Moses is on a proverbial cloud nine, everything he could ever ask for, except being let off the hook of being in charge of Israel as an advocate on the Lord's behalf. But when Moses broke the covenant of the two tablets, Moses was acting on God's behalf because the people were in sin and their own actions broke the covenant.

What the Lord showed to me was the reason Moses had to chisel out two new tablets, like the first was for God and man to be working together for the Lord's blessing to be made available to man. God had done numerous miracles for Israel, and yes, the stone tablets could have been reassembled as quick as a lick, but the Lord wants us to see the truth of His Son, Jesus, and how we are to respond to Him, to receive His provisions. The work then becomes ours instead of just mine.

Exodus 34:2–3 says, "Be ready in the morning, and then come up on Mount Sinai. Present yourself to Me there on top of the mountain. No one is to come with you or be seen anywhere on the mountain; not even the flocks and herds may graze in front of the mountain."

So bright and early tomorrow morning, have those two stone tablets chiseled out, and then come up to the top of Mount Sinai. The current Mount Sinai is about 7,300 feet, and I know at that time there were no particular paths, but rather Moses had to climb all of that distance. In verse 3, the Lord states that no one—not Aaron, Joshua, anyone, or animals—are to even graze in front of the mountain. "You, Moses, come up the mountain alone."

That is how we see God. We come as an individual doing what He has instructed, and no matter how hard it may seem, we as His body do what He has asked of us. The thing that I think about Moses is that he was ecstatic, and for me also, Moses was probably whistling "whistle while you work" and humming to himself about just how good God is. And in a few hours, it would be quite a few hours to climb up seven thousand feet. But I believe Moses was ready to go and at least had something to do to pass the time until the morning.

Can I also say that the Lord was also giving Moses the opportunity to back out of His request? If the Lord asked me to chisel out two stone tablets and then climb to the top of Mount Sinai and I just gotten done interceding for all my people, I might be thinking that I was back in Egypt and a slave. But the Lord is like, "If you want it, then come and get it." For the Lord to know and to let Moses know his own heart and what resides there, are you willing to give it all?

Exodus 34:4 *reads,* *"So Moses chiseled out two stone tablets like the first ones and went up Mount Sinai early in the morning, as The LORD, Yahweh had commanded him; and he carried the two stone tablets in his hands."*

I believe that Moses' heart was just full to overflowing. He was the happiest man on earth. I am going to see the Lord my God in His glory.

Exodus 34:5–6 states, "Then The LORD, Yahweh came down in the cloud and stood there with him and proclaimed his name, Yahweh. And He passed in front of Moses, proclaiming, 'Yahweh, Yahweh, The compassionate and gracious God, slow to anger, abounding in love and faithfulness.'"

The Lord came down in a cloud. Well, isn't that the same as every other encounter—cloud by day and fire by night? I believe that once the Lord passed in front of Moses, then the cloud lifted because the Lord had just said the previous day, "once My glory passed by." I have taken many indulgences with Scripture and these three chapters, but I would also like to express Yahweh's revelation to Moses in the first person, as I think it happened to Moses. *"Yahweh, I Am Yahweh, the compassionate and gracious God/El (strong and mighty one), slow to anger, and abounding in love and faithfulness."*

Exodus 34:7 says, "I maintain love to thousands, and forgive wickedness, rebellion and sin. Yet I do not leave the guilty unpunished; I punish the children and their children for the sin of the fathers to the third and fourth generation."

Ahhh! Hit the brakes. What does God mean to the third and fourth generation? What if my grandfather were a good and righteous man, whom I knew and loved for those very reasons, but my old man was a dog. He sinned every day of his life according to Mom. My dad sinned more than he ate, and he never missed a meal. I'm doomed!

But back in *Exodus 20:4–6*, the LORD clears it up. I, the Lord God, am a jealous God, punishing the children for the sin of the parents to the third and fourth generation <u>of those who hate Me</u> but showing love to a thousand generations of those who love Me and keep My commandments. Whew! Praise God.

Exodus 34:8 reads, "Moses bowed to the ground at once and worshiped."

The reality is "the Lord God." That is all you can do.

Exodus 34:9 *states, "O Lord/Adonai (submissively and reverently addressed), if I have found favor in Your eyes,' he said, 'then let The Lord/Adonai go with us. Although this is a stiff-necked people, forgive our wickedness and our sin, and take us as Your inheritance."*

After all the intimacy between the Lord and Moses, Moses falls to his face, and in reverent fear, he asks to be forgiven along with the children of Israel for their sin, reciting back to the Lord His very words, "And take us, not just them, but, us, the nation, as Your inheritance."

Exodus 34:10 *states,* *"Then The Lord, Yahweh said: 'I am making a Covenant with you. Before all your people I will do wonders never before done in any nation in all the world. The people you live among will see how awesome is the work that I, Yahweh, will do for you.'"*

Since Scripture is for all of us, who have been born again, then these very same promises are for us all. I Am making a solemn promise with you, Moses, and your people. In verse 11, it says, "It is conditional, and you must obey Me."

Review ***John 14:15, 23***. *(15. "If you love Me, keep My Commands." 23. Jesus replied, "Anyone who loves Me will obey My teaching. My Father will love them, and We will come to them and make Our home {or dwell} with them. Anyone who does not love Me will not obey My teaching. These Words you hear are not My Own; they belong to The Father who sent Me.")*

Exodus 34:11 *reads,* ***"Obey what I command you today."***

K : The Smack

Ok, so imagine that one day you are sitting at home—wife, husband, and children—and an unknown entity enters your house without a "Please or may I borrow a cup of sugar, ma'am?" It's a complete stranger, not a sibling, relation, or friend, but he just steps in off the street and commences to flip over end tables, chairs, and your own child's high chair in front of your astonished eyeballs. He takes items from your cupboards, looks them over, and proceeds to toss them without regard over his shoulder and onto the floor, smashing them without a care. He's just carelessly and casually walking over the fragments.

Some of the things being destroyed are family heirlooms and cannot be replaced. Finally, as a last straw and insult, the individual grabs a hold of your youngest child and smacks him in the head. Then he turns and leaves without a backward glance or show of concern.

Now we Christians have been taught repeatedly to turn our other cheek, whether we like it or not, since our Father is so merciful toward us. I also see in the gospel of Luke that if someone asks for our shirt, we are to give our coat as well. Jesus did likewise in offering me salvation, but my point here is not whether it is good or bad to allow someone into your home to destroy it and family and your own flesh and blood is crying because a stranger has just clubbed him in the noggin.

But in a Christian home, I see that at times we allow "the enemy" to come right in, mess up a relationship with our spouse, have us children of God not speaking to one another, and have the Holy Spirit work overtime on us to get us to reconcile with that which God Himself has brought together.

In the small analogy above, if I were to ask, what would you do if someone came into your home to do those things? I would get many responses: shoot first and ask questions later, boot the individual out on the end of my size-ten Chuck Taylors, or, at the very least, just say, "Get out and do not come back ever!" We would do most anything to protect wives, children, and homes against intrusion. "The enemy of our soul can catch the last plane to Clarksville. Who needs em?"

But our enemy is instead granted immediate access into our imagination, and we then take about three days to three years working out the problem. In my life, I was cheap and told that I was stupid. I was abandoned and beat, and as Johnny Cash said in "A Boy Named Sue," my daddy left home when I was three.

The enemy wants our attention to be off the Lord and onto ourselves. Can I state that every single life that pulls a breath on this planet has difficult days or is at present knee-deep in them? We are just looking at other lives, and how easy we think that they have it from our perspective. So they somehow have it so much better than the life I've been given and daily must tread out. And why does my treading always seem to be heading uphill?

A part of that is not true since we all get life, good with bad, hard with easy, and sometime we seem to get all of it in a very short period of time. And then the residual of my bad day or life is that now I am left to deal with it alone or to restore the kitchen that someone else obliterated. And I did not ask for any of it in the first place.

Now to cheer you up, we also have our developing relationship with our Lord via the Holy Spirit, and God our Father comes along and grants us a living relationship with Him for our good and His joy. For me it is a matter of seeing what is really the truth, when I am blind to that truth.

I also see from my life that almost every single problem that the enemy throws at the Christian is seen, or rather we see it coming in one sense or another. Sometimes we duck, and other times we just turn our backs and get hit with the unexpected in the unprotected.

Now my own heart immediately speaks to me when I say something unkind to my wife, whom I've noticed is the closest individual that I'll ever know, while walking out these daily events called my life. When I look at it, the enemy was attacking my heart and where I am insecure, so I once again defend myself and allow her to suffer the slings and arrows of my uncontrolled tongue.

If I thought about it, my insecure heart can rest better in her love than trying to prove how much while in that tempest I am in and then desire for some odd reason that I don't need her or do not want to need her. So I can see that it is I myself who desires to be in a disagreement with the one who honestly wants to be there for my betterment instead of her being on the receiving end of all the wisdom I want to throw at her that I believe I quite naturally possess.

So that analogy about some schmo coming into my house to mess up my belongings is the Christian allowing the enemy to grab our attention away from God and placing our imaginations back on ourselves. If we saw it, then of course we would put an immediate end to the intrusion because it's our adversary. Also because we do not see it with our eyes, we then turn inward and start to blame our spouse, children, siblings, pastors, friends, bosses, and so on and so on as the individual on the earth who wants to wreck my life.

We have power over the unseen world, with the same amount of authority as the actual or carnal world. The Lord God said in Genesis that everything that moves along the ground. Although I cannot readily see the enemy who is coming to mess up my relationship with the Lord, I personally am on the ground. So if it is near, then I have authority over it.

I can say of myself that I should not be so easily baited. In **Genesis 4:6-7**, 'The Lord said to Cain, *"Why are you angry? Why is your face downcast? If you do what is right will you not be accepted? But if you do not do what is right, sin is crouching at your door, and it desires to have you, but you must rule over it."*

And so we should, with all diligence, for our relationships with the Lord and humanity.

L: A Quiver Full of Arrows

John 17:11, 20–23 (NIV) reads,

> *"Holy Father, keep through Your Name those who You have given Me, that they may be one as We are ... I do not pray for these alone, but also for those who will believe in Me through their word; that they all may be one, as You, Father, are in Me, and I in You; that they also may be One in Us, that the world may believe that You sent Me. And the glory which You gave Me I have given them, that they may be one just as We are One—I in them, and You in Me—so that they may be brought to complete unity. Then the world will know that You have sent Me, and have loved them even as You have loved Me."* Amen

Amen. In my imagination, I saw the Lord Jesus and me in a large field, and I had a bow with a quiver full of arrows. The Lord was standing nearby giving instruction on how to use said bow and arrows. I was currently taking aim at a target with its concentric rings in large black-and-white circles growing smaller to the actual red bull's-eye at the center. The target was about thirty yards away from us. I was looking at the target with my bow fully drawn back and about ready to let the arrow fly, peripherally checking on the Lord to see if I were doing it correctly.

The Lord looked me over and gently but with surety suggested that I move a slight bit to the left, which I did. Jesus in the same manner tapped under my right elbow and said, "Up just a little," and knowing Him to be in the right, I adjusted my sights a tiny bit higher, keeping the target in view. I let the arrow fly and missed the bull's-eye, but I at least hit the target, just barely though.

I apologized but was also pleased with myself for hitting the target at all. This was my first encounter with a bow and arrow, outside of when I was a child and we used to break off a large tree branch, string our sneaker laces to it, and then try to find somewhat straight single branches to make them our arrows. This was way back when we used to play Cowboys and Indians. Almost every child wanted to be an Indian, and if we could, we were able to scalp one another and allow our souls to float up and into the heavens. It is amazing the things you can do with a Popsicle stick to have it become your very own Bowie knife.

I obviously did not want to disappoint our Lord God. So I notched another arrow and drew that one back, concentrating more on the target.

The Lord said, "David, that was a fair shot. You must keep your eyes on the bull's-eye and clear all of the other objects out of your mind."

I spread my feet and brought the bow and arrow back up to my right cheek. The Lord repeated Himself by tapping under my right elbow.

"Your arrow will not travel in a straight path to the target. Raise it up to accommodate gravity, David. You are also turning a bit too much to your left. My Word is to guide you, but you must be the one to shoot the arrow."

I thought that perhaps I was overcompensating because I was left handed and wanted most definitely to appease His supervision.

The Lord then said, "Bend your knees a bit, and draw back a little further on the bow to put a little more oomph into your shot."

I smiled hearing the actual Word, used the word *oomph*, and pulled back a little more, which I did not believe I could even do. My muscles were straining, but He said do it, and so I did.

"I am trying my best, Lord. I'm just not used to a bow and arrow."

"Your best, David, is a lot better than what you are showing Me. I happen to know you quite well."

"Ok, Lord, I'm ready." I squinted my eyes tight, felt like I was concentrating more, and was about to let the arrow fly, thinking, which I have a tendency to overdo. But I'd been standing here for about an hour, all William Tell and whatnot, when Jesus stepped close to me once again and lightly tapped my right elbow.

"A bit higher and a touch to your right."

I guess the Lord was training me for the heavenly Olympics. I took a deep breath, let it out, and released the arrow with a twang. I still missed the bull's-eye but was about six inches closer than my last attempt.

A smile spread across my face. "How's that, Lord?"

"It is closer, David, but My expectation for every arrow is that it hits the bull's-eye."

"Well, Lord, Your expectations for me are greater than my ability, uhhh, from my own perspective, that is."

The Lord shook His head in the negative. "Allow Me to use your bow and arrows for a moment."

I handed Jesus the bow and removed the quiver from my left shoulder, and the Lord took the quiver and slung it over His right shoulder casually. The Lord looked at the target and smiled broadly, just a happy grin. He let three arrows fly faster than I could blink. I could hear the three thumps as the arrows pierced the bull's-eye. It amazed me. I saw that the three arrows were embedded in the exact center of the bull's-eye, and each arrow perfectly pierced the proceeding arrow. And all of that took about a second and a half.

My jaw was just hanging open. The first word I thought of was a curse, so I considered keeping that to myself. I was astounded at the skill. I know who Jesus is, but still to see Him in action is just unbelievable. In a cartoon or a superhero movie, you would see the same, but even if watching those, you know it is not the individual's skill but rather Hollywood magic. The Lord put any and every legend six feet under, movie magic or not.

I had to say what I was also thinking. "Well, Lord, You're not going to miss the target after all." I pointed my left index finger at Him. "You're God!"

"You, David, are also a son of the Most High God, our Father, exactly as I Am. That is what salvation is. You, David, are a son. What do you think? We are going to spend eternity together, you are just a human, and I am just God. How could you ever hope to measure up? How can there be unity, to be one in Us?"

"To be quite honest, Lord, I always thought you would fix that. Once I got home to be in heaven, then I would be transformed in my heart to know you exactly as You and our Father are."

"That process is taking place, right here, right now. Once you get there, then you will know Me fully, but nothing stops you but you from knowing Me fully now. It is just belief. You know Me because you've given yourself to Me, but to completely know Me demands that you completely give yourself, as the church states, 'surrender' yourself to Me. So whatever you see blocking our relationship is equal to what you are holding onto for and of yourself. My own perspective is that we are One, just as My Father and I are One. You are just like Me while still being you. You are His son, David. That is from My Father's command. The problem is you like seeing things from a human standpoint, which has been corrupted with Adam." The Lord laughed to Himself. "Why in the world would you depend on that?"

"Well, it is how I was trained. After all, Lord, I am a human being. So I am not exactly the same as You, Lord. You are the one and only Son of God. There is no other, and yes, I am a son, but a lowercase s. I've been adopted, but you, man oh man, You're God and His Son!"

"Your view of who you are keeps you from believing Me, as you stated lowercase. But whose view do you think is superior: yours or My Father's? His view of you is certain. So right at this moment, you are asking yourself, 'How do I hit the bull's-eye?' The important things we are discussing require belief and work on your part. You think it is far less demanding just to agree, a simple yes or no, hit the bull's-eye or don't. The real work is in building the relationship with and in our Father, God.

"But I'll give you what you don't need, the desire of your heart. I see that target as My Father, and I see the bull's-eye as His heart. I Am the arrow being placed in His heart. Not as a weapon or a philosophy, but love. And for your understanding, the love is a reverent love and longing to please His perfect will, to obey Him. Just like you want His love, I want you, David, and My bride to know just how marvelous His heart is, how true He is. The requirement for that takes work— surrender, belief, love, trust, and faith, to name a few.

"Each of those works is a character trait, and character rebuilding requires work. The more you trust or believe Me, the easier the work is. And so the harder you find the work, it shows less belief, no faith, and no action, the sluggard. That is just the tip of the iceberg of any unbelief, commonly called insecurity.

"My Word states in **Romans 8:14–17**, *'For those who are led by The Spirit of God are the Children of God. The Spirit you received does not make you slaves, so that you live in fear again; rather, The Spirit you received brought about your adoption to Sonship. And by Him we cry, 'Abba, Father. The Spirit Himself testifies with our spirit that we are God's Children. Now if we are children, then we are heirs—heirs of God and co-heirs with Me, if indeed you share in My sufferings in order that you may also share in My glory.'*

"As His child, the requirement is that you have faith in our Father, just as any child first learns to have love faith in his own parents. So for you to be His child necessitates that you put that into action. What am I to be like? Well, if a child of God, then you have no other Father, and so you are to be just like Him, which requires a positive action, which is faith on your part, David. But in your heart, you hear those words and say to yourself, 'Well, good. I am a son of the living God. But then why do I also have to suffer since after all I am a son and You, Lord, have already done the suffering?"

"It is true, Lord. Why in the world do we have to suffer? You already suffered for us. Why repeat that process? What's accomplished?"

"I am purifying individuals, My wife, My bride, to remove all of the worldliness, those impurities from what you were born with. The reason is obvious and is so that we can share eternity together, tomorrow, and today. Why do you think the living God is in you? Just to have someone to talk to. No, it is to revive you so you are His very own child. I mean, really, I gave My life not just to bring you to heaven, but to bring heaven to earth, the same way our Father planned it from the beginning, with Him being sovereign and reigning in your heart and life so everything will work together for good because He is God, righteous, and true. What more can you possibly want?"

"Well, for it to be easier … The more you work, the more there is to do, Lord. Sometimes it is like pushing a boulder up Mount Everest with ice under your feet. It is a windy day, and the wind just happens to be blowing against me."

"First, the wind is blowing in you, David. You are a son of God. You have been born anew and have His power to accomplish His will. Once you realize that there is work to be done, that is when the fire gets lit. The gold or the precious things that you, mankind, which is of our Father, gets placed into the furnace so the unclean or worldly can be removed and made holy, just as He is holy. If you think that God has nothing to work with or He is wasting His time working on you, then why do you think He rested on the seventh day? My Father and I rested to show mankind that they too need to rest in Him and not just to catch forty winks. The rest is in Him alone. That is where you are renewed, and the work is then not so much a chore, a demand on your time and body, but instead brings you the individual joy. And just a note for you, David, but that seventh day was Adam's first full day of being alive. Adam's first day was a day of rest in and with God. Mankind was meant to find complete rest in God. You began from a place of communion. Then the work began on the eighth day, or a day of new beginnings."

"Man, Lord, You're blowing my mind, but now I see that You still did the work and then came the rest."

"Ah, so now you are beginning to see that My Spirit is inside of you to work. So you now see why We said in the Scriptures *[Romans 5:1–5]*, *'Therefore, since we have been justified through faith, we have peace with God through Me, Your Lord Jesus Christ, through Whom we have gained access by faith into this grace in which we now stand/ live. And we boast in the hope of the glory of God. Not only so, but we also glory in our sufferings, because we know that suffering produces perseverance; perseverance, character; and character, hope. And hope does not put us to shame, because God's love has been poured out into our hearts through the Holy Spirit, who has been given to us.'"*

"Ok, so why the bow and arrow? That is not my thing. You might have better been able to teach me these things with a sling or a football?"

"I know what speaks to your heart, David. I know that you would not give up trying with your own skills until you hit the bull's-eye more than once, to remove from your own mind that it was not just a single coincidence. But to know My Father and your Father well, that is more than treasure, more than life. I'll use a parable here. If an individual came to you stating that somewhere on the two acres of land you live on that, long before a home was ever built there, a treasure chest of money was buried on your piece of land. The individual believed it was true but was not sure. The value of this treasure was well over two million dollars at the time that the letter was written, over forty years ago, so worth a lot more in your time and season.

"Now you know that your house is taking up a portion of those two acres. Your library, your septic tank, and all the trees also have a portion. You also know that at some past point in time, soil was distributed over the whole lot so grass could grow on top of the lime and sandstone.

"Now if you thought it was going to be too much work, then you would not begin. But if you wanted that treasure, then you would pick a spot and start to dig. My Father is a treasure far, far more valuable than any other. I know intimately and value our relationship, more than creation and life. If you want to know our Father as I do, then you must search for Him exactly as if there were a small fortune buried in your yard. If you worked on your yard with perseverance, not giving up, then eventually you would find that treasure. And after every hole had been dug, you would then be closer to your goal/gold. The blood, sweat, and tears poured into knowing our Father has a reward, which is Him and to know Him just exactly as He is—He in your heart and you in His heart. For you, the man, His presence, His heart, is where your natural desire longs to be, so just like Adam who was once able to do there on your Planet Earth. It is to stand before Our Father, naked and unashamed, without any fear naturally.

"So, David, I Am the bow." Jesus pointed directly at me. "You are the arrow, and I am aiming all of you into My Father's heart. The reward is relationship. The more you want it, the more of that relationship you receive. The less you desire it, the less you will receive. Let Me be your bow so you get to place yourself into My hands for His purpose. So, David, do not deny Me My quiver of arrows.

"**Romans 6:19–23** says, *'I am using an example from everyday life because of your human limitation. Just as you used to offer yourselves as slaves to impurity and to ever-increasing wickedness, so now offer yourselves as slaves to righteousness leading to holiness. When you were slaves to sin, you were free from the control of righteousness. What benefit did you reap at that time from the things you are now ashamed of? Those things result in death! But now that you have been set free from sin and have become slaves of God, the benefit you reap leads to holiness, and the result is eternal life. For the wages or payment of sin is death, but the gift of God is eternal life in or through Christ Jesus our Lord.'*

"**John 14:19–24** states, *'On that day you will realize that I AM in My Father, and you are in Me, and that I AM in you. Whoever has My commands and keeps them is the one who loves Me. Anyone who loves Me will be loved by My Father, and I too will love them and show Myself to them.* Then Judas (not Judas Iscariot) said, *'But, Lord, why do You intend to show Yourself to us, and not to the world?'* Jesus replied, *'Anyone who loves Me will obey My teaching. My Father will love them, and We will come to them and make Our home with them. Anyone who does not love Me will not obey My teaching. These Words you hear are not My own, they belong to The Father Who sent Me.'*

"The love of the Father cannot be separated from the Son. **Ephesians 2:1–10** reads, *'As for you, you were dead in your transgressions and* *sins, in which you use to live when you followed the ways of this world and of the ruler of the kingdom of the air, the spirit who is now at work in those who are disobedient. All of us also lived among them at one time, gratifying the cravings of our sinful nature and following its desires and thoughts. Like the rest, we were by nature deserving of wrath. But because of His great love for us, God, who is rich in mercy, made us alive with Christ even when we were dead in transgressions—it is by grace you have been Saved. And God raised us up with Christ and seated us with Him in the heavenly realms in Christ Jesus, in order that in the coming ages He might show the incomparable riches of His grace, expressed in His kindness to us in Christ Jesus. For it is by grace you have been Saved, through faith—and this is not from yourselves, it is the gift of God—not by works, so that no one can boast. For we are God's handiwork, created in Christ Jesus to do good works, which God prepared in advanced for us to do.'"*

M : What Do I Believe

Ok, so here we go. Each Sunday I have work to do in my church in San Antonio, and that is to read Scripture. I have other things I do, but those are ways to serve the body of Christ and not to toot my own horn. So they do not need to be brought up. But in this story, in my imagination, it proceeds like so.

I was explaining to the body of Jehovah Perazim Christian Fellowship that we are vulnerable in the power of God because although we hear His Word often or sometimes read the Word for ourselves, we do not practice what we preach or get taught.

In this story I was telling the body on Sunday, our pastor declared that Scripture states that we should test God to see if this/He is true. That statement is contrary to other statements that say to not test the Lord God, such as *Matthew 4:7* (AMPC). *"Jesus said to him, On the other hand, it is written also, You shall not tempt, test thoroughly, or try exceedingly the Lord your God."*

Jesus is quoting His Word *(Deut. 6:13–19)* and *1 Corinthians 10:6–13*. But *Malachi 3* always gets quoted when tithing is the subject, but *Malachi 3:6–12 (NIV)* states,

> *I the Lord do not change. So, you, the descendants of Jacob* [and since we, the church are the offspring of Abraham, then we too are descendants of Jacob] *are not destroyed. Ever since the time of your ancestors you have turned away*

from My decrees and have not kept them. Return to Me, and I will return to you, says the Lord Almighty. But you ask, "How are we to return?" Will a mere mortal rob God? Yet you rob Me. But you will ask, "How are we robbing You?" In tithes and offerings. You are under a curse—your whole nation—because you are robbing Me. Bring the whole tithe into the store-house, that there may be food in My house. Test Me in this, says the Lord Almighty, and see if I will not throw open the floodgates of heaven and pour out so much blessing that there will not be room enough to store it. I will prevent pests from devouring your crops, and the vines in your fields will not drop their fruit before it is ripe, says the Lord Almighty. Then all the nations will call you blessed, for yours will be a delightful land, Says the Lord Almighty.

Also review **2 Chronicles 31:9–10, Psalm 51:16–17,** and **Isaiah 58:5–9 (NIV)** for the answer.

So if I believe God and His Word (Jesus), then I can test God by standing in faith to what He has said. This is the point my pastor was making, although not explaining because you first have to know to explain, but—and this is a big but—if I do not believe God and His Word, then I can ask for just about anything. If I get it, good for me, and if not, then God fell short and did not really hear me. He must have been busy with the end of the world or something.

But there is always a but with me. As I was talking, I noticed a few hundred-dollar bills lying on the floor where all the people who make it out to church on Sundays at 10:30 a.m. Being on time is a big issue, which is part of the point in Malachi. Is God really that important to me, the individual?

I have a point about my church, JPCF, because that is where I attend, but we say that when I gave my heart to the Lord, then God gave me His Holy Spirit to come and dwell within me. So if that is true and according to Scripture it is, then how can I be late for church? My pastor was speaking to the men one Monday a few years ago and said something important, but he said that if I am late for Bible study or church, there could be a very valid reason, like I had a flat tire, I did not get up on time, I lost my keys, or one of my children was sick and I did not want to duff my wife with the responsibility. It's something, but if I am consistently late, then the problem is with me. I really do not care. I have my habits or routines that work for me. You actually should be happy that I even come to church at all.

Now back to the Holy Spirit within me. If He, the Holy Spirit, is within me, then God is in me. And if God is in me and those who have asked Jesus to be their Lord and Savior, when I ignore them, when it is my time and not His, then I am in reality telling the living God that it really is all about me, that I am God and "Who cares what You, Lord, think?"

I would like to refer to many scriptures here, but one group of verses from the epistle of *1 John 4:7–21 (NIV)* states a whole lot of truth but underlines what is stated above concerning how we treat each other in the body of Christ.

> *Dear friends, let us love one another, for love comes from God. Everyone who loves has been born of God and knows God. Whoever does not love does not know God, because God is Love. This is how God showed His Love among us: He sent His one and only Son into the world that we might live through Him. This is love: not that we loved God, but the He Loved us and sent His Son as an atoning sacrifice for our sins. Dear friends, since God so Loved us, we also ought to Love one another. No one has ever seen God; but if we Love one another, God lives in us and His love is made complete in us. This is how we know that we live in Him and He in us: He has given us of His Spirit. And we have seen and testify that the Father has sent His Son to be the Savior of the world. If anyone acknowledges that Jesus is the Son of God, God lives in them, and they in God. And so,*

we know and rely on the Love God has for us. God is Love. Whoever lives in Love lives in God, and God in them. This is how Love is made complete among us so that we will have confidence on the Day of Judgment: In this world we are like Jesus. There is no fear in love. But perfect Love drives out fear, because fear has to do with punishment. The one who fears is not made perfect in Love. We Love because He first Loved us. If we say we Love God yet hate a Brother or Sister, we are liars. For if we do not love a fellow believer, whom we have seen, we cannot Love God, whom we have not seen. And He has given us this command: Those who Love God must also love one another.

I look up at the congregation thinking that they will be jumping out of their seats to retrieve some of these hundred-dollar bills for themselves because my congregation is not an affluent one, but they also show respect for whoever is talking from the pulpit. At the moment though, I can easily see a couple grand spread out in no specific manner, on the seats, under the seats, or on individuals' shoes. It's as if a money bomb went off and bills just landed haphazardly all over the place. But I'm no fool, and I start to walk around still speaking.

At the same time, I too bend over and clutch a few of those hundreds. I stack about seven of them in my hand, fold them over, and place those in my pocket. And as I go to work picking up these hundred-dollar bills, I clearly see emeralds, rubies, and chunks of gold spread around. In my spirit, I know that this is the Lord's gracious provision. So I am trying to control my thoughts and not start thinking about going out and purchasing a brand-new car, truck, or both for that matter. It is God's money, so He has a better plan for it. As I pick up a few rubies, I think, *What do you actually do with a ruby?*

I start to tell the congregation how important it is for us, the body of Christ, to work with the Lord and that God has come to work with us and not to work for us. Each time I bend or squat down, more of the Lord's treasure appears. Or rather I can just see it more clearly.

The amount is overwhelming. Previously I had thought it only a few thousand at the most, but now figured it was in the upper millions. My pants pockets were full of bills, and I had been dropping emeralds and rubies down the front of my shirt.

I had no idea what the individuals who were there were thinking because the Word was ok, but why all this movement? I went to grab one of the hundred-dollar bills from a seat, next to Sister Perez, but she placed her hand on it, looked me in the eye, and said, "I see what you're doing, but these here by my husband and me are mine."

I thought, *Well, praise the Lord! At least someone else was seeing all of this provision.* I told her to take all she wanted since it was not mine but the Lord's, and you just must be willing to do the work. In this case, just pick it up.

So you see that the treasure of the Lord is everywhere and available to everyone. I was not purposed by God to be the only beneficiary of His love; rather every one of us is. We must see His blessings to receive His blessings and then bend over and pick up what He has placed there, which is the fundamentals of faith. There is work to be done. This treasure begins with the church and is then transferred out into the public. In His provision, He is the source of all for mankind. As long as we give and do His will, the righteous will never be forsaken, nor His seed, children, loved ones, begging for bread.

There is not a thing that I know of that is superior to God. He is the key to every treasure *(Isa. 33:5–6 NIV)*.

N : Chick-Fil-Argument

I was thinking. It is a thing I occasionally do, but it entails an argument concerning homosexuality and just as a thought what I see through my own two eyeballs relating to this subject. My argument is not homosexuality, but rather prejudice and our thoughts and desires that somehow we are in the right and the rest of the world needs to be on board and to agree with me. And since it is prejudice, it can be that way and, as a consequence, to disregard my own and our fellow human beings as individuals who have been endowed with the same rights that I want shown to me daily.

First off, I do believe in equality for all individuals. For me, the world was not created so my own opinion is what everyone else on this planet should exist by. I am not God. I am far, far from perfect, just like the rest of us. So what I've learned is the simple fact that if God is perfect, then His own opinions are for everyone's good, and it is first for those who know Him through Jesus Christ how very unceasingly wonderful and awesome our Father God is. To know Him is to love Him.

So it is not me first and what I want or like, but just in the overall way that I grew up and have gone through life. I find that mankind, every single one of us, are incredibly unique and special. There is also the other side of the coin. We are messed up without salvation beyond what any of us can possibly begin to imagine. Messed up is the human condition.

A very common wish for mankind is that we as a race will advance to a next level, a more aware yet unassailable human being will emerge, and that we as an entire race will all somehow have a major shift in our spiritual perceptions of life and everything in creation, a better way for all of humanity to relate to that which is not centered on this planet. I'm starting a new cult here. It is the desire of all of us to just be better than we are.

Currently it is February 2016, and in my opinion, the political climate is a complete disaster. A large group of adults' only ability to lead a nation is on calling their opponents names as if they, every one of them, were back in early grade school. And now it is not who is best qualified to be a parent to this great nation and its individuals, but rather who you like best out of the worse this country has in the running. It is as if I want to eat an apple and I go to my fruit basket for that apple and find that every one of them is decayed. So now I am choosing between them to find an unobjectionable or eatable piece of fruit, one I might be able to digest.

But enough of the preliminary underpinning and on with the show.

Several years ago, I was driving my daughter Aleece to the airport in San Antonio. It is forty-five minutes to an hour away from my house, but Aleece and I were having a heated discussion on homosexuality. My daughter has a heart for their community, and she feels that she should be an advocate for the unfairness of equality not being shown to them as a people. I would also like to say that when President Barack Obama made it law that everyone should be shown equal rights, the president was correct. Although I do not biblically agree with the decision, I also see that if President Obama said that equality should only be shown to the Caucasian race, well, since I am one, then I would be like, "Ok, great law, pres!"

So then the money, jobs, education, retirement, and social programs all belonged to me and basically my people. But when you say everyone has these same opportunities, then he or she would have to apply that law as a standard to every single person, no matter whom he or she is or who we think that he or she is. Equality is only equal when it applies to all fairly. You thought I was going to say *equally*, didn't you?

I would also like to say that when I was a teenager, as an example, I had taken a bus into the Port Authority in New York City. I was on my way to catch my last bus back to Paterson, New Jersey. While I was winding my way through the large crowd of individuals catching their own transportation to a new destination, a young man a few years older than myself stopped me. He was asking for a donation for the Black Panther party and asked if I could spare a few bucks. Well, I just did not own any bucks and probably just had a few spare cents to my name, which I gave to him, not for any other reason than that he asked.

But we just got along with each other. We talked for a few minutes. I gave him what I had to support his cause, and I was off to hop on a bus to my home and slums. Now up until that time, I had only heard of the Black Panthers, their political, rebellious, and against-the-status quo. At least that was what the news was broadcasting back in the 1970s. But having just met an individual Black Panther, I found him to be intelligent, well spoken, and passionate about what he gave himself to, basically dispelling any of my previous anxieties from the evening news and the half-insane crazy men the news media had figured the Black Panthers to be.

If I myself had the will for it at that time, I would have grabbed a coffee can and went around the Port Authority and asked for money for myself, telling anyone who would listen that I did not enjoy in any way being poor. So could you support me in changing that?

So my daughter and I were still in a dispute on the way to the San Antonio airport and our different attitudes about the homosexual lifestyle. As my daughter was once again defending their position, the Holy Spirit gave me the following.

"Aleece, are you a homosexual?"

"No, no, I'm not, but what does that have to do with anything?"

"Well, I'm not a homosexual either. I've been a heterosexual all my life."

"So what's your point, Rags?" Aleece likes to call me that. I do not know where it comes from, but I call her Wheezy.

"Well, my point is that we are arguing points without experience. My position is from what I've seen and heard from friends, coworkers, and associates, but for myself, I don't know what it's like. I and you have drawn an imagined conclusion about something we personally have not lived. If I have not walked in their shoes, then what is my opinion based upon?

"More so, what is my opinion worth? You want these individuals to have equality, so you will support their cause. But I am your parent, and I know you love me. But somehow we are debating opinions, and neither is giving ground. And worse, we do not even disagree. You want me to accept your hypothesis, and I want you to accept mine.

"Let us take the homosexual out of the conversation and instead let us talk about a diabetic. I have diabetes, as you well know, but let us say that some Christian somewhere states to me, 'Your diabetes is due to sin, and the reason, although you may be saved, is that somewhere in your life you have not surrendered your diabetes over to the Lord, and so you are still a diabetic.' Now I can argue the point with this imaginary Christian since I have diabetes, and he does not. But when I read Scripture, I can clearly see in **John 3:16** that God so loved the world that He gave His only begotten Son. There is no open parenthesis stating what does not apply to God so loving the world.

It would seem to me that anybody who is alive in the world can also know God's love.

"It is a pretty broad brushstroke because He does have rules He has placed on human beings, but I must know Him first. And then He can tell me what I need to get rid of because whatever it is, that thing is holding me back from knowing Him better. I personally believe that homosexuality is a spiritual issue."

My daughter started to object, but I put my finger over my lips to quiet her. But I also believe that everything that keeps us, everyone in the entire world, from knowing Jesus Christ as Lord and God is a spiritual issue, which only He can free us from. That is what salvation is, freedom to know Him. Then He has access to the inner person, and He and I become intimate companions. That is why I love Him so much. He is individually involved with the individual, but I have found that it all begins with Jesus. It is Jesus, and His life, death, and resurrection made a way into that relationship.

If I am holding onto my diabetes more than Him, then I will continue to have diabetes, as the imaginary Christian stated. If I give Him the diabetes, then He can remove it since I no longer own it because He is not a thief. The same is true with anything the human being has. But I can only speak about me.

The homosexual as well as the heterosexual both need salvation. If I am assigning more wrong to one and less wrong to another of which I am not a member, then I am prejudice. *Ecclesiastes 12:13–14 (NIV)* states, *"Now all has been heard; here is the conclusion of the matter; Fear God and keep His commandments, for this is the duty of every human being. For God will bring every deed into judgment, including every hidden thing, whether it is good or bad."*

One other point on the title, but that is how the conversation started on humanity's right or wrong opinion on homosexuality. My daughter said she would no longer eat at Chick-Fil-A because of their prejudice, but when she stated that, I thought, *Well, that is what prejudice is.* You will not involve yourself with an entity, namely Chick-Fil-A, and its views of what a traditional family is. But my thought was that Chick-Fil-A has many individuals working for them, especially here in the United States and I do not doubt around the world. But once I begin to disregard any individual's rights, then I am prejudice. And with that opinion comes me exercising my rights as being more important than yours or theirs.

Now for myself, at that time, I had never eaten at Chick-Fil-A, so I really did not have an outlook, but once I did eat there, I was going to go back. So whatever opinion or influence my daughter had on me concerning her right to not eat there, mine was transformed by eating one of their chicken sandwiches and really enjoying it. So any chance of a prejudice developing was overruled by my stomach and taste buds.

This thing called opinion changed because of the experience of having gone to Chick-Fil-A. But the greater issue is a natural concern for people. In today's climate of people not caring for what other people think, the issue is that we no longer listen. We just post an opinion, a view, basically my view, which of course I believe to be the best view.

The homosexual individual, just like me, needs Jesus. If my opinion is against that individual, then I am the roadblock to that person finding Jesus and His answer for this person's troubled life. By the way, every life has trouble. No one group of humanity is exempt from it.

This point brings us back to **John 3:16** that God so generously had charity toward the world that He gave His one and only Son as the cure for it. Everyone in the entire world is included in the Lord's eyes. We—all of us—need, need, need Him!

O: The Olympics

This short one came about when thinking about my own church and how each week those who are in a position to teach, such as Sunday school or Bible study, or to pray on Sundays over the body and read Scripture to the congregation. We who are in the process of doing that are also hopeful that what is spoken is also taking root.

Since I do not personally know what is going on in someone else's heart, then I cannot say with any certainty that what was said is causing growth. And so we just keep it ongoing, each of us in our own various ways. So we use everything from simple explaining to yelling or praising. We who do teach want to see the body of Christ edified, built up, and made ready to touch the world; basic Christian maturity.

God is at work on the individual of course, but He is also working on the entire body on this earth to prove Himself God. Listen, you must be God to have this many different and unique men and women working as one unit and fully committed to Him. That is a goal of God the Father, but it starts and ends in Him alone. I sure don't have a plan, but I know He does, and He desires that I be included.

But what I was thinking was that I love to swim. Swimming was a big thing with my family while growing up. Although I was never really taught how to swim, the basics were there, and through trial and error or great need, I learned how to master it. Almost any body of water, from a swimming pool to an ocean, was an open invitation for enjoyment. For me, the bigger the body of water, the better and the more exciting. So an ocean is naturally my favorite place to take a dip, and hopefully it is warm because I'm old.

Now let us imagine that when I was a child and my mom or dad began their instructions for me on the how-to-swim concept. They might have given examples, such as, "This is how you, David, are to move your arms and legs, and you can move your head to the side to catch a breath. And all of these are to be in a constant rhythm. This is how you do the doggie paddle, the side stroke, and backstroke, and when you need to rest, you can flip over onto your back and float slowly, keeping your feet moving to give you direction and necessary momentum."

But then as time passed, every time we as a family went to a beach, lake, river, and so forth, I just stood on the shoreline watching everyone else enjoy himself or herself in the water, splashing, diving, and running, but just having a great day at the beach. Now in my youthful mind I had swimming pretty much down pat but had never set foot into the larger body of water. All my stuff with water came from my time in the bathtub, and that was probably once a week, if that. I was a boy at that time.

Since in my imagination I just knew how to swim, I never worried about it. And then one day in the future, I go out on a fishing boat, and we are about a mile offshore. I put some meat on a hook and cast my line into the ocean. Further west I can see a storm brewing off in the distance. The waves are picking up, and the water is getting a bit choppy. But I am not feeling seasick because I have not eaten anything yet.

Suddenly a large wave hits the boat on the side, and I lose my balance and stumble over a cooler. I flip over the bow of the boat, and even though it's stated in my imagination, "I know how to swim," I instead begin to sink like a lead weight. And even though I have head knowledge on swimming, I proceed to drown.

So the needed info, the words pressed into me by my parents on how to stay afloat, is of no use. The Word is given, but if it is not exercised and made a reality within my everyday life, then drowning is the predictable consequence. Swimming sounded easy enough. But now that I am drowning, then what I was told did not matter at all. I am a lead brick.

Now we have heard that these are those final days, an older hip-hop song by Ugly Duckling, "Everything's Alright," contains this chorus, "If the end is near, then send it here." Not many are going to argue the fact that the end is near. As a matter of fact, since Jesus came to this earth and was crucified, buried, and, praise the Lord, raised up from the dead, then everything that has occurred in the last two thousand years has marked these final days as those that are last.

My point is that we—you and I—sit in some kind of church service at least once a week. We see God at work, not only on me, which is the easiest one for me to observe, but also on those whom I serve within my own church. I can see God at work or grace displayed when I see growth in the Spirit. But concerning the swimming metaphor, I may have received a great deal of instruction on how to do this godly work and, at the same time, have never put a foot into the water. Then I have not put into practice what the Spirit has placed into me.

Now the boat can be the world, and it is sinking. "If the end is near, then send it here." Well, it is here. If the boat sinks, then many who are trying to keep afloat and looking to be S/saved from a sure death are also dead weights, because they have had no instruction on swimming for themselves. Now if I cannot even save myself and the gifts that the Holy Spirit has ventured to work through me haven't even gotten my fingerprints on them, so my brain tells me to swim, but my experience is asking, "What should I do?!"

I am going to sink like a lead brick. Then I shame God because what good is my own salvation if not put into practice in this world. It would be a treasure put into the ground because I thought that God was asking too much of me instead of sharing that treasure and so increasing what He has turned over to me.

Now if I can only do the doggy paddle, then I may be able to save myself, but anyone else thrashing around in the water is surely going to perish because I am way too busy with saving me. Now if I have exercised what the Spirit has placed into me, then I am no longer concerned about myself.

Since I can swim (have been saved), now I am looking to help others find the way to a piece of debris or to flip them over onto their backs so they can relax while I go to help another individual. I can tell them or point them to Jesus who actually does the saving, and He does that far better than anyone, anywhere, at any time. Although I have to exercise what the Spirit has placed into me, I also realize that He is the one who does the actual teaching on how to save. It is His to begin with. I am only an expression of what He is doing with reality. But the doing it, that is mine because He Himself is teaching me.

Jesus changes that hip-hop lyric of "If the end is near, then send it here" to "If the end is near, then bring them here." Jesus is the answer and the author of life. There will be no sinking in the deep on His shift. If an individual wants to be S/saved, he or she will be.

This is the other side of that, and that is the individual who wants a different lifeguard or wants to depend on a worldly system instead of the divine. Or some make believe God instead of the divine. Hey, I am just an average man, but I am going to choose the best. His name is Jesus. Saving is as natural to Him as breathing life.

So my brothers and sisters, exercise what has been placed into each one of you for the salvation of those who are heading for sure destruction without Him. "If the end is near, then bring them here."

Proverbs 24:10–12 (NIV) reads, *"If you falter in a time of trouble, how small is your strength! Rescue those being led away to death; hold back those staggering toward slaughter. If you say, but we knew nothing about this, does not He who weighs the heart perceive it? Does not He who guards your life know it? Will He not repay everyone according to what they have done?"*

Proverbs 24:30–34 (NIV) says, *"I went past the field of a sluggard, past the vineyard of someone who has no sense; thorns had come up everywhere, the ground was covered with weeds, and the stone wall was in ruins. I applied my heart to what I observed and learned a lesson from what I saw; A little sleep, a little slumber, a little folding of the hands to rest—and poverty will come on you like a thief and scarcity like an armed man."*

Proverbs 28:4 (NIV) states, *"Those who forsake instruction praise the wicked, but those who heed it resist them."*

P: A Merry-Go-Round of Sin

It's a statement somewhat like Dr. Martin Luther King's, but "I had a dream." In this dream, I saw myself with many other individuals sitting on those very stationary mockeries of brightly colored chairs and animals having been placed on a large mechanical carousel.

The dream has been influenced by my stepfather, Jack Egan, who really enjoyed working the carnivals when they came to New Jersey in the 1960s. Jack worked all of the rides, but for me at that time, it was a merry-go-round. My stepdad would always warn us boys that we should avoid any games of chance, that they were all rigged against the individual who wanted to be a sucker. "In this life, nothing is easy" and "For my kids, it is not to be duped by any hayseed manning a game of chance."

Jack Egan was a good dad but not such a great husband. He was more in love with getting inebriated than with his marriage vows. My stepdad told us boys, "The winner of those games of chance were usually controlled by the individual who oversaw the game itself." That statement later in my life was proved to be exactly true in my early teenage years, long after my mom had thrown my stepdad out for the last time, but we Egan's had the opportunity to go down to Seaside Heights and the Atlantic ocean in New Jersey.

There was a young lady who was our next-door neighbor, but we became friends for the week that we were down there and out of the slums of Paterson. So anyway, she and I would talk, and she invited me to visit her while she worked one of those games of chance. Just a word, I'll get back on point soon, but my mom played Bingo almost every day. When the lottery was approved in New Jersey, she sent me to the candy store to get her a ticket. And if you lived a life where most of your luck was consistently bad, well, you kind of hoped that at some point that had to change. But our lives are not a game of chance. So I had two opposing teachings on chance, one from my mom and another from my dad.

My acquaintance worked her game of chance, and her prizes were any type of candy that was popular in the late sixties, so a Hershey or a 3 Musketeers bar. And if you hit the harder-to-get numbers or the fewer-on-the-wheel numbers, you might pay a quarter for a quarter candy bar, but if you hit the higher rate, then you would walk away with a box of those Hershey bars or whatever your favorite was. Mine was a Payday, but I am not sure they had it back then. Old memories here.

So my friend, the young lady, was manning this candy roulette wheel. It was early morning, and there were not many people hitting the booths to see if they could win a teddy bear for baby or a psychedelic poster, "Fly United," or an air blaster bazooka. Those parents were mostly on the beach with their kids, soaking up the sun or watching their children play in the Atlantic, telling them not to go out to far and watch out for sharks, jellyfish, and undertow! Just a pleasant day at the seaside.

As we talked, she nonchalantly asked me if I wanted to play her game and win myself a candy bar. I was stone-cold poor. The fact that we were down at the shore was due to someone else's benevolence. Poor folk avoided us and looked down on us, and they warned their kids not to play with those Egan boys. The few quarters I did have were scrounged up by those same Egan boys going under the boardwalk and sifting through the sand to find change that had fallen out of the pedestrians who did have moolah in their pockets and which had fallen through those same spaces on the boardwalk above. Kinda like pennies, nickels, dimes, and quarters from heaven.

Yet I was still young and led primarily about by my testosterone, lower brain functions, so I pulled out a quarter and placed it on a number. I thought to myself what pretty eyes she had. She spun the wheel while saying something I could not remember after I walked home. I know that the odds of me winning were impossible. At least if there were other individuals, it would be my luck versus theirs. But I already knew way back then that I had been born under a bad sign. But today, I think how amazing it is that God looks at the poor in spirit and calls us/them into a relationship with Himself. So no matter how hard my life may have been, He, the glorious He, was waiting on me to call on Him. Winner!!

But on this day, my number came up, and I won a full box of candy. She asked me to play again. Hey, once is enough. You don't tempt fate. She smiled and told me to take a chance. So I took my last quarter, placed it on the same number, and told her to let it rip, which she did. And once again I won! Now I had two boxes of candy. This diabetic was heading for the emergency room. Hot dog!

The point of that is just to state what my father had been telling me, "They're fixed. They'll take your money, and you won't have anything to show for it." It was almost true.

Now for the merry-go-round of sin: In my dream as stated earlier, I was on an indoor merry-go-round, yet I was an adult, although a young adult, and I was riding on a pony, a camel, or a hippo, but something of the four-legged variety with a copper pole through its center to anchor it to the floor. People, most adults and some children, were just doing the circles, and after a few repetitions, I grew curious because I noticed that people were trying to grab a gold ring.

When I circled by, I too tried to grab it, but it was just out of reach. If I really wanted to grab that ring, I was going to have to do some serious stretching. But now I had a challenge, and on my next time around the same circle, I kept my left hand attached to the reins and reached out as far as I thought possible and just barely missed the gold ring once again. I looked around now at the other passengers since almost all of them were still on the merry-go-round. I noticed that about half had lost interest in the gold ring since to me it seemed near impossible to grab a hold of it, unless of course I was Lew Alcindor.

There was such a contrast in the people trying. The youth were more energetic and willing to take chances, hanging a leg around the pole and leaning out as far as they could while the older folk had split into groups. The first was "If I hang too far off my post, will I slip off and break something? But I am going to try anyway." Or the others were thinking a bit like me on "How can I reach it?" Others hadn't achieved anything as far as I could see.

I knew I was going to get that circle of gold, no matter what. I had no idea what would happen once I achieved this desired goal, but deep inside me, I knew it was mine. But the how was not forthcoming.

Now I realized just anyone in the whole wide world that the merry-go-round that I was attached to was sin. The sign above the ride did not state in plain English that I was just sitting around on my own desires and going along for the ride. But I knew that deep down inside of me, just as we all do, that something with me and the world in general was not quite right. There just had to be better, but where?

I know because I know me. That sin is not, let us say, murder, and since I have not murdered anyone, then I am good to get into heaven. I also know that as an unsaved individual, I was comparing myself against the rest of humanity, where I was better than most of those others, yet at the same time not the best, which only proved to me how humble I was. But for sure and without question, I was not the worse, I mean, Charles Manson, the Unabomber, Hitler, and almost anyone who shows up on your evening news.

After salvation and after these many years, I have discovered that it is not the rest of humanity that I should compare myself to, but rather it is Jesus. He is the example that God our Father uses to sum me up against—and not whether I am saved or unsaved. So it then changes from good or bad. I am without a doubt not as good as He, Jesus, is. He is good; I am bad. I can never measure up.

Jesus is the one who gets you off that merry-go-round, that futile endless day in and day out. It is Jesus who paid my debt of rebellion against God's holiness. And since I now know that He created man, He, Father God, is our Father since He is the originator of the race. I see that sin or any type of actions that are against His character or nature is sin. Since it is self-indulgent or self-desire, what I want is regardless of what anyone else wants.

As that unique child of God, what I find is that I am not showing to myself, my family, and all of mankind who my actual Father is. The requirements are impossible to obtain because my very nature acknowledges that I am incapable of reaching that high plateau of holiness. Salvation though gives me hope since God, by His grace, nature, or character, placed Himself within me to reach the goal of knowing Him.

With God and man working together, then holiness can be achieved since He is holy and happens to live within me. I know I will have to work at it, but since His goals have become my goals, then achieving them will be a reward for us both. I'll be happy because all the things I endeavor to do will be done out of respect for our Father. It is His glory that I now want and not my own.

But that statement is a hard one because I know how insecure my own heart is, and so hero worship, some other human being/child of Adam besides me, will alleviate those insecurities with any type of praise. So it is apparent to me that I must stay with the Lord so I do not turn back to myself for what I feel I need at and desire at various moments in life. So around I go, trying to figure out how I can grab a hold of that gold ring. I know I need it, but how do I get it?

Innumerable plans go through my imagination since that is what I do naturally, and I even put a few into action but without success. The more I push myself, the closer I get, but so far there's no gold ring in my hand. It is just out of my reach. I try some of the more bizarre thoughts that I've had, but they too do not bring me success. I am thinking that on the next pass that I will just jump off my ride and onto the wooden rod hammered into the ground with the gold ring dangling off it.

In the back of my mind, I am worried that if I get off the merry-go-round that I will not be allowed back on. Some lucky person will immediately take my place. I am now thinking to myself that this, although it does not seem like much, just a gold ring, I did not have it when I sat down, so nothing ventured, nothing gained. But I cannot deny what my heart is telling me, so I know that I must have that gold ring, no matter what!

"Oh God, I cannot do it alone. I know it is only a ring on a string, but I need you to help me reach it. Please God, help."

Suddenly the dream splits in half, and I see that I make a lavish attempt at grabbing the gold ring and miss, and now my shoulders are slumped down. I sigh and grab the reins for a few more repetitions on my make-believe animal. I am just another passenger on the merry-go-round of sin. On the other half, I see that the Father has moved the wooden stake closer so I could take a hold of that gold ring. And now that I see Him, I do not know why I have not seen Him before since He was always there, right here with me. But now there was not anything that could prevent me from getting that gold ring.

So now once I had it by itself, it was slipped onto the second finger of my left hand. I am now His, and He has always been each one of ours. It now seems so simple, but all I had to do was to give up on me doing the work and trusting Him without knowing I could. God cures the merry-go-round of sin, and that gold ring dangling from that wooden stake was who I needed.

Q: I Surrender All

Luke 9:23 (NIV) says, *"Then He said to them all: 'Whoever wants to be my disciple must deny themselves and take up their cross daily and follow Me.'"*

Ok, this one the Holy Spirit gave me several years ago, and I thought you might like it. The church that I was a member of was having a retreat, and this story was my last discussion for the three days while we were in attendance. While growing up, getting to this point in my life, I've had many songs move up and down the ladder of what I considered my favorites. There was a point in time when "Ave Maria" or "Hail Mary" was a favorite. I think it is a beautiful melody and lyrics for an individual or a choir. Another is "Oh How He Loves Me," but these Christian songs have a great deal to do with where we are in our walk with the Lord. But for me, one song has spoken to me because it developed into a story or a narrative, "I Surrender All."

Chorus 1

I surrender all, I surrender all, All to Thee my blessed Savior, I surrender all.

Verse 1

All to Jesus I surrender, All to Him I freely give; I will ever love and trust Him, In His presence daily live.

So instead of me singing that to you and having you run back home as quickly as possible, I'll relate the following narrative: I am the worst criminal on the North American continent. I take great pride in being number one on the FBI's most-wanted list. In my life, I have done everything from stealing a pack of gum from a drugstore to the larger point of walking up to a total stranger and then reaching into my pocket to pull out a gun, shoot the individual in the head, reach into his pocket to remove his wallet to pull out the two or three dollars, take all the plastic, and put that into my own pocket without a care as to whether the individual life I had just taken had children or a wife who loved him. I just didn't have any care at all as to the impact that same life had on the world in general.

I just cared about what I wanted, and really it was all just about me. I personally took a great deal of pride in being a sinner. Charles Manson is an apostle compared to me, and I glory in my depravity. I'm a bad man. The things I have not done yet are to undermine the government, but only because I am not that ambitious and feel that they might make me a saint instead of condemning my actions against society. I dislike the human race, all of them, and when I think about myself and them, I still prefer to be alone and un-annoyed by their daily intake of breath.

A personal quote that I keep in my noggin is from Ebenezer Scrooge telling the two portly gentlemen who had come to request charity from him at Christmastime. "If they would rather die," said Scrooge, "they had better do it, and decrease the surplus population."

I own a house in a small town in Texas. I own numerous homes around the country and a couple in other places. Real estate is a quick way to get cash if the need arises.

My favorite outside of Texas is down in Bora Bora, Tahiti. I keep to myself just in case someone somewhere might recognize me and use his or her cell phone to take a quick shot of me and say "Snap!" Then it's posted online where anyone anywhere might place me at the scene of a crime I've committed, except of course in Tahiti, because there you are just another individual who has come to ogle our woman and go to swim with the sharks.

Back in the States, it would not take long for my name to come up on the radar of the news, the police, and most likely the FBI. And soon hopefully there would be a manhunt out for my immediate arrest. And let us also imagine that they knew that I lived right here in Spring Branch and sent out their individual task forces to bring me in, dead or alive, but most likely far better off dead. So they surround my house.

All are on edge because they have been told and have themselves been watching the news, and they know I will most likely take whomever I can along with me when they send me off to the fiery lake in a handbasket. Let us also say that the news media has gotten wind of this because it has become our very nature to gossip about everything, and I want to be praised for being such a good rumormonger. It would seem that every bad characteristic of our human natures has now become something that I can personally brag about.

So this Wild West showdown will bring that ratings boost to their individual news outlets. The big four or five (NBC, CBS, ABC, and Fox), along with CNN and anyone and everyone, are present, hoping that it will be messy and worth their time, effort, and money.

As I review what is set against me from my personal cameras that I have set around the exterior of my property for such an event, I know I have completely underestimated the force sent against me. I may be able to take out one or two dozen, but sooner rather than later, I'm gonna be a chunk of chewed-up Swiss cheese.

Subsequently, with a great deal of reluctance, I figure that instead of a Bonnie and Clyde shootout with me having more holes than the two of them together, I should just up and surrender. Logic tells me that after the first gunshot, the volley of bullets descending on me and my house, will undoubtedly be the end of me. I am crooked but not stupid.

I have my laptop with its few terabytes on my lap and checking out all the available entrances into my place and see bodies moving around to get the best shot at me while not offering up the same. Suddenly a loudspeaker barks, "David Weaver, we have you surrounded. Come out with your hands up high. We have the police, SWAT, the FBI, and a good number of individuals who want to see you dead and gone. Give it up, and come out immediately!"

Now everyone has been told to chill because of the press. You do not want to be making a martyr of this clown and then having copycats all over the world and every terrorist group having this idiot as a pinup boy. So unless of course he gets goofy, then hold your fire. Now I also realize that my only two possible chances of escape are to either pump a few rounds into my propane tank out back, and that would clear that side of the house. I could have the shower running upstairs to soak myself down and to slip out of my dining room window. And then I could hold out in the woods for a few minutes and hopefully make my great escape by heading off into the woods or just by simply surrendering because I really do not many choices.

I pick surrender because I don't have any other real ideas as to how much damage will be created when I pump a few rounds into my great big propane tank, which would cause a desired distraction, by incinerating my house with me in it.

So I go to the backdoor, crack it open a few inches, and tell them that I am coming out, so hold your fire. I kick the door all the way open, take a deep calming breath, and come out with a gun in my hand over my head in a defensive stance. They do not think that is exactly what they meant by surrendering, and they open fire, faster than a mosquito on a bleeding arm, and I am gone in a hail of blunt chunks of heavy metal, travelling at a very high rate of speed.

Rewind. I figure that I should surrender, so I do the same, calling out to the law enforcement agencies, telling them I am going to surrender. But once I kick the door open, I come out with my hands behind my back just because in my imagination I figure that they are going to slap some handcuffs on me. So why make them work for it? The law does not know what I may be hiding back there, so once again they do not wait for Christmas to come. They open fire, and once again, there is one less bell to answer, one less egg to fry.

Final rewind: I finally come out and completely surrender because my very existence depends upon it. I come out of the open door with my hands high above my head, take two steps, and fall flat on my face with my hands outstretched and say, "I surrender all. I surrender all, all to Thee my blessed Savior I surrender all."

So what the Lord showed me is that surrender is not exactly how I envision it, holding on to the things that I imagine I might need—my money, my personal strength, or my knowledge—but rather it is Him and only Him. The second type of surrender is when I think I have a little bit better plan than the living God and I am surrendering, but in my own way to help Him out. Because of course God actually needs my help. The thing I have found is it is only Him; He is God, and I am man. It is so much easier to believe and do what He is asking of me, which is commonly referred to as faith.

R : A Thought

This is a short one. I was thinking that in **Genesis 12:1–9**, but the Lord tells Abram that his descendants will inherit all the land, which was Canaan. But from that point unto the actual point where the children of Israel go into the land to first conquer it, well that took a lot of time and events in history. A small note on Scripture, but what I see are individual events happening to many individuals. It would be impossible to mention each and every event of just Adam. He could have said, 'I named this bird *meshuganah* because it is always banging its head into every tree it lands on.'.

Eve is like, "Well, Adam, why don't we name it a woodpecker? I think it is tapping its head against that tree to find something to eat."

God gives us the highlights for things that speak to numerous individuals so we can see Him while we also see ourselves.

So Israel took a lot of hard history in all of Scripture as well as the bride of Jesus Christ. Likewise, Isaac had a hard time with many trials and errors, then up to Jacob with Lanban, his uncle, in trying to get the wife he wanted and getting more than he asked for, along with his relationship with Esau, his mother, and dad. We see Jacob, that his life had far more highlights than the few that we are given in Scripture. But Scripture shows us God and us; with expectations from both sides.

For example, consider Israel's loss of Joseph with his own brothers selling Joseph into slavery. Each one of them lived with the consequences of that action daily. I can see that Israel as a people in Egypt and their subsequent slavery was because of their actions toward Joseph. Israel was freed and under the leadership of God and Moses, along with their trials to get to the promise of God made to Abram before he had any children. It was a long and very hard road to transverse, but a life lived especially with God is necessary.

So when I claim a promise of God and my expectation is that it should have been fulfilled yesterday, then I am not looking at how God brings about change in His people. It is usually a long and hard road, but praise God, He is walking that road along with me. And since He lives here within me, then He knows exactly what my life feels like. If I say to Jesus, "Lord, you do not know how badly this wound hurts!" He is in my heart where I relate to pain, sorrow, or life. And He is walking that out with me and you every inch and step along the way.

My point is that most times it takes time for the Lord's things to be fulfilled because we are in the process of changing into Jesus while still being David or whoever you are. The second point here is that Scripture is giving the Lord's side of the story along with mankind's. It cannot all be there because even the Word of God would become boring. If we had every nuance of David trying to figure out a way to get Bathsheba, we might be taking notes to do the same, and if Bathsheba does not interest us, then we might just skip some chapters that are extremely important to me, and you. It is all important, but we must inquire so as to know Him, and me.

S: Marriage and So First Things First

Matthew 6:33–34 (NIV) reads, *"If you in all things first seek the kingdom of God, and His righteousness then all these things will be added unto you; Therefore, do not worry about tomorrow, for tomorrow will worry about itself. Each day has enough trouble of its own."*

In Scripture, there is a balance, and from what I've seen, there is also an explanation. So the second set of Scriptures to remember or write down means that you, the individual, are using to get God into you.

That which concerns a treasure, so *Proverbs 2:4–5 (NIV)* says, *"And if you look for it as for silver and search for it as for hidden treasure, then you will understand the fear of The Lord and find the knowledge of God."*

And *Isaiah 33:6 (NIV)* states, *"He will be the sure foundation for your times, a rich store of salvation and wisdom and knowledge; the fear of The LORD is the key to this treasure."*

Also review *Matthew 6:19–21, 13:44–45, 52.*

There are many scriptures for treasure, but this is one more that I like a great deal, *Colossians 2:2–3 (NIV)*, *"My goal is that they may be encouraged in heart and united in love, so that they may have the full riches of complete understanding, in order that they may know the mystery of God, namely, Christ, in whom is hidden all the treasures of wisdom and knowledge."*

The last of these three would then be faith. Faith is the actual believing God, putting into action what the Lord has placed in your heart, mostly when you cannot see the beginning or end of the work that is taking place. Not based on the emotional, the soul, but rather to just do Jesus.

So for me, marriage is just like that in the fact that I knew that I loved my wife before I married her, but I had no idea of the challenges that marriage would present. But I can tell you that if anyone had told me how much I would grow in our relationship and how very much I love her today, then just in my natural mind, way back in 1977, I would have thought you to be the biggest liar who ever spoke in a human tongue.

There is no limit in what God does that honors Him. We, Gisele and I, both come from broken homes. Both of us had an alcoholic father. My mother was pretty close to being one herself, but she had more of an addictive personality. And just as an aside, those personality traits, good and bad, are the actual lessons that your children are learning because they believe what they see. Actions always do speak louder than words.

Now you can very well try to beat the sin out of your own child, but then your own child, when he or she becomes an adult, will try to beat the sin out of his or her child instead of trying to beat the sin out of myself, where the real problem exists.

Even though Gisele and I did not really know if we would make it, we did trust Jesus, and basically each of us in our own individual life turned our marriage over to Him. Even though we were young, we could plainly see that most had failed at the task of making their own marriage work.

I would like to also say that just as much as Jesus and our relationship with His and our Father God is the for-real treasure, every marriage is predominately a visual for the whole wide world to see who God in all His majesty is. Marriage shows that I love my wife more than I love me. But once again Jesus is the key. The more we serve Jesus our Lord, the more valuable not only are my relationships but people in general, all people, since you all are family and have the very real reality that all can be a part of His family. Then I have the deeper and the more conflicting emotions toward you all.

Just as a point in my marriage, I certainly did not marry myself. If I had, the marriage would never have lasted, even if I put all my determination into that marriage of the individual who had each one of my personality traits. That marriage would never last because I would always see the faults that I have yet to deal with in myself, as I surrender or release each to God. This is basic grace, God at work.

I thank God that Gisele is much different than I am, and one of the major things that I see is that in a marriage we complement each other. Where I don't, she does. Where I'm weak, she is strong. And vice versa. That is also where the struggle in a marriage lies. Why doesn't she do these things? Doesn't she see that is the right thing to do? Or from her perspective, "How can you say you love me when you won't even put out the garbage, raise the toilet seat, or paint the living room?"

On this planet, I have no better friend because she still loves me in all my apparent weaknesses. My blood sugar was low the other evening, and I was in bed. I'm the early-to-bed individual, and Gisele was still up, but while in bed, I was thinking about the future and how the church was going to be persecuted. I also was thinking in the extremely abstract way that my mind goes to when my sugar is low, but I just felt the need to get up and be with my wife because it may not always be that way.

So I came trotting out into the living room in my draws, insulin pump hanging off to the side. I sat down next to her and just held her hand,

and I did not want to let go because of the limited time we might have together. But Gisele thought that was just so sweet. All of that is just to show in a tiny peek how much of a treasure our spouse is to us if we only allow it in Christ Jesus. She will drive you crazy with her personality, just the same way I drive her crazy more times than not. We are two extremely different individuals that God in His wisdom could not stand to be apart, but united making a singularly unique example of who He is, especially when we as a couple are walking or living our lives in accordance with His divine will. *Isaiah 53:10 (NIV)* reads, *"and the will of the LORD will prosper in His hand."*

Talking about Jesus, when we are in the Lord's plans for our life, we prosper because our Holy Father wants His will to divinely grow as we are obedient to Him. Dead wood is burned away; new life is added to grow by.

Did I always know that? Of course not! Can the relationship we have as husband and wife grow? Of course it can. Love never maxes out, but you and I cannot come to the end of it, love in Jesus our Lord. But the negative of that is that desire, which is self-fulfilling. Well, that will always max out and get to be tiresome. And as soon as that happens, then we start to find the other party not as comely as we once did. Because the for-real problem is with ourselves, which we cannot get rid of; I need the fix and find that the problem does not have anything to do with my spouse.

Relationship is everything to God. First and foremost is our relationship to Him and, after that, with our fellow human beings, my wife being the primary one for me and then my children. And because I have different types of relationships, the more familiar or the better I know an individual, the deeper our relationship becomes. And that, as a note, is what *koinonia* is.

Unity (*2 Chron. 30:12; Ps. 133; John 17:23; Eph. 4:3–13; Col 3:12–17*)

Psalm 133:2 (NIV) reads, "Precious oil poured abundantly on Aaron's beard, on the collar of his robe." The oil of Aaron's anointing saturated all of him. This signifies for us and Aaron as well our total consecration to the Lord's holy service. In the same way, communal harmony or harmony in the church of Jesus sanctifies God's people. It works from above since it is poured out on his or our head, from above to below. His will is for it to work, and it works with a husband and his wife. And it works with the body of Christ as we put our best foot forward for each other's very best, giving our all for someone else's betterment, basically *agape*.

Coming Together in Unity *(Col. 2:2–3 NIV)*

Unity is defined as being one; combining into one; something whole or complete by combining or joining separate things or entities to form one (Encarta Dictionary).

Harmony *(Matt. 18:19 and Amos 3:3 NIV)*

Harmony is happy agreement; a situation in which there is agreement (Encarta Dictionary).

Agreement is the act or state of agreeing, the reaching of sharing of the same opinion that somebody or others hold (Encarta Dictionary).

How Do We Get There? (From NIV)

1. Choose Jesus Christ as your first love *(Matt. 22:37–40)*.
2. Fear the Lord *(Ex. 20:20; 1 Peter 1:13–17; Isa. 33:6)*.
3. Believe Him and love *(Heb. 11:1, 5–6; 1 Cor. 13:4–8)*.
4. Walk it out in love by faith *(James 2:26)*.

T: In Beginning

This is a subject that I've been meditating on concerning the similarities between the Lord's birth on this planet and how our new birth through the Spirit of God comes about. I hope that it shows to me first the importance that God places on every one of us who has received Jesus Christ as Savior, God, and King. I see through Scripture that Jesus not only wants the individual to know intimately who His Father is, but also in that knowing that I think of God with all due respect and honor for His glory and not to minimize Him trying to promote my own magnificence. In reality I know that I do not have any glory, except to be seen once again in His own eyes, according to His example, which is Jesus.

Also for me is that the very life of God on the cross was never meant to be minimal to any of us and greater still to God, it being the greatest sacrifice any being can give, to redeem that which by its own choice duffed Him. I also see from *John 3:16* that God the Father so loved the world that He gave His only begotten Son. But God did not tithe of Himself, only giving 10 percent. He gave everything that He cared for, His only Son. So if I want to be like God and Jesus, then I should be willing to give my all, holding nothing back as was and is both of Their examples.

So to begin, I have a natural and supernatural predisposition to study Scripture. If someone states something that I have not read in the Bible, then once I am back at home, I will scrutinize the Word of God to get an understanding. I know that I too can be wide of the mark. I for one have not memorized all of the Word of God, but if an item comes up and in my mind I say to me, "Hey, I've never heard that!" then I will pop open my TNIV Study Bible, which is on its last legs, and search for that scripture and then study the substance in context. I have also asked my Father God since I was created with a need to know and to find out what is lurking underneath the rock. But I have truly asked our Lord to just download the entirety of Scripture into my heart.

Now my reasoning for this is so I do not personally get His Word wrong and then start to teach someone that incorrectness. In my imagination, I can see God the Father placing His hand on my head and speaking the name of Jesus to cram every nuance of His Holy Word into my heart. Plus, that would make studying so much easier. I say to me that if God downloads, then He too will leave no stone unturned. And therefore, "I will know."

But that is just not what has happened. I, just like you, must study, and I, like most, do not find the time to do just that. Either I am busy with this or that or have too much on my plate, or I am just in the mood for me and not for Him. I hate to say it, but habits are bad and are human. Although I love the Lord, I also find that at most times I am also much more in love with me. Basically I am not denying myself, nor taking up my cross and not following Him, even though I am saved and positively know within me that I am. There are times individuals doubt the words that are being spoken.

Accordingly, you may ask, what does this have to do with reading Scripture or my own study habits? I'm glad you asked. For me, since I'm the writer, I have found in my daily life that the more I do study Jesus, the Word of God, the more opposition I find on what I consider my free time, to be diligent on the things of God. Consequently the more I do study Scripture, the more I really see Him and come to know the character or, better, the individual who is the Lord our God.

So the Word of God keeps me on track on "in Seeking first the kingdom of God," who just happens to be my own King. Hence the Word of God, again in my life, speaks to me on how the relationship between God and man works in covenant relationship, or communion. I see the rules of how I am to walk that out in the reality of also living in a world that in its natural state is in rebellion to who He/God is. There is so much in the spirit world that I do not see.

Thus, the first step, in a logical perspective, would be to see how and where all of Scripture then applies to me, the individual who is seeking to know.

I would like to use two—or possibly three—sets of scripture that from the surface do not apply to me because from a commonsense look at these scriptures they seem to be speaking of something quite different than this human being's existence. The third set might be a bit iffy though. We will see together what is revealed.

Genesis 1:1–5 (NIV) reads, *"In the beginning God created the heavens and the earth. Now the earth was formless and empty, or void, darkness was over the face of the deep, and the Spirit of God was hovering over the waters. And God said, 'Let there be light,' and there was light. God saw that the light was good, and He separated the light from the darkness. God called the light 'day,' and the darkness He called 'night.' And there was evening, and there was morning—the first day."*

Now to examine the evidence: First, in Hebrew that word for "In Beginning" is *Bereshit*. In American English, it's "in the beginning," God. So that made me look at the last word in Scripture, in **Revelation 22:21 (NIV)**, which is *amen*. Amen is also Hebrew and means "Let it be, as You, Lord have said," my own interpretation of *amen*.

May I say—and for the many who already know—that the majority of what is commonly called the Old Testament is Hebrew and the majority of the New Testament is in Greek from today's perspective.

Aramaic was more common and influenced much of what the common community read. I can see from those languages that God's desire was for the natural man to understand Scripture. I personally do not have the education nor the wherewithal to debate other languages. I have more than enough trouble with American, and I've lived here my entire life. My point is that the Hebrew of the Old Testament was for Israel and their common language so that everyone could understand it, Scripture.

Now the New Testament was written in a language that was good for the common people so they too could understand the Word of God. So then the Word of God was written by the Holy Spirit through human beings because we get each other, and God also wants us, as a result, to get Him.

I always have another point, but for the Old Testament and New, there is no really separating them. It is only one book, covering who God actually is and who man actually is and how we need Him to be free to have a relationship with Him. We are unable to come up and keep up a plan to have a relationship with God without Him being a part of said relationship. When I tell you how you should worship God, that is religion, and from a world perspective, religion wants basically to destroy whoever does not agree with it. *2 Peter 3:9* reads, *"The LORD is not slow in keeping His promise, as some understand slowness. Instead He is patient with you, not wanting anyone to perish, but everyone to come to repentance."*

That is the message of the entire Bible. Jesus never once quoted the New Testament. Jesus brought understanding or light to the Old for our betterment. The difference I see for myself is that the law was done away with so the relationship could begin. But the Old and New Testaments show how to walk that out. If I want to know how to love God correctly, my first step would be not to have any other gods, including myself, before Him.

So with Scripture comes comprehension, and a consequence of understanding is found when my own mouth says "Amen." Then I am in agreement with God my Father on what He has spoken through Jesus, who is the Word. So all of the promises He has spoken over me attach themselves to me if I am in a loving and obedient, along with a reverent fear, which develops the relationship with Him being God. The bonus of salvation is that He, God, also gave the cure for my rebellion, His own obedient Son. So if I know that I should be compliant to Him, out of that very same love and reverence, this puts the relationship with God on a proper track, as it would with any relationship.

Yet at the exact same time, if I am in a rebellious association, then I can also comprehend that all the negative stuff the Lord has stated also would apply to me. That is why Jesus, the Son, rejected sin. He wanted His Father to be glorified in everything He, the Lord Jesus, did. Goose equals gander.

Now I, just like in Genesis 1, had an "In the beginning" moment, and that is when I was twenty-one years old. I did not want to make it to twenty-two. There were way too many things vying for my attention, and since before salvation, I was so into the occult that I thought I would just die and pay the penalty for that action and come back for another shot at the title of being a god. But that is a whole different story and full of junk or worldly and worthless philosophies. God took the time by the Spirit of God to hover over the surface of my own deep darkness, namely me.

But one day while in that darkness, one of my closest friends, Javier Marquez, had given his heart to the Lord. I did not know this, but as the Lord was working on me, my brother Barry had decided that we should go and visit Javier or the whole Marquez family down in southern California. Since Jav and I had so many things in common, he was anxious to tell me of his personal experience with Jesus. I told Jav to take a hike, but he continued to pray for me, I am sure.

And once we got back home, Barry also started to go to church, and he too gave his heart to the Lord. Consequently he kept asking or bugging me to go to the First Baptist Church of Half Moon Bay with him. And the Spirit of God also at that time had an elderly reverend by the name of John Thrasher praying for me, along with my girlfriend, who is currently my wife, Gisele.

Now even though way back then I was a human being and still am one, I was still formless and void. Formless to me has no definitive shape to it. A circle is a shape with dimension, along with a square or a triangle, but formless is as if I took a pencil and scribbled on a sheet of paper. It may have a form, but it cannot be repeated, except with a Xerox or a piece of software that would define all the nuances of said scribble. But if you asked me the scribbler to repeat that scribble, then I would not be able to do so and would be therefore formless, not defined as yet.

Now void, or empty, although alive, eating, sleeping, and affecting the world, I was void of life. I also think that from Scripture that a good example would be Sarah, Abraham's wife from the book of Genesis, on what void meant to me. Now Sarah was a beautiful woman. When she was in her late eighties and nineties, dudes were still attracted to her and wanting to catch a rap. I'm old school. But she, Sarah, still did not bear any fruit for her husband; therefore she was void, exactly as I was.

I was alive, but since I had not given my life or surrendered my life to Jesus yet, I was still heading eagerly to the depths of Sheol, even though I had no definite idea of what that entailed. So what I see now is that the Spirit of God had been hovering over me, brooding, caring, and wanting me to wake from my coma, which I call alive, but without life and without Jesus—therefore void.

As a result, God, as in **Genesis 1**, came and spoke His Son's name over me and said, *"Let there be light/Jesus." And there was light.*

I said to myself, "Oh, look, light and truth, I think I'll choose the light/Jesus."

Then God, when He saw me acquiesce, separated the light from the darkness and, in me, called the light Jesus and the darkness David. The Lord also gave me an invitation to join Him in that light, which I kind of saw as His truth or character. And God saw that the light was good, good for me, needful for me, we, and every single one of us. And that was my first day of being a new creation, a new being born of the Spirit, designed for God and by God for His own personal use as a member of His family. That was how I had life placed inside of me by the Lord's Spirit.

Because that is so miraculous, then all I can say is, "Thank You, Lord!"

The hard thing for me is separating the darkness in me from the light and truth. But God wants us to work together on that project, so He came to live in me to get that work done. It is not Him alone; nor is it me alone. Scripture states that I must die to the things of sin, Romans 6: clearly state this. And the second part is to live for God.

Once again if you look at that Scripture, there was evening, and there was morning the first day, evening and dawn. To me, I have a combination of light and dark, so I see that Jesus needs to rise within me so that all who look will only see Him *(Malachi 4:2)*.

Even when God got to the final day of that first week and sin had not begun with self-desire, what I see is that the light/Jesus coexisted with the darkness, me. But since Jesus is light and He then calls me to be where He is, so that I would enter His rest, which is His way.

Now that first requires the relationship, Jesus, to be with me. When I see Him as God, then I am in awe that He could be so loving as to search me out of the entire population of the Planet Earth and then to invite me into a bigger communion/community with His Father and Spirit. But that is a whole different writing, which is a book unto itself, which the Lord already wrote, called the Bible. Please read it.

So once again, if we review those verses of Scripture found in **Genesis 1:1–5**, I find that they start and end with the Lord. I can conclude that He will finish the work He has started, just as He did when He finished the work of creation and took Adam and his wife, Eve, and entered into His rest, for the work of creation was over on that seventh day. And the work of living was no longer void because He had filled in all of creation with life (fish, birds, animals, and mankind with His breath). I now had purpose, Him.

Then my life began with a new beginning, my own eighth day (or first day in God) and in the desires of His heart. It is easy to write since the Holy Spirit gives it to me, but it is a bit harder to do since the task of changing my own character into God's character requires more work than relaying every single brick and stone in the Great Wall of China. But that is why God put His Spirit within me to make His seemingly impossible stuff possible with a human. I already know that I am incapable of doing anything without Him. Yet faith says, "do."

You can see how God spoke creation into existence and how that same piece of scripture from Genesis applies to you and me. Another note on this one, but I started to think about knowledge along with understanding.

Proverbs 4:7 (NIV) reads, *"The beginning of wisdom is this: Get wisdom. Though it cost you all you have, get understanding,"* or *"In all your getting, get understanding or whatever else you get; get understanding."* That statement is very important to me. In my mind, knowledge is head knowing; but knowledge is to know through experience. It is not just heart or head knowing, and that I have pulled data into me carelessly or with purpose file it for later use. It is putting it into use through exercise, and exercise of The Spirit.

I enjoy the study of science, so I will use science as an example for wisdom and understanding. I can state that evolution is the way of the world as stated by science and Chuck Darwin. I can also state that evolution has multiple similarities to religion, in a sense from a knowledge platform. I do not personally know what evolution is since I only know from what I see and from what I have experienced in these sixty-three years of life, so evolution is more about what I think and not what I know from experience of my life and from what I have lived.

I may agree, but just like science, I do not know or understand because none of us have lived it. Like I said, I am currently sixty-three years old. The things that science has stated as being absolutely true have changed dramatically since the decades ago when I was a child. So now, the more common announcement from science is that when new data is available, then our ideas will adapt to them. Well then, if my head knowledge is always in flux, which it is, then why in the world should I put any credence in it, science, since I can depend that it will change with time, which I can say from personal experience, it has?

Therefore, when those same rules are challenged by people with questions, then other people go back to the rule book and then state, "This is why" or "That is why." And once again we are left with the argument of what is in my individual noggin and not really what the Lord God is stating is the truth.

Or is the truth my own head knowledge? I know this, and you know that. I believe I am correct and that you are therefore incorrect, if perchance you do not agree with me. What I have seen in Scripture is that God does not like that approach either, so He wants you and I to know Him. Thus, we have Jesus, who is the verb of the proof of what has been stated from Scripture as to what His character is. I have found that He is the Truth, but to better understand what God states, because now I know Him. And He, God, overwhelmingly accepts me when I come to Him with a question. The Lord does not just drop an answer into me, but many times He has led me to Scripture or to a better understanding to Jesus, where I can see the proof for myself because I now know Him. This is the major difference between science/religion and having been born again. It is Jesus, and I have a personal relationship with Him. He is reality, and I know Jesus exists far more than my own life and reality or even the fact that I am drawing breath.

Jesus is God and yet is also man. Better yet, He, Jesus, is man. Jesus is the model of what God knows a human being can be once the relationship is begun and allowed to grow, just as any other relationship can grow on this planet.

We all have the ups and downs, the closeness of fellowship and parting of ways due to disagreements. For me, there is the bonus that He helps me with, and that is that I also get to release all the Adamic stuff, whose destiny is to die **(Genesis 2:17)**.

I stated earlier that I had knowledge because I was occasionally sent to church as a child and young adult, but when I actually gave my life, heart, and mind on that February day in 1977, then a real relationship began. And now I could say within me, "Ahhh, now I understand. He, the living God, does love me and does expect better from me because since I am in a relationship with Him, then other people who do not know Him will see the truth of who He is by my actions. It is something every other human being can relate to, one of their own, but not by my own will. But more because of who He is, I am a better man, and since I have been called and now know Him, He requires a greater purpose from the life He gave to and for me. Therefore, my actions should be His actions, my love His, my marriage His, and so on."

But what I have also found is that I do not have the strength of character to live a God life because by my very nature I am corrupt, or flawed, but now since I am His kin or have a kinship and He is within me, then I can come to Him and say I need help in living His life, His way, which I do often. He will not ask me to do anything that I am not capable of doing. But at the same time, as I said, Jesus is the Father's plan of what a human can be, the more of Him, the less of me.

But to fill that out, from God's perspective, the more of Him, then naturally the more there is of me, if that is what I truly want. Many times I do not because of the work that is involved, but the more intimate we become, the more the work becomes a joy and far less the chore that I think it is.

I hope this statement will help you to better understand it. But until I had children, then I just had head knowledge on how I would parent a child. Once I had children, and still do, now head knowledge is for the birds because being a parent is a hard job. Nobody is giving us any cash monies for doing that job, being a parent. But the rewards for the effort, no matter how hard it may get or, for that matter, how wonderful it is. Parenting is so much worth the effort, along with anything on this planet that is for the good of another. It requires effort. But for children to become good adults is a treasure to a parent. That is far, far greater than any lotto cash dividend. Now I understand what being a parent is, and my own heart at times now goes out to the Father because I only have two kids. The Father's love and concern is for every single one of us, no matter who or where we are in this world. Each one of us has a will to choose Him or not. See *John 3:16–21*.

Concerning my own children, I now have understanding and knowledge. I would put my money, if I were a betting man, on the one who loves and has found salvation for himself or herself. But I would not want the child who has yet to arrive to miss knowing the Lord because I love them both with all my heart, as every parent does for his or her own. Ultimately, if I understand an item, that insight now trumps and somehow at the same time completes knowledge for me. Whew! That was an extended thought!

Finally the second set of scriptures is going to be on the birth of our Lord, Jesus Christ, He who is the anointed One. *John 1:10–14 (NIV)* reads, *"He was in the world, and though the world was made through Him, the world did not recognize Him. He came to that which was His own, but His own did not receive Him. Yet to all who received Him, to those who believed in His Name, He gave the right to become children of God His Father—children born not of natural descent, nor of human decision or a husband's will, but born of God. The Word became flesh and made His dwelling among us. We have seen His glory, the glory of the One and Only, who came from The Father, full of grace and truth."*

And the text I am going to use is primarily from *Luke 1:26–38 (NIV)*.

> *In the sixth month of Elizabeth's pregnancy, God sent the angel Gabriel*/Man of God, or hero of God; *to Nazareth, a town in Galilee, to a virgin pledged to be married to a man named Joseph* [to add or let him add]; *a descendant of David. The virgin's name was Mary* [their Rebellion, obstinacy, rebelliousness]. *The angel went to her and said, "Greetings, you who are highly favored! The LORD is with you. Blessed are you among women." Mary was greatly troubled at his words and wondered what kind of greeting this might be. But the angel said to her, "Do not be afraid, Mary; you have found favor with God. You will conceive and give birth to a Son, and you are to call Him Jesus. He will be great and will be called The Son of The Most High. The LORD God will give Him the throne of His father David, and He will reign over the house of Jacob forever; His Kingdom will never end." "How will this be," Mary asked the angel, since I am a virgin?" The angel answered, "The Holy Spirit will come on you, and the power of the Most High will overshadow* [a bright cloud signifying the presence of God; *Ex. 13:21; Gen 1:2 (NIV)*; moved or hovered over the face of the waters [Strong's concordance states to be moved affected, with a feeling, of tender love,

> hence to cherish] *you. So, The Holy One to be born will*
> *be called The Son of God. Even Elizabeth your relative is*
> *going to have a child in her old age, and she who was said*
> *to be unable to conceive is in her sixth month.* **For no Word**
> **from God will ever fail.**" "I am the LORD's servant,"
> *Mary answered. "May it be to me according to your word."*
> *Then the angel left her.*

So the unique birth of our Lord Jesus onto the Planet Earth, how does that act of God relate to me? Well once again, I'm glad I asked.

Now first off, let's get the junk, or the carnal thoughts, out of the way. I do not think that in any way that when Gabriel told Mary, "The Holy Spirit will come upon you, and the power of the Most High will overshadow you" the Holy He had a bottle of Dom Perignon on ice and pulled from the future, my past, Marvin Gaye singing, "Let's Get It On." That is just not the nature of our God, but it is the nature of imagination.

Although off track once again, do you find it interesting how the individual acceptance of salvation is never discussed in Scripture. The closest individual act that I see is Paul's conversion, but even for Paul, it shows how Jesus showed up while Saul was on his way to Damascus to continue his job of destroying or, at the least, slowing down what had begun in Jerusalem with the eleven apostles and what God had initiated in the life of His one and only Son, Jesus.

Paul had asked who it was, but that one act of being transferred from having been born of Adam, to being born of God got recorded a bit later in **Acts 22**. My personal belief is that the act of salvation is an individual experience. The Holy Spirit comes to me, invisible, but still comes and asks if I want to know God. For me once again, it is like the reverse of the Tree of Knowledge. Now I act in faith to what God has said without any proof. The proof becomes self-evident once I accept it as being valid before I know intimately that it is legitimate, before salvation was offered.

Once I have accepted it and in my own heart know it or rather know Him to be true, now I have some choices to make. The first is, "No, I like things the way they are," or "Yes, I agree that I need You, even if I do not really know You at this moment. Even if I've studied all my life about You, I still do not know You personally."

There is the second option, and that is that I say, "Yes, I need You, but then find in my life that the things I am doing with everyday life are far more important than taking my life and placing it in the Lord's hands and working with Him on His plans for this earth."

In **Matthew 21:28–32 (NIV)**, Jesus uses a parable concerning the owner of a field who has two sons. The father goes to his first son and asks for assistance on working their property. The first son states that he will not but a little later changes his mind and helps his father. But while the answer is still no from the first son, the father goes to his second child and asks him the exact same thing. The second son says, "Yes, sir, I will," and yet does not do what he has said with his own mouth that the second adult child has agreed to. The Father still wants help with the field though, or else He would not ask.

For me, what I see is that salvation is an agreement between God and the individual to do the things of God, which from my view is the opposite of what took place with Adam at the Tree of Knowledge. So first and what has the most priority would be to establish the relationship. If I obey the Lord my God, then I agree with His heart for how I am designed to interact with His creation via His Son and Spirit. The relationship deepens as I get to know Him better, just as any standard human relationship develops. I can now see that God and I are working together on the same conclusion, namely that the relationship grows and produces fruit.

I put in a great deal of effort to avoid Him as an individual all my life until salvation, and now that the relationship is alive and thriving once again as if Adam had never fallen, then with the divine Him being my sovereign, I, just like Adam, now have choices to make concerning His will for me. I am in a sense like Jesus, one of the Father's children, that I should be humble and seeking only what the Father desires and don't have my own personal junk or agenda getting in His way. Since the better I know Him, the more I understand His heart's desire, His heart's passion, which is humankind and their betterment.

There is so much in those verses, but back to the point, which is salvation is unique. Each one of us has a choice, but how that choice is given to us is different and especially what we do with salvation once we've made the decision. Once again, I am back to the Father, who is asking me for help on His estate. I say one thing and then do another.

Some of us are desperate and cry out. Some have accepted salvation and little by little come more and more into the relationship, weeding out the worldly garbage. Sin is junk since no one really wants it. Even if we desire it, we call them our flaws, but since everyone has some, then these are mine. And they ain't so bad when I think about me. It is funny, but they are big flaws/problems when I think of those attributes in anyone else.

Accordingly, if I am extremely introspective, then I'll acknowledge that I am playing a part, but the other person does need to change. My wife would hate it if I had a drinking problem because, if I did, then I would show her that I was more concerned with me than her that I was far more in love with me than the woman whom I married. Relationships always suffer when any individual is self-centered, self-absorbed, or self in love rather than in love with whomever the individual that the relationship is supposed to be in love with.

Love's outlook is for the other and their benefit and not for oneself. That is the basic problem with any relationship. "Do I love you more than I love me?" Yes. No. Maybe. I don't know. All are the slings and arrows of outrageous thought. I have a parting thought on this subject, but we Christians are in a relationship with God, and I see that how my relationship with my spouse continuously demonstrates to me what my relationship to Jesus should look like. I can be virtuous and forgiving if my wife were having an affair, but do we ask ourselves how often we are loving this world system more than Jesus. And if it is Jesus whom we are cheating on, then I am also cheating on His Father since that is what an affair would be and His Spirit.

But that is a question we all must ask ourselves, especially concerning God. How do I walk out the reality of the living God who decided to live in my very own heart, emotions, intellect, body and spirit? He is God. I know it is true, and yet I cannot believe it to have happened to me. Who am I that the Lord God should take notice of me? The Spirit says to us all, "You are His!"

Once again, I am trying to get back on point. In *Luke 1:26–38*, I see that the Holy Spirit brought completion to Mary's womb by bringing life to it. The most common method is how I was born, a man. My dad and mother came together and combined their perspective parts, sperm and egg, DNA, and hence me. The Holy Spirit completed the process much later in my life by God and His will.

It's a touchy subject, but in the natural, that which is dying, a man comes together in unity with that which is also dying, a woman, to create something new, but is also destined for death since each one of us has that destiny. We know this, but almost all do not want it. I know because currently at sixty-three years of age, I am so much closer to the end zone than ever before, and the prospect is very exciting. But what I see is that when the Spirit of God works, His intention is life.

The method that we human beings use—our physical strength, natural abilities, and intellect—will not work for the long haul since those things will decay and die. Only Jesus makes the eternal work. I heard it stated this way, "The Lord puts the super into the natural," which is God's plan in His sacrifice. He, God, is working life in humans by planting seeds of His Son by His Spirit and not by religion, but rather through a relationship with Him.

The seed, Jesus, is planted within us to bear fruit that has the character, shape, and substance of God. The Father's character, which Jesus Christ fully displayed, lets us know by looking at Him if we are on track or not. So Jesus's seed becomes my new character, but I can say to change character in this human being called David is hard work. I may have the will to change for the better, to better my heart physically and my mind by study. And when I attempt these changes, by nature, my body, Adam, naturally rebels and seeks death. I can exercise for a week, and then at the first opportunity, I throw in the towel, and I am back to sitting on the couch.

It's the same with study. If it is well-written fiction, I will enjoy it far more than almost anything else. This is especially true if what I am studying is a subject that I do not enjoy. May I also state at this point that is why God gave me and you saved ones the Holy Spirit. He knows that I hate the work, but at the exact same time, I tend to do the task given to me well.

All this that is being written is the Holy Spirit telling the reader about God's very character by one of their own, who is not qualified to speak about His nature if I did not personally know Him. That is the primary reason I use capitals for pronouns or His name because He, Jesus, God, the Father, and the Holy Spirit are so much greater than I am.

Shoot, I was thrown out of high school as a freshman because I hated being there. The school did not want to waste your tax-paying dollars on someone who was not interested in studying at all. But God can see potential when no one, including myself, can. May I also say that every single individual on this planet has a potential to fulfill God's desire. He, the Father, gave Jesus to bring that about. I need Him every day, and I'm saved.

That is the whole point of this second set of scriptures. Jesus was placed into Mary a human so that God's full potential could be seen through the life of a human being. Salvation makes the human being brand new, yet that very newness, no matter how bad the life looked before salvation is changed, because the relationship has been restored by Jesus taking the blame and punishment that I personally earned onto Himself. And that was not the end of it because now He wants me to be a son to His Father/Dad/Abba, exactly the same as He is.

Only God would consider asking that of us, which in my opinion is an impossibly difficult task. Since He also wants us to meet with Him in fellowship, placed within me, by His Spirit, to bring that about as we work together in unity, exactly as a marriage that works, works. It is both the man and the woman working for the other individual and what best affects their mate and future and not at all concerned about what I only want for me.

He, Jesus, was placed in a human being to bring relationship about in a world that wants the relationship, but each one of us wants to set up the rules/standards/boundaries on how the relationship is going to get better. What I have found is that His living Word, Jesus, is the only thing that works. God gets the glory and honor because He is doing the work. I am just a human destined for death as stated earlier. I cannot bring life to anything, least of all, for another human being or myself, but He sure can. **Psalm 22:31 (NIV)** reads, *"They or us will proclaim His righteousness, declaring to a people yet unborn."* **He has done it!**

So the potential of God the Father has been planted within this man, the same as it was for Mary. Jesus needs to get out of me to affect the world with God choices, with God's character. Since the Spirit is in fellowship with me, then the more I surrender my will to Him, not thinking just of what I desire from this life called human, then the more He can do to affect the world, just as Jesus did.

"Mary answered. 'May it be to me as you have said.'"

From *Luke*, Jesus stated numerous times in the Gospels that this was true. But even I can see that what is asked of me by God, let us say from the Sermon on the Mount from *Matthew*, chapters **5–7** and from *Luke* **6:27–38** (and as a bonus for the difficult, the rest of those verses **6:39–49**), that I cannot possibly do them nor would I want to consistently, especially if what is asked of me is from *Luke* **6**. I may be good for today, and when tomorrow arrives, I will not even care to think that this is what God the Father expects from His very own child, a sixty-three-year-old, uneducated, uncompassionate man.

I am not trying to be humble, or this is what a good Christian says, but I am a realist. I know me and the fact that God loves me is unbelievable to me, but He does and desires the best for each and every one of us. It is made a reality through Jesus the Christ. He anoints with life, which is His own blood, DNA, alive with life in it, in me.

In the long term, I cannot do God without God, but since He is, then I believe I can. And believing Him then adds faith to what I consider. And because I have faith in His ability to accomplish His will as I put His desires into practice, I read His Word. Then I find to my own amazement that He has shown and created Himself in my heart, the same as He did for Mary in the Gospels. Jesus wants to be released onto the world scene, and since the Lord put me in charge of me, just as He did with Adam while in the garden of Eden, then the more I trust Him as my own sovereign Lord, the more we can do together. The less I trust Him, then once again the Lord and His creation are back at the Tree of the Knowledge of Good and Evil. And in my heart, there will seem to be a better plan composed by me than the one God has in His heart for me. The book of Genesis is a great book of the Bible if you want to know how the human being's heart works.

Luke **2:39–40 (NIV)** states, *"When Joseph and Mary had done everything required by the Law of The LORD, they returned to Galilee*

to their own town of Nazareth. And The Child grew and became strong;
He was filled with wisdom, and the grace of God was on Him."

John 3:3–6 (NIV) reads, *"Jesus replied, 'Very truly I tell you, no one*
can see the Kingdom of God without being <u>born again</u>; or born from
above.' 'How can anyone be born when they are old?' Nicodemus
asked. 'Surely they cannot enter a second time into their mother's
womb to be born!' Jesus answered, 'Very truly I tell you, no one can
enter the Kingdom of God without being born of water and The Spirit.
Flesh gives birth to flesh, **but the Spirit gives birth to spirit.'"**

Now we humans know that we, every one of us, are born or take shape
in the embryonic sack in our mother's womb. Even Nick at night
knew that well over two thousand years ago. Can I also state that
each birth is not the same, especially now with the world's scientific
knowledge. But the standard model is that we are conceived and that
we grow for a period within water. My point is that everyone can also
be born again, but now the second part needs to take place. And that
is to be led by the Holy Spirit, so that He, in love, can place the seed,
who Jesus is, within us.

Once that initial step in obedience to God the Father's will is done,
then a new life, His life, begins. So that also shows me that it is not
because I was such a good individual before I gave my heart to the
Lord, and for me, since I know me pretty well, the opposite was the
truth. I was in rebellion against every form of authority. But what I
can plainly see now was that God was asking me to join Him. "Well,
my mom didn't raise no fool," so I then said yes to God, just like
Mary. "Let it be to me, as You Lord have said."

Another point I would like to make is that I did not see any physical
difference in myself. I did not look any different—I was no taller. I
had no more muscles. I was not more intelligent. I did not have less
testosterone. I was not less obstinate (more a character trait, but it
was a major part of my everyday life). But there was an incredible

character change that naturally affected my physical body since I was now trying, given that I was an infant, but I knew that God was present. I still had difficulty because naturally I wanted to show the world who I was and not who God is.

In that state of me versus God, even though I was a new man, there was an instinctive conflict because I grew up in a world that accepts as true that believing in God is just plain foolishness and is why we as the human cannot move onto a more enlightened or extraterrestrial existence, even though we are going to take ourselves with us wherever we go. If we thought about it, how can we become God when at the same time we refuse to actually know God? And even though He gave His own life to win us back from us, we then state that real love is just a myth that misguided people put forth for other fools to follow. And at the same time, they believe that they are more or by far better than those Christians who only want people to know Him as He is.

Religion, no matter the name or where in the world that religion had its foundation, is not of God. It is us doing what we have been told to do, to make us right with God. But I lived most of those false religions, and when I asked Jesus into my heart, He arrived. Nothing more was required. God wants relationship. He wants us to know Him, and in knowing Him, we want to be just like Him. He, the Lord God, makes all that possible. Sorry, got a little carried away again.

What I found, little by little, was that God already knew what the right or righteous course of action was. I mean, He has always been God. What I also see or saw and wrote about this in an earlier story was that fact that when I gave my life over to the Lord on my day of salvation, I gave the Lord my entire life because I did not have anything worth keeping, which would have the slightest bit of a chance on making me a better man. All the resources for that better man can only be found in Jesus Christ. So, as I said, I surrendered my own life to Him, and He took it. And then since it originally belonged to me, the Lord God gave it back to me and put me in charge of this piece of real estate.

There is no other piece of real estate in my jurisdiction, although I have a wife and two grown children. The Lord did make me a priest to serve Him first and His body, my family, second. But those are different subjects to discuss, but He is God first.

The Lord did this so the work being done on David could be shared. Now the church, the body of Jesus, works the same way. If I want to devastate His piece of real estate, my life, then I will fully take the only actions for this life into my own hands since I would believe it only belongs to me. But like the church when we are not willing to work, to put our hands to the plow or for me to pick up my cross and to daily bear it with the Lord God and to be willing to take His lead for this individual life, then there is the church, His body, which must do the same, to be completely surrendered to His wonderful will. Then we are being directed by God, who just happens to work all things together for good *(Romans 8:28–30)*.

I see that our new birth is the Lord being born again in a human being, in this case, me, and, in your own case, you, to change the world so they, the world, can see the true character of God our Father in a being they can relate to, called human. This is what Jesus did while here. He did not exalt Himself; rather Jesus exalted or glorified His Father and His Father's plans or desires. God's desires never led to sin, but God's desires are only for the good of all. His love is profound and beyond comprehension. The point of being born again is to know Him, and as that relationship grows, then I can say through my experience, "Lord God, You are full of mercy. You are good and faithful, and You are kind to me. Yet at the same time, You are holy and just in everything You do."

The better I know the Lord God, the more of His character is revealed to my own heart. He is more real than the chair I am sitting on now, typing these out. And the additional benefit is that I can know Him better still. There is no end in sight of who He, the living God, is while here on this earth or when I get home to Him in heaven. He is endless in who He is. If I think the universe is big, then knowing who He is, is far greater, much bigger, and so much more astonishing.

Now being born again, as Jesus was born into the world, opens the way for us, the individuals, to be in a relationship to the Father, just as Jesus the Son and the Holy Spirit are in relationship. Their relationship is an example for how I am to be with Him, and His body; the relationship is the same. You and I, for that matter, may say, "Well, that relationship is unique, and I cannot just prance my way into the Holy of Holies, pull up a chair next to Our Father God, and then just say 'Good morning, Lord.'" But that is exactly what being born again does mean, and it is not only my own desire to know Him, but it is exactly what He wants, desires, and planned for in the sacrifice of His beloved Son, Jesus Christ.

So being born again is not only to have God dwell within us, but it is so we who are the voluntary slaves of Christ, due to our own love for Him, that we Christians can dwell with Him, which is the goal that is spoken to us in **Revelations 20:1–7 [2 Cor. 6:16–7, 1; 1 Peter 2:4–6; Eph. 2:19–22 NIV]** for dwelling.

Ephesians 2:4–7 (NIV) says, *"But because of His great love for us, God, who is rich in mercy, made us alive with Christ even when we were dead in transgressions—it is by grace you have been Saved. And God raised us up with Christ and <u>seated us with Him in the heavenly realms in Christ Jesus</u>, in order that in the coming ages He might show the incomparable riches of His grace, expressed in His kindness to us in Christ Jesus. (Eph. 1:3–5 NIV)."* The living Word of God says it much better than I ever could.

One more scripture written out for your benefit is **Ephesians 1:15–23 (NIV).**

> *For this reason, ever since I heard about your faith in The Lord Jesus and your love for all of His people, I have not*

stopped giving thanks for you, remembering you in my
prayers. I keep asking that The God of our Lord Jesus
Christ, The glorious Father, may give you the Spirit of
wisdom and revelation, so that you may know Him better. I
pray that the eyes of your heart may be enlightened in order
that you may know the hope to which He has called you,
the riches of His glorious inheritance in His people, and His
incomparably great power for us who believe. That power is
the same as the mighty strength He exerted when He raised
Christ from the dead and seated Him at His right hand
in the heavenly realms, far above all rule and authority,
power and dominion, and every name that can be invoked,
not only in this present age but also in the one to come. And
God placed all things under His feet and appointed Him to
be head over everything for The Church, which is His Body,
the fullness of Him who fills everything in every way.

This should be the final point on **Luke 1:26–38**. I spoke a lot about being born again. I would like the reader to consider how that new birth applies to you and me, and what are God's desires with us as by-products of having been born again?

If I know and I set my heart to do what the scriptures state who the Seed of God, the Father, is, His name is Jesus Christ, who has been planted within me, the truth who His Word is. Then why don't I think of other Christians as having had that same thing taking place on the inside of them?

An example, if I see with my eyes an individual who is perhaps unwashed with clothes that are un-ironed and dirty and I cannot make heads nor tails out of his or her speech, I in my mind categorize this person, which is what prejudiced is. Webster's Ninth New Collegiate Dictionary states, "Preconceived judgment or opinion or an adverse opinion or leaning formed without just grounds or before sufficient knowledge." For me, it is to put any individual into a pre-constructed category without prior knowledge or more to the point and personal relationship with that person.

For many, certainly not all, we see in fellow Christians that the Holy Spirit is at work with them. We can see their growth, more interest in the Word of God, and fruit of the Spirit being produced in the individual's life, and yet still we judge. But Scripture tells me in **John 14:23–24 (NIV)**, *"Jesus replied, 'Anyone who loves Me will obey My Teaching. My Father will love them, and We will come to them and make Our home with them. Anyone who does not love Me will not obey My Teaching. These words you hear are not my Own; they belong to The Father who sent Me.'"*

What I gather from that scripture is that when I accepted Jesus as my Savior, He placed His Spirit within me. So with God being in me the Lord God has come to tabernacle or to set up His tent of dwelling. I was not the best individual whoever drew a breath on the Planet Earth, with sin being my master, but Jesus changed that and continues to sanctify me out of His personal love.

But that is to be our goal for every human being, to love and care for him or her, just as God did for me. Also for me is that I am, by nature, self-aware, and since I think it is all about me, then I also assume over mankind that is how it should be, my way or the highway.

God's intention though is Jesus

We have been saved from Adam's line of descent and what that entails into God's line or family and therefore what that entails. It is impossible to live His life. I, for one, am not consistently good enough. But if God delivered me from Adam's line, then He also delivered me so that I now with His Spirit have the ability to live a godly life. Many would say, "Hey, I'm already doing that!"

Well, yes indeedie, so here is another example. But if I'm on Facebook and see a statement from an individual who has a post with something like "Today everyone who says *Amen* will be healed, so say amen," well because I read Scripture, God has requirements. They are to obey His Word and not just to think about obeying Him. But the other side of that is that once we have been saved, then our relationship with God has been healed; Jesus is the example of what that healing looks like.

I've been a type 1 diabetic all my life, yet I have been healed, so Amen and Amen. I am not to judge the individual because he or she is not living my standards. Rather I can pray for this person and ask the Lord to show me and him or her what relationship in You requires. Another that gets to me is that we judge those who have become successful in Christianity, have loads of money and mansions, and are selling literature in every bookstore around the world. But success in America is not grounds to judge. I do not know any of them personally. I also need to say that I have been married to the girl I love more than any other and still find after all this time something new. She still dumbfounds me with her life. God is the only judge who as Scripture states in **Psalm 96:10–13** who judges in equity or complete fairness because His nature is righteous and faithful. And above all, He is good.

I have never had a billion dollars. If the Lord wants to bless me that way, then bring it! But I can see that He has always been there for me. Even before I gave Him my heart, He had already given me His. If I am going to fall under peoples' contempt because of what God has done in me, then bring that too. But He is God, and I know that He knows what He is doing. God is the only one who can judge a Christian. If we are doing that while online or only in my own imagination, then I am judging God and the very reason why He went to the cross. If I accuse a brother or sister, then I am in league with the enemy. Since satan is the accuser of the brethren **(Rev. 12:10)**, then if I am judging those He loves, I have chosen a side to make an allegiance to. Whether I believe I am right or not does not matter.

Like I said earlier, I've known my wife for forty-one years, so how can I possibly state what someone whom I have never met is doing and why he or she is doing it? And somehow I know exactly the reason why this person is acting in that peculiar way. If I do not like his or her actions, then pray for myself first and ask the Lord to reveal the truth to me and to pray for whomever so that he or she is kept on track for what the Lord is working out in their life.

If God died for those individual/individuals, then who am I to judge Him, with Him being in them? I have never thought that my Father God was an idiot for saving me. Then why should I judge you when I do not even live in that house? I've been a Christian since 1977, and our Father is still working garbage out of me. And that is because He loves me and does not want to see me fall back to sin/Egypt, not the location, but the slavery.

Some scriptures exist for this. So please study them: *Proverbs 4:20–27, 16:2, 18:19–21; Matthew 12:34–37, 15:16–20;* and *James 3*.

So that is the supernatural seed of God that has been planted within every Christian, Jesus, the Son, exactly as we are intended to be. We are one in a relationship, complete unity with the Father, Son, and Holy Spirit for you and me. So get busy and grow.

U : Repentance

I am a man, the seed of Adam, and even though I have been saved by the mercy and love of the living God, I still need repentance.

This day brought that home to my heart. I am a man, arrogant, foolish, and more self-aware than Jesus aware. I am hardly worthy to be called a Son of God, and it is not just me, but all of humanity. "Forgive Lord and make me humble before You."

I have recently been praying for different nations and states around the world, using a calendar from *The Voice of the Martyrs*. I have only just begun. It is January 2017. But because I want to know what I am praying for, I do a little research on the nation itself before I pray. With my worldview widened seeing what is taking place in Africa, the Middle East, Burma, and the Philippines, to name just a few, but to see how a world without Jesus tends to exist.

I can also say since I live here in the United States that it is no different. The overall philosophy is "I rule, and you are subject to what has been decreed," a common theme. So far it does not matter if it is Christian, Islam, Buddhist, Hindu, or other. Once in control or basically the majority, then it is in their power as that majority that has the last word to say as to what takes place where the individual lives are concerned.

I am talking about me, but if I am one member of the LDS church and am stating my belief to a million Baptists, then my subjective opinion has little or no value except to me. But if I am one of the million, then my opinion has a much greater value and import. And so it carries more weight, and hence for me and mine, it now becomes our worldview. So once in control, the majority wants to tell the minority how they should live. If you do not agree with the majority, then you will suffer the consequences of you not agreeing with me, the majority. These rules to live by are carried out in various ways, everything from stoning, being pelted with rocks until you are no longer alive. There is also the fact that you can live, but you cannot go to school and be educated, or you cannot get a decent job opportunity. In some way the majority subjugates the minority, and of course they believe they have a God-given right to treat you in the opposite way then I would like to be treated.

Now there are a billion nuances of that taking place in the world today, and whether I live in a democracy or monarchy, whoever is in power as a majority makes life as he or she sees it should be endured, and of course this is for our national well-being.

Accordingly, if you do not fully agree with this fictitious majority, then there may be loss of jobs, home, freedom, and life basically. "I will make you do what I want through fear of reprisal. I am also in a position of not having a thing to worry about except being in the right." Please do not misunderstand me. The answer is not some individual who is strong enough to not only be the answer to every question and who can bring peace to the straight and homosexual communities, set a straight path for the pro-life and pro-abortion, bring about the freedom to smoke marijuana, remain Republican or Democrat, have belief in God, or be atheist. We all have our individual life that we are living and have some type of code that we as that individual exist by, to hold anarchy or chaos at bay.

Here is where it gets tricky though, but all of us need a relationship with Jesus that does not consist of a religion. What is a do or don't or what I say is a right or wrong? But rather what does He, Jesus, say?

In relationship you ask Him. And because I trust Him to be true and I trust that when my back is against the wall, I will think about me and not Him. But as our relationship grows and deepens, then my own heart is for what He wants. It just so happens to be for the good of all mankind, and I am of that race of animals.

I need Him, and so do you. But if I am making up how that is to be accomplished, then you have every right to call me a nut. When you know Him and not just about Him, then you can just ask Him, "What is it You, Lord, want me to do?" The Bible is a perfect guide for this, but for the moment, I do not want to tie religion into these statements.

Therefore, if you know about Him but at the same time have never met Him, then you can honestly state that is just a Christian's code of ethics, what he has been taught at some denominational institution, such as, look both ways before you cross the street, respect your parents, and don't cheat (because you will get caught). That is religion because by my own will and efforts I can make God pleased with me while I think that I'm pleasing Him.

I said in an earlier story, "The more you work, the more there is to do, Lord. Sometimes it is like pushing a boulder up Mount Everest with ice under your feet and it is a windy day and the wind just happens to be blowing against you." Since religion is more work than we ourselves can do, then we transfer the burden onto our family and friends. "If you do this and if you would just start doing that, then you will not fall under the wrath of God. I am only asking you to change for your own good because I love you."

But the relationship with the living God changes that in such a big way. He, the living only real God, who out of His mercy and forgiving nature, says to us all, "Come to me because I've paid for your entire debt of guilt. Whatever was in your heart that made you say to yourself that you do not measure up has been taken out of the way. I want you to know Me exactly as I Am just as I know you for exactly who you are, and I still want you to be Mine. It is a relationship, the more you work on it, the better the relationship will be. Consequently, the less you work on us, the weaker the relationship will be."

Basically religion is my rules that you will live by. Relationship is the Lord personally coming to you to know you for exactly who you are. He desires to know me, and as a bonus, He wants to see better from me. And because we are in a relationship, I can disagree with Him, and He does not call me an idiot or a fool, and He does not seek to terminate the relationship. Rather He draws me closer to His heart, and I know how He feels and what is accomplished through that death, hardship, or even the good stuff like a big raise at work. The better I know Him (and any and every relationship has room for growth), then the more comfortable I become with Him. He is still my God, but He is also my Dad. I may disagree with a life decision, but no matter what, He is still the very best Dad anywhere. Relationship brings life to love, and it, love, just grows.

Back to the point. But these large worldviews are not only for me, but for you also. For this world problem where the majority does make the rules, then I need someone who I can love and who I know loves me in return and that I can go to, too get the answer. It is Jesus and not religion. I do not want to be the bully, but I do want someone who can bring the two opposing parties to a peaceful resolution or just to bring peace to my mind because I cannot begin to comprehend why people do the things they do. I live with my own heart, thank God, and have trouble with the, "Why did I do that? Why did I say that? What in the whole wide world is wrong with me?"

Now my reason for repentance is because I do not see that depth all the time. I look through my own worldview. At times I care more about what I am feeling and not asking the Lord Jesus how He feels. The prayers I offer for the world now include every nation whether they are on the Martyrs list or not. The United States is not on the

Martyrs list, but I pray for President Trump as well as my fellow Americans. This is where I live, and we need Jesus, just as any other nation does.

In *Jeremiah 29:4–9 (NIV)*, Jeremiah sent a letter to the Israelites taken as captives to Babylon. But the Lord is telling His people to pray for the prosperity of Babylon because if they prosper, you too will prosper. I lost sight of that and say to all, "Please forgive me."

The Lord our God always has a worldview. He cares for everyone everywhere and wants them to know Him. Now that I see that truth, I now pray more earnestly for everyone since that is His desire, that we all know Jesus for ourselves.

Know Him! Know Him! Know Him!

V: Current Events without Jesus

(2 Timothy 4:1–8, Titus 1:10–16, 1 Timothy 6:3–5)

Without salvation we naturally turn inward or are concerned primarily just for ourselves. I would also point out that no individual is an island. Each one of us helps or supports with our time and monies causes or charities. We are human and do care for others. It is as much the human condition as breathing. What I see easily enough is those who give more of themselves to a thing: AIDS research, cure for any cancer or diabetes, social injustice, the plight of the innocent and children, slavery, St. Jude's, entire nations perishing, or not getting a glass of clean water. It is endless, but those who give of themselves, Christian or not, seem to be more satisfied with their lives. Their reaching out has given back to them. This is not a commercial so that you can be inspired to donate some moolah to me. Therefore, you can relax.

With that being said, our other negative tendency is to be overtly self-orientated. Now if I have a propensity to be concerned only about what I think, feel, want, or basically desire, then subsequently those who are not for me are naturally against me. And since it is only about me, then why can't they see that truth. "Cus sumtin' must be wrong with 'em!"

To me, not just for the United States but the world, we are only seeing what we want to know and have embedded within our minds as a natural part of growing old, without doing the work to understand how that conclusion came about within us. If I do not agree, even if it is with someone I care deeply for, I begin to categorize the individual, as not being truly aware or not quite bright enough to understand to nuisances of daily life. Because the individual disagrees with me, then I no longer have compassion or heart for him or her. I do not want to hear what this person has to say and have lost all patience and empathy toward him or her or, for that matter, to pay attention to what his or her own heart is stating that he or she sees as his or her own truth *(James 1:19–27; 1 John 2:15–17)*.

In my opinion, I think that the reason for all of this is fear, fear of being punished for having done something wrong and then called to account. As fear dominates, then we fortify against anyone's intrusion because we do not want to be seen as being vulnerable, and we therefore will not allow incursion into our hearts. Anyone anywhere who has surrendered himself or herself to change knows how hard that endeavor can be. It may start in my mind, but after continuing for a short time, the change ends up at my heart, soul, and inner being. But I never wanted my heart to be broken. Then I spent a great deal of time with brick and mortar, building a very solid wall around my heart so I could keep it safe and unimpaled. Words can wound just as much as a spear thrust.

Since these are the last days, then internally we desire someone who can make our self-desire more secure. Basically, a superhero, who cannot be beaten but if I side with, can beat anyone who comes against him (antichrist) and me since "it" would satisfy my intrinsic desire for sanctuary or security. The world system is pretty much setting itself up for the antichrist since from a perspective without the Lord Jesus, our hope needs to be in something or someone that we can see, hear, or know in our coconuts that this guy means business. And whoever stands against him/us will not be standing for very long.

1 John 2:18–27 and Revelation 13:3b–4

People, you and I, if we are expecting a world leader to rise out of the calamity that is currently taking place in the political, economic, and racial tensions being aroused the world over, not just here in the States but everywhere, then whoever does come on the world scene will be applauded and most welcomed. If we have been going to church most of our lives, we believe the antichrist will be all sinister and easy to spot on the horizon, just by the fact that he will have two horns, sport a long-pointed tail, and wear a red Speedo. I'm being facetious.

But when this guy does show up, he is not going to be so easy to recognize, just by the very fact that we mankind are going to be in such need of a savior, someone who can speak, and we will listen. Basically we are like children with a strong need a strong father figure. "Ok, you kids, enough roughhousing and breaking your mom's things. I want you to stop now!" We are looking for character and not just a strong hand. We need character we admire, not a strong hand we rebel against because no one enjoys a whoppin'.

Now for me, I am a Christian. No one ranks higher than Him, and since I know and love Him, I also have a strong confidence that no one is better than Him. But a lot of what was in the previous statement sounds a great deal like God, whom I know. We want someone who will be godlike and at the same time, not God. The thing about knowing God is that once I am in His presence, His Word, or worship, I naturally regret my own sin. I want to change because He is so good. I desire the Lord's happiness well above my own.

Exodus 20:18–21 (NIV) gives us a good example of this point. *"When the people saw the thunder, and the lightening and heard the trumpet and saw the mountain in smoke they trembled with fear. They stayed at a distance and said to Moses, 'Speak to us yourself and we will listen. But do not have God speak to us or we will die.' Moses said to the people 'Do not be afraid. God has come to test you, so that the fear of God will be with you to keep you from sinning.' The people remained at a distance, while Moses approached the thick darkness where God was."*

In Jesus, we find this to be true as the relationship grows. I now find that He, the Spirit, now resides in my heart, and since He is God, then what do I really have to fear—as a matter of fact, death—now becomes my most prized possession since that is where my heart/ Jesus is. And at the exact same time, He resides and lives in this tent called David, here with His body commonly referred to as the church. Since God is the only one who can change a heart for the better and as I desire His will in my life, I find us working together on His poignant desires for me, the individual.

Now I find that my need for security has been met because Jesus is all that I am going to need. Even though I still get hungry, still get scraped up, catch a cold every now and then, or for some unknown reason have a disagreement with the wife, whom I love more than any other, principally life is still ongoing.

I also see in my life that He rises my head up to look around, and now I see that since I have been thoroughly taken care of, now my concerns are to be about everyone else. Since outreach just feels good, then give that five to five hundred bucks, walk those miles, or go to their place of suffering to bring the only cure for humanity, Jesus. I know within my heart that He is alive and well and has restored me to relationship with Himself and His Father. So all my needs have been satisfied in Jesus, the Christ. Knowing Him changes us all for the better. We not only become children of God, but now we, as His, get to show His personality to a world piled knee deep in religions and basic heartache.

The only way that I have found to make a clear distinction as to who is right or wrong is by knowing Him. Then He alone can say to me, "I know you and love you." I am not me telling you how you can be acceptable to God and not living the very thing I say; rather it is you knowing Him by Himself, you and Him, one on One.

That point brings up another topic, but I have heard many times that the reason I do not attend a church is that they treated me badly as a child or I watch any Christian, Muslim, or LDS show on TV, computer, and so forth. I sure don't need them. I'm much happier with the Lord and me—and no one else. But can I say that is not God's nature? I mean, after all He is God, totally secure in who He is, but He so loved the world that whoever wants to can know Him as He is. So if that is true of Him, then it must also apply to us. The body or the church need each other, to be about His purpose, to stop playing at religion, and to unite.

In my life, I have found that this can only be possible through the life, death, and resurrection of His One and only Son, Jesus. I spent a great deal of my life searching for a way to be satisfied in God without Jesus, and although I believed in those other systems with all my heart, there was always something lacking. But when I found Him, then I had the answer. His name is Jesus!

By God's will, my self-desire becomes His desire, for individuals to know who God is in their reality. God wants us to know Him, and by a continuous relationship, we learn more and more about each other. Religion has a large set of rules in place that may possibly bring me closer to God. But the Lord makes it much easier and harder at the same time.

If you want to know Me, then you will know Me. Then and there, the religious things get pushed out of the way, along with the meditations, the denial, and the self-incriminations. Now it is about Him. Since God is so perfect, the more I know Him, the more there is to know. And because I just love Him so much and want to be just like Him, He alone is bringing life to a dying world. I find that my personal ego is removed from the picture, and now my heart just wants Him to be glorified. I mean, after all, God did all the work. The last phrase of **Psalm 22:31 (NIV)** states, *"He has done it!"*

There are a ton of scriptures on these matters for the positive. To seek Him, try **Deuteronomy 4:29–31, 33:13; 1 Kings 22:4–5;**

1 Chronicles 28:9–10; 2 Chronicles 7:11–22; Malachi 3:6–7, 16–18; Jeremiah 29:4–14; and *Romans 6*.

When speaking on God's will for us, review *Ephesians 2:6–10*, which also goes the step further. It is not our works, but rather His works He has planned for us to do.

Titus 2:11–14 shows us that grace is not just a gift from God … period. Rather something that we live continuously proves God is alive and well and has set up shop inside of me to show other humans what a relationship with Him looks like. So far His plans have yet to fall short of His intentions when we work together with each other and with Him.

A Contrast:

Use *2 Corinthians 5:1–8, 9–11, 15–21* and *Acts 2:42–47* and *3:1–10* as an example of Christianity. The scriptures are all to be read and not just lightly to be passed over. The, "I'll do that later when I have some time." Read His words. They bring light.

Numbers 33:3–4 reads, *"The LORD brought judgment on Egypt's gods, but on the people, who believed their imaginary gods were better."*

Deuteronomy 1:15–18, states, *"Do not show partiality in judging; hear both small and great alike. Do not be afraid of anyone, for judgment belongs to God."* The elders or judges were not to show partiality to anyone because they were to act with justice just as God does, for Israel as well as for the rest of humanity.

Deuteronomy 32:40–47 speaks about judgment on those who hate the Lord, but for us, what does 'hate the Lord mean'? *Exodus 20:4–6* reveals that God is a jealous God, and for anything that I love more than Him is hatred toward Him. It is not that I want to blow up a church or even shoot Christians, although these things would tell me where my heart is. But it is to desire useless things more than Him, the living One. The opposite is also true, that loving Him is not picking Him flowers and reciting poetry about His wonders, although if that is my heart, then good. But rather it is wanting my best to show off His best and keeping His commands, which Jesus repeats in *John 14:13–15*. This shows faith because even though I do not see Him, I have my heart set on what He has said to be true and walk that out in my daily life. I pray.

W: A Tenth.

About a year or so ago, I was trying to find in the New Testament scriptures concerning tithing and why we as Christians tithe or should not. There is the same story in two different gospels where Jesus is condemning the Pharisees, as in **Matthew 23:23–24 (NIV)**. *"Woe to you, teachers of the law and Pharisees, you hypocrites! You give a tenth of your spices—mint, dill and cumin. But you have neglected the more important matters of the law—justice, mercy and faithfulness. You should have practiced the latter without neglecting the former. You blind guides! You strain out a gnat but swallow a camel."*

The Holy Spirit through Paul and the other writers of the New Testament spoke a great deal about generosity and charity, to put it bluntly, to have grace for your fellow human beings. So based upon those statements, I thought that I no longer had to tithe and I was good to go. No tithe but be generous. After a few months, that thought became a philosophy, but then one Sunday morning while getting ready to go to church, I turned on the radio for our dogs to listen to while away from home, and there was Dr. David Jeremiah speaking about tithing.

So I listened, and he brought up a very valid point. He too said that tithing was not a New Testament ordinance, but when compared to what Jesus gave us and the very valid way He gave salvation to us, then we as Christians should be required, although we are not, to give more and surely not less in everything and in every way. So I thought while waiting for Gisele to get ready, *He is right. What can I possibly give? And not a miserly 10 percent, but more or my all, my all for Him and the purpose of His kingdom to grow here on earth.* That is, I surrender all for Him, Jesus.

Now all of that to say this, **2 Corinthians 9:6–15 (NIV)**.

> *Remember this: Whoever sows sparingly will also reap sparingly, and whoever sows generously will also reap generously. Each of you should give what you have decided in your heart to give, not reluctantly or under compulsion, for God,* Himself, *loves a cheerful giver. And God is able to bless you abundantly, so that in all things at all times, having all that you need, you will abound in every good work. As it is written: "They have scattered abroad their gifts to the poor; their righteousness endures forever"* **[Ps. 112:9 NIV]**. *Now He who supplies seed to the sower and bread for food will also supply and increase your store of seed and will enlarge the harvest of your righteousness. You will be made rich,* [In the right things of God] *in every way so that you can be generous on every occasion, and through us your generosity will result in thanksgiving to God. This service that you perform is not only supplying the needs of the Lord's people but is also overflowing in many expressions of thanks to God. Because of the service by which you have proved yourselves, people,* [all people] *will praise God for your obedience that accompanies your confession of the gospel of Christ, and for your generosity in sharing with them and with everyone else. And in their prayers for you their hearts will go out to you, because of the surpassing grace God has given you. Thanks be to God for His indescribable gift!*

Malachi 3:10, which many in the church quote on Sunday mornings, states that if you tithe, then the Lord will throw open the windows of heaven and shower you with His abundance, but that is what happens when we only look at the Word of God for the 'more' we can get for ourselves.

I also see in **Malachi 3:1–5 (NIV)**, which I'll write for both of our benefits.

> I will send my messenger, who will prepare the way before Me. Then suddenly The LORD you are seeking will come to His temple; The Messenger of the covenant, whom you desire, will come," says The LORD Almighty. But who can endure the day of His coming? Who can stand when He appears? For He will be like a refiner's fire or a launderer's soap, [both used to make an object clean.] He will sit as a refiner and purifier of silver; He will purify the Levites, [the church] and refine them like gold and silver. Then The LORD will have **men who will bring offerings in righteousness and the offerings of Judah and Jerusalem will be acceptable to The LORD, as in days gone by, as in former years.** So, I will come and put you on trial. I will be quick to testify against sorcerers, adulterers and perjurers, against those who defraud laborers of their wages, who oppress the widowers and the fatherless, and deprive the foreigners among you of justice but do not fear Me, says The LORD Almighty.

Although the Lord God provides all that we need and more, will He not also give to us, as Scripture states in the world that is to come, where we will spend eternity together? One other note: Jesus also said in **Matthew 5:17–20** that basically all the Old Testament is intact until all things are fulfilled, which we Christians are still waiting for. So it is not the Old and New, but the entire word that is equally important to the Christian and not just because we may be religious, but more on how God's heart beats for what He sees as correct. Without knowing the Old, how can we understand the New? It is one book and not two different halves of different pies coming together to make a new dessert.

My point is that we as Christians sometimes think that I gave my heart to the Lord. "Once I die, I am going to go home to be in heaven, get my mansion, and kick my feet up forever. I'll plant a garden, eat some grapes, and watch my grass grow on my very large estate. All of this work stuff is now over with. Praise God!"

When I look at Scripture, I see that God the Father, God the Son, and God the Holy Spirit are always at work. They are always active, and if He is setting up His new kingdom with Jesus as Lord, then Scripture states that if I do well with the gifts He has given me while here on earth, He will put me in charge of His things when He arrives once again.

Matthew 25:14–46 states that *He gave to each according to their ability, **and later on, for those who did something with what was given to them, they are told,** "Come and share your Master's happiness."*

Luke 19:11–27 (NIV) is where Jesus states that He will put them in charge of cities. Our Lord gives more to those who do more with what they have been given. In the *Luke 19* statement, the individual who did the most with what was placed in his hands was then given ten cities, so basically that individual was made a prince. All the statements are centered in Him, along with ourselves in service to Him. Even in *Matthew 7:24 (NIV)*, specifically it says, *"Therefore everyone who hears these words of Mine and puts them into practice is like the wise man who builds his house on a rock." It is not that God built the house on a rock, but whoever puts the Word into practice will build his own house/life on the Rock.* *Psalm 89 (NIV)* states, *"You are My Father, My God, The Rock My Savior."*

Matthew 19:26–30, Revelation 5:8–14, Romans 14:10–18, and *Psalm 96:10–13, 112* speaks *"their righteousness endures forever."*

The value of the cross is inestimable to the Father. He gave 100 percent of His heart and not only a small portion, as in 10 percent. As Scripture states, He will judge what we as the redeemed have done with Him while here on this earth. *Ecclesiastes 12:13–14* speaks "for all of humanity." Also review *Matthew 12:33–37, 1 Corinthians 3:10–15, 16–23, and 2 Corinthians 5:6–10*. I also know that there is much more concerning judgment.

But if I look at my life and how it relates to God and what He has planted within me, then what comes next is of equal importance to what I did with my time here and now. How did I do the things that I do, and was the Lord Jesus exalted in them *(John 12:32)* because I will stand before Him? My life as a Christian will be tested by fire, along with the foundation I walked out, the proof of my life, and what I think I believed because He lives. I live in Him and represent Him to individuals here and everywhere on all of the spiritual planes.

The first part on judgment sets up the second part on *Acts 2:42–47* or what am I doing with the opportunities God has given me.

Each of us who have been born again and have been chosen by God to fulfill His purpose on earth. And just as He lives 100 percent for us daily, likewise we should be doing the same for Him in return. Once again that is easy to say but harder to do, but in *Luke 9:23–26 (NIV)*, it states *"to deny themselves, take up their cross, and daily follow Me."*

The thing that the Lord wants me and you to see is that all things do actually work together for good when we are fully involved with Him. So this unity of the body of Christ, mind, and s/Spirit brings about life to the general populous since Jesus is life. We are all of us equal in the eyes of God and have the exact same responsibilities as Jesus since we are also children of God.

Whoever the pastor is should be promoting salvation through the sacrifice of God for humanity. But that is also my job and yours. The unity of the body after Pentecost was that the individuals were all on the same page and brought God's profound love to everyone. They started someplace, let us say, San Antonio, and worked outward as the Spirit led those whom He could trust. We see Peter and John in Acts 3, providing healing in Jesus's name. And that healed individual was then jumping up and down, proclaiming how great God is to everyone in the vicinity. Also *Acts 4:32–35, 5:12–16, 8:4–8, 26–39* shows what Christianity is like when led by the Spirit, as with Philip, the Spirit, and the Ethiopian. These are only a few, but what it shows is that when we as the individual, with the individual being a part of Jesus Christ's body, agrees with the Lord and His purpose, since we are in unity, we can do whatever pleases Him and of course not just for ourselves.

If our/my concern is only about me, then how will the Temple of God be made known to those who need to know Him for themselves? I see that if it is all about me, then it will be I, whom they will know. That is what the individual will see. I already know that I could not save myself. I needed Jesus as much as any other soul on this planet.

He chose you for Himself because of all the potential you have in you to further His kingdom on this earth. And even though we are doing what He has asked of us, yet according to the previous discussion on judgment, He will also reward us for the sacrifice of our time, monies, family, and whatever I think of as mine. It is for Him. He is so good.

So a tenth is the absolute smallest amount I can give to further His kingdom since I can plainly see that He gave 100 percent of Himself to further His kingdom by including me in it. It is not enough to say, "Yes, I agree," but more to walk out the things of God in each one of our daily lives *(Luke 12:8–34)*.

X : Peace (A True Story).

I want to raise my hand and yet I do not want to interrupt what this group of peers are considering. It's a simple request really. A folk singer feeling in the groove had asked the audience if they would like to create a song together. The gathering is small, about twenty tops, with a smattering of children watching the show. Now it is obvious that children enjoy music, no matter what is being played, which is an entirely different subject.

The folk singer, Chris, asks us, "So what'll we create? Anyone just pick a subject matter, and the rest will be up to us!"

She states this option with a demure smile, looking over her silent admirers like a mom waiting for her child to repeat the word *mommy* for her husband to hear, lips drawn in a slight smile, eyebrows arched expectantly. Finally someone speaks up, the husband of the wife, Trish, who is throwing this little get-together for this not-yet famous young woman who writes and sings her heart's lessons, her life's poetry, actually her truth.

"Let's sing about Peace."

Brave man, I think. I was thinking about gorillas, but that is just my sense of humor. Now I capitalize Peace throughout only because it is one of those things, like Love, Unity, and Brotherhood that makes the human being human.

Someone says, "Give Peace a chance." Still each of us know quite well that Mr. Lennon patented that one, and he was right and wrong, as will be explained. No one is forthcoming with lyrics to a robust folk tune. One of the main reasons, I believe, is that many of us are complete strangers and are not going to throw our hearts out there for the birds to peck at. Now we know that image is not completely true, but we perceive through the lens of our own heart, and not many of us stand in line to get it hurt.

A few lines are uttered here and there, but nothing you can wrap three chords around. The issue at hand to me is not really Peace, but stopping the war or the invasion of Iraq, which had just happened and was a highlight of the nightly news services. Those are two completely different subjects and have nothing to do with Peace. As a matter of fact, both are anathema to Peace.

There was no success in creating an impromptu Peace song a few faints and parries, but no blood was drawn, and here is the reason why. I believe Chris should have known that when she writes, she writes mainly from her life's experience, drawing on moments that struck her heart, experiences with friends, family, loves, lovers, and losses. Her being a tumbleweed or a wanderer, which is also a well-known song, but then again, all the above is.

Peace for those that have it is not a subject that is high on the priority list; it is not our heart's quest. There is also defining Peace. The cessation of war would not necessarily bring about peace, but it would stop war. Man cannot be at peace except for those moments when he is contented within. For example, if my family's lives were being destroyed daily and I just wanted an hour to mourn them and was then granted two, would I then have peace or grief? I do not believe that war is in any way correct, but there is an Everest of events that sculpt the human being when under duress—positive and negative but definitely change—and that is the human condition. Without life, which is the perpetrator of most of our unique catch-22s, what would be the reason for change, and how could we possibly seek Peace if chaos were not there to present the arrow?

So as I looked over the crowd of unspoken word, it struck me that Peace would not be a prominent subject for a very liberal group of middle- to upper-class Caucasians because it is an undefined experience. We can grab our Encarta Dictionary and tell you exactly what Peace means, but since I do not understand its value, then I am not competent to dictate how anyone else is to depend on it. And that is just Peace.

We each consider Peace to be ours by right when I say things like my wife, my house, and my city, Half Moon Bay. It's like almost everyone else is claiming ownership. With ownership comes our personal value system of what we deem correct standards by which all humans should act. Therefore, Peace would be my perception and not truly Peace because no one else is democratically voting on what can bring this about. I am not truly looking through the eyes of my fellow human being, but rather judging them and my undefined value of what Peace should be, like "don't kill your neighbor, me," "don't take a whiz on my lawn," "it is my wife and my family," or "don't touch, and do not hurt."

Along that same subject, this is my problem with those who think that our African American brothers don't deserve more, not welfare, but a break or true equality. We, White America, own the military, educational, and financial systems. We even print the stuff, and much of land we stole from those individuals that settled it. We also kidnapped the ancestors of these individuals, and now say if you work hard and get a good education, you can be ... me!

That definitely won't bring about Peace because if our view is only through our own eyes, then how we see other nationalities, religions, and people will only be distorted because the view is one-sided and not based on experience or concern for the other individual's experience.

So if I were to try to describe Peace, I would think of it in two very different ways from personal experience, the first as a very young child when visiting my maternal grandfather's house. And on waking up very early in the morning, I was lying there watching the dust motes floating on the rays of sunbeams streaming through the window of his spare bedroom that my older sister and younger brother were sharing and dreaming our less than innocent dreams. As I was lying there, I listened to the early-morning birds singing sweet songs outside and the slight slow sounds of traffic moving slowly about the exterior of our Grandpa Anderson's house. And I had a child's knowledge that there would be no fighting between my mom and dad at Grandpa's house, it gave me at that moment the most complete sense of Peace that ever struck a human heart. It was more than an epiphany. It was truth realized in the fiber of my being! The serenity of that moment is etched within my core, but reality or the enemy soon realized the dilemma that I might think to seek after Peace and find it in Jesus.

Also because I wanted everyone to see what I saw, in my zeal, I woke my sister to share this amazing insight. Without a moment's hesitation, she cuffed me in the side of my head for waking her so abruptly. Then she closed her eyes, rolled back over onto her side to ignore me, and tried to regain her own Peace, which I had totally trampled upon without concern.

The second event happened many years later when I was around twenty-one years of age and standing on the bluffs of the Pacific Ocean in Half Moon Bay, watching the sun set over that endless sea. This was a very beautiful and familiar spot, one of those magnetic spiritual centers that you might come across if you are sensitive to it. But that same area has now become part of a golf course, which has been covered over with purposed greenery and gated for those individuals that can afford a stay at the Ritz-Carlton and more than likely miss that peaceful moment trying to sink a birdie or taking a swim in the oversized saltwater Olympic pool with the Pacific Ocean watching not fifty yards away.

So maybe this is the song that Chris had hoped for:

As I stood watching the evening clouds alter shades of crimson, orange, then pink,

and, down below, the five or six families just having a day at the beach,

I sat with knees pulled high to share a kiss between the shore and the tide,

watching it striding ever onward and then closer.

I watched and felt the sun bearing down to slip behind the lip of the world as the eyelids of darkness and dreams unfurled

the children laughing and enjoying life, the Frisbee floating by, seagulls in flight,

the dog barking and joyfully biting at waves, and the lovers holding hands totally amazed, and the cacophony of Peace ablaze.

Amazing is our God, I thought, and so stood, amazed.

Z : It Is Well.

If we, from our own perspective of the truth, thought about Jesus and His glory in going to the cross on our and my behalf, then we would quite naturally be overwhelmed. But I believe that for myself since the cross was never a requirement from God for me. Then it lets me off the hook, and I look at Jesus and with sincerity say, "Thank You, Lord, for salvation!"

For the church, that event in space-time is something that we on Planet Earth do not even have to consider. I can also say that the cross of Jesus is also not out of our hearts since we all, every one of us who have been born again, have an invested knowledge of how far God went to redeem our individual lives from certain separation from Him. So I am not denying the truth of the event, but since the punishment of the cross was suffered by another, then it is off my radar, in the inner heart sense of issues.

I recall the classic psalm/song, "It is well with my soul." But one of the lyrics speaks to me. "My sin, oh, the bliss of this glorious thought, My sin, not in part but the whole, Is nailed to the cross, and I bear it no more, Praise the Lord, praise the Lord, o my soul. It is well (it is well), with my soul (with my soul), It is well, it is well with my soul."

Still in speaking of the cross, Jesus knew that it was the conclusion of a life lived totally for the glory of His Father, but it was still God's wrath against sin or my distrust in His very nature and the consequences of having misgivings about who God in all of His glory is. Sin came solely to rest on the One and only Son of the living God, on yours as well as my own behalf. Even if I did not have to suffer God's justified wrath perpetrated by me against Himself, against His character and person, the event itself should give me an opportunity to pause and think of His sacrifice by the nature of that incident/death.

I would like to give you a parable on that event, the cross, and how I would translate it as to what I could perhaps have done in similar circumstances. Let us say that I drive up to my house after having gone to the store and find my front door opened and my dogs in a panic on the front lawn. I enter and see that my home has been destroyed, and calling for my wife, I hear moans coming from the rear of our house. I immediately phone 9-1-1. My wife has been molested, beaten, and humiliated.

Then the bathroom door opens, and out steps the culprit of this event against the woman that I love more than any other. He is drying his hands on one of our hand towels and casts it over his shoulder onto the floor without a care in the world. He looks to be proud of what he did with what I call mine.

I want to murder this intruder in worse ways than my imagination can contemplate, but I can see in his eyes the genuine disregard for her, my wife. The police do arrive after what seems to be hours, but I have no concept of time passing, only that the unspeakable has happened in my home. The police see what has happened and grab us both and handcuff us. I tell them who I am and that this other is the perpetrator of the attack. He freely admits it and proceeds to tell the police that he just got bored and didn't have anything else to do, so he just picked a house randomly and decided to destroy a life, basically a terrorist who just happened to be in my neighborhood. He only drove a few short blocks and said to himself, "Eeny, meeny, miny, moe," and chose us.

A little time passes as the court date is set, and since I'm the one who found him in my home, then I have become the primary witness against him. My wife has since the occurrence, passed away, partly from the abuse, but the act so broke her heart against humanity that she just no longer cared to fight against life. She had become afraid of every human being, whether male or female, old or young. She just did not trust anyone any longer. Her love for the child in every human was one of the character traits that I most treasured about her and which had been destroyed by the architect of this individual's self-desire. So this criminal in my mind had become the opposite of the character of my wife. I know her, and I also know that she saw every human in need of love and encouragement to better the world in which he or she lived.

The legal case is opened and closed. He freely admitted to the crime and was almost bragging about the act. Now the judge had him, and since the individual had not committed suicide or had the law enforcement agencies do the deed for him, the judge was going to throw the entire book of the law at him, not only because of his nonchalance, "I did it, and I'm fine with that," but also to show any others who may be contemplating similar actions what they could expect. He receives life imprisonment, along with two consecutive ninety-nine-year intervals after life had been added at his soon-to-be home in Colorado, The "Alcatraz of the Rockies, ADX."

Now because of my love for my wife and my Savior, I tell the judge that I will stand in for the perpetrator. I will take the full weight of the verdict on his behalf. The judge knows I am not guilty of this crime in any way. The evidence is sitting about fifteen feet away and is as nonchalant as if he were fishing on a lake at his estate. Now the judge knows that I am not guilty, but someone is going to pay and will. So I will receive no mercy. I get the prison time in full. I am to bear all of the hard labor, the embarrassment, and the ridicule, along with the hate from the guards up to the warden for being such a fool and letting the guilty party off the hook as well as to show anyone else what the punishment for that type of mercy from the world at large is going to get you. Oh, thou fool!

I could keep the short story above going, but I believe you get the point. Jesus chose to suffer the full penalty for my own sin against His Father, whom He loves far more than I love my wife, and we see that it is not a past tense thing. Jesus loves His Father now, just as He did when He came to earth and just as much as Jesus did while on the cross bearing for the first time their separation that my sin caused. That point was made in many of the earlier writings, but when I was born with Adam's sin or seed inside of my nature, I was destined to die the death of a sinner. Scripture states in Genesis 2 that God told the man Adam straight up the following verses, "And The Lord God commanded the man, 'You are free to eat from any tree in the garden; but you must not eat from the tree of the knowledge of good and evil, for when you eat of it you will certainly die.'" Now since we are Adam's offspring, then just like dear old dad, we will also die. That seed, death, is continuously being passed along.

It took a bit, but now I would like to flesh this whole point out for our mutual enlightenment. I would like to say that many Christians say of themselves, "I was the worst individual that God ever saved and gave His life for." Even on the day of my salvation, I was still caught up in my philosophy that Jesus was a man who lived about two thousand years ago and a bunch of other individuals were so in awe of the guy that they perpetrated this Jewish-based religion called Christianity.

But then in February 1977, I asked Jesus into my heart, and He showed up immediately. He, blessed am I, did not believe in my useless philosophy. Even my own salvation proved to me that the Word of the Lord was true even if I did not actually believe it. He saved me, but I sure did not save Him. I could not, even if Jesus were in need. I am not equipped to save God. Now I know that God never sinned because that is what salvation is, coming into a relationship with God.

The entire trinity is God, and He has provided a means to come back to Him as if I personally had never committed an act against Him. Salvation is the fact that Jesus took His holy life and gave it in exchange for my sin-filled life. Since the act was a transaction, He exchanged Himself in place of my relationship to Adam so I could now be just like Him, able to approach Father God as His own DNA or seed.

Now the wisdom involved in those statements above is simple yet more complex than string theory. If I really thought about it, God could have very easily asked every individual that when he or she was approaching death, he or she as the individual would be required to suffer the cross for himself or herself. And that would still be fair, although there would certainly not be as many Christians as there currently seem to be. I mean, really I know that my sin separated me from a loving and truthful relationship with God, so why should I not pay the penalty for my own actions? But if, say, me and some other person died at the same time and I saw what type of wrath God, who is and has always been holy, saw as the just consequence for the individual actions against His character, I then watch that individual suffer exactly as Jesus did. Then I might be inclined to think about whether heaven was such a great place to live out eternity because really I'm not getting nailed to a cross, even if only for myself and eternity.

When I think about sin, I used to ask myself, "Well, why is God so upset with my actions? It isn't as if God is a sinner and therefore hates what He used to be like." He, the living God, has never sinned, distrusted His own thoughts, or was envious or prideful of another. The same loving Father that I know today has always been that way.

When I look back at infancy, if I had an itch from a diaper rash, being dumb as a brick, I could not communicate to anyone that I needed to get that itch scratched. My own hands were most likely balled up into fists, and I was crying my eyes out. If my mom knew what the problem was and tossed some powder onto my hiney, then things calmed down. But that is the human experience: we learn as we grow older in some cases. But God is full and whole. He was never one thing and then became another thing. He never started out as a thought and developed into a consciousness and then a God. He is exactly who He is, The I Am.

But then I am back to the thought: Why does God our Father, His Son, Jesus, and the Holy Spirit hate sin so much? The Lord showed me a while ago when I originally asked Him that, but it is what sin does to the individual. Sin in effect makes us aware that we have done something wrong and that we deserve to be punished for our actions, not knowing what that specific punishment will entail. When I was a child and I had done something wrong, my mom told me that when my father got home, he was going to basically punish me for language used, things stolen, beating up a sibling, lying, and so on.

The list can go on till another book is written. But I was going to pay a penalty for what I had done against what my parents had perceived to be correct character and behavior for someone who supposedly represented them to the world. I also saw that deep in my heart I feared punishment from God and not because He was going to throw me across His lap and tan my behind, but I feared all punishment because of my own actions against Him. Now I only know because now I know Him. Before knowing Him, I just did not want to be caught, so I feared a great, great deal. And so I wanted power over those things that I feared.

What I also found was that because I feared things, then more and more things got added to the list. Desire wants more things to play with and brings me, the individual, further and further away from God, whom I need more than what I crave. Sin is where the world is at today, if thought about. But insane actions are taking place every single day. We need Jesus. We need an answer to our individual sin.

Now if I do not even know God, then all these sin things are due to overpopulation, food shortages, the ozone disappearing, our fellow human beings wanting to kill us for no apparent reason, the weather, the world, and so on. Sin brings fear, but the multifaceted complications emerges from my first sin until my last hurt me and everyone I encountered. Now God in an extreme use of mercy cured that problem by the cross. Jesus suffered the weight of the punishment that I earned on Himself so a relationship with God, His perfect Dad, could begin. And I think that the relationship is the cure for sin.

But that disregard for God's nature had horrible consequences, hence the cross. He, my Lord, went to the cross for everyone, but since He would never force anyone to accept such a wonderful gift, then it has been placed into our own laps to receive or refuse. And now the consequences of my life actions are placed back into my hands. I can deny Christ, but then I must pay for my sin against myself as well as those other individuals that came across my path while being alive and living in daily fear and heart shame, even if I were not aware of it.

This also explains why we as individuals look at our own effects on humanity and have so much mercy over our actions. I could say of myself, "I know I'm bad, but I am certainly not the worst of over seven billion people. Whoever God might be, he'll be more than happy to have me to come and live with Him in His home."

Can I say that when I think about God, Scripture tells me that heaven is His throne and the earth is His footstool (*Isa. 66:1–2*), but God wants to live in our hearts. The moment I gave my life to Jesus, the Holy Spirit came and took up residence within me. This also tells me that God has a lot of nerve because I am being sanctified, yet on my worse day as His own child, He has never abandoned me. The same way that I love my own adult children, they can do almost anything good or bad, but I cannot stop loving them. They are both a part of me, no matter how goofy they may get or good they may be. I, as their father, want to see character and not crazy.

So for me and sin, it begins with life, blood, and our parents, Adam and Eve, in **Genesis 3**, but when the Lord came down in the cool of the day to fellowship with His children, Adam and Eve hid themselves because they now realized that they were naked and could not stand in the Lord's holy presence. But at the same time, God still came. But now in Jesus, since we have the forgiveness of sins, we can now come boldly into our Father's holy presence. So now we can stand before God, naked and unafraid. The purpose of standing in His presence naked and unafraid is because the relationship has been repaired by His own sacrifice on the cross.

It is a nice thing to say, but the reality is that once the debt of our own rebellion against the character of God has been met, out of love going in both directions from the Father through Jesus and then to mankind and once it gets into us, His presence then goes outward to people from people, to bring those same people back to God so once again we can be in His presence in who He in all of reality is. There is nothing that can hinder us. He is a loving, caring Father. I believe that statement deserves an Amen!

A1 : *Numbers 14:10–45.* So much for Choices

The issue that I see is not so much what our individual choices determine, but rather are our choices God's? Just for Christians, but if I looked at Scripture and said to myself, "Look, David, how many times do you see the Sabbath mentioned? It, the Sabbath, is number four on the Ten Commandments and separates the relationship of God and man, to man with man, and with God. But so what? I'm a part of the New Testament people, and the law does not bind me to this world. I have been set free in Jesus Christ!"

The conclusion I would draw from my own statement is, "I have been set free in Jesus Christ!" So if free and in Him, then for what specifically? "In Him" also brings to my mind *John 14:20.* "On that day you will realize that I Am in My Father, and you are in Me, and I Am in you."

A short comment on the Sabbath, but if I honored the Sabbath by setting aside one day out of seven to be completely at God's disposal for anything that He desires, then that Sabbath day would not only give me rest and restoration but would also keep me God aware because I've entered into Him and He is genuinely life. Can I also say that if I set aside twenty-four hours to spend with the Lord, then after a few shots at that, I would find us growing closer. And because of that closeness, then that twenty-four would soon evolve into forty-eight and then more and more.

It begins with that first step of love and obedience. The Sabbath is important because the relationship is developed and advanced; He becomes through experience more God, and I become more Christ-like because I model that which I perceive. Malachi 3–4 speaks to this thought, but **Malachi 3:6–7 (NIV)** states, "I The Lord do not change. So, you, the descendants of Jacob, are not destroyed. Ever since the time of your ancestors you have turned away from my decrees and have not kept them. <u>Return to Me, and I will return to you</u>."

I see this in myself primarily, but there is so much that God wants us to know about Himself and, on top of that, to animate a life that measures up to Jesus. If I say to myself that there is just no way that I can measure up to Jesus, that He is God and that I am only a man, then I miss the point of having become a child of the only living God. Per Scripture I see that Jesus was a man and that when John the Baptist baptized Jesus, the Holy Spirit settled on Him and did not depart. I can also see from Scripture that everything Jesus did was in God, His Father's will.

Isaiah 11:3 (NIV) reads, "And He/Jesus will delight in the fear of The Lord." Jesus did what any man can do, having first given oneself to God so that every aspect of Him can be shown to humanity, the angelic host, and all of heaven and earth. God is the three shown to those that basically have a hard time getting that. That God is fully whole and complete and does not need nor want to change. He is sound and dependable in who He is.

I am not starting a cult. Jesus is and was God and became a man those two thousand years ago. Part of His purpose though was to show those of the new covenant how the relationship with God and without religion in truth works. God's holiness, His character, gets magnifies in us as the intimacy in the relationship also expands. The better I know Him, the more glorious my entire being slowly but surely comprehends Him (*1 Cor. 2:10–12*).

In these statements, I am going to try to apply them only to myself, without the continuous pointing out to you, the reader, where you may be falling short of God the Father's example, His Son, Jesus. I know me. You, I am sorry to say, I do not really know, so I cannot therefore tell you how you should walk out your own life experience with God. But if I am a child of God who was born again by the Spirit and more so having His own Spirit placed within me, then I asked myself, "Why? Why did Jesus, the Son of God, suffer for me? Was it just to get me into heaven where we could hang out together, that somehow God, the eternal living God, found heaven to be boring without me?"

That, for me, is more impossible to believe than anything—unicorns, dragons, aliens from other worlds, time travel, unique dimensions, multiple earths, and so on. I find it distinctive that God is one, or singular, and yet I know Him to be three individuals: God the Father whom I love and know, Jesus, His Son whom I love and know, and the Holy Spirit whom I also love and know. But then how can they be one? For me, since I ask the Holy Spirit all these questions, is that they are one in agreement, one in heart, one in unity of purpose. They are one in love.

For me, I am not talking about anyone else, but for me, I love God the Father, but when I think about my own salvation, then I could never in truth have known the Father without first having made Jesus my Lord through an invitation that my own mouth spoke when asking Jesus to be my Savior, and on top of that, I never, ever would have asked Jesus to be my God if the Holy Spirit had not been drawing me closer to Him, the living God.

God's harmony of purpose invites everyone to get the opportunity to know Him, to understand Him, to be in a unique relationship as a father is to his child, as is a man to his wife, as friends who say about each other, "Oh yeah, David is not only my friend, but he is my best friend, closer than my own brother." That is how Jesus and His and our Father and the Holy Spirit operate. God wants all of us to know Him for whom He really is and not to be terrified of coming close to Him because He Himself fixed that by going to the cross and taking my willing separation and its consequences onto Himself. God does not lessen Himself to make Himself available to mankind. What salvation is to me is that God made me able to approach Him in all of His power, truth, righteousness, holiness, and love, just so we could all know Him intimately.

He also provided the means for me to clear the junk out of my soul, body, and spirit so I would not be in continuous pain, knowing that He and I are multiple universes different in our physical beings. God is clearing the junk/sin (present tense) with my agreement to unite with Him in His work of love. Yes, I know that God is a Spirit. Totally off the subject, many years ago, after having gone to bed and falling asleep, I opened my eyes in my sleep.

I was in the middle of a wrestling match with a demon. It was bigger and stronger than I was, but we were grappling with each other. It was a titanic physical struggle. Finally I got that demon in a headlock and would not let it go for nothin'. Then while holding onto it, I thought, *Hey, get the demon to tell me its name, and then I can send it to depths God created for it.*

So I started to demand the demon's name from it. The demon then picked me up with my arms still wrapped tightly around its head and threw me like a five-pound bag of potatoes straight back into my sleeping body, and I hit my body so hard that I was almost flung out of our queen-sized bed. I was no longer lying down but near to standing up. Luckily my wife was still up and watching TV in the living room.

Now the point of all that is to say that I was not physically there, wherever there was, but my spirit was there. I also believe and have tested that demons or angels are not flesh and blood, like your average

Joe. So when someone states that God is a spirit, I do not see someone who is invisible and all Casper the Friendly Ghost like, but rather someone who is physically real. He is exactly who He is, but He is real, tangible, and physical. If I had the opportunity, I would jump onto His lap and hug Him around the neck with all my might, and I'm sixty-three years old.

Have I done that? No, but I also have that desire. That is also a much larger truth about what Jesus gave us. God is our Father. He wants the very best for us. I would love it if God just gave me everything I ever wanted, but what I've found is that as my Father, He wants me to grow up and become a man and not just any man like Paul, Peter, Moses, or Abraham, but rather Jesus, who is the perfect man.

You have to be God to expect that from the human being, but He has made provision for that to be accomplished. Only God would think of the impossible and make it a reality. It is Him and I—or you and Him—working together. We can both say. Whew, that's an awful lot to think about, but I have more in store.

I would like to also say that we all have individuals who are Christians in our lives who teach us about God and what we are supposed to be doing about His kingdom here on Planet Earth. Those pastors, teachers, preachers, deacons, bishops, reverends, priests, popes, apostles, parents, grandparents, and siblings, all of them are inputting Him into you, and in truth I pray.

But I have been a Christian for at least forty-one years, and just like myself, I have made errors. I am not saying you need to get out of your church or to stop being a part of the family of God. But to truly grow as His child, you need Him, God, the Holy Spirit, for that. Maturity comes through Him and Him alone, but because He is God and He is invested in the lives of His children, then we all should have things to share with each other for our betterment.

Somehow we all take God out of His exalted sovereign position as God and then try to run things on our own. For myself I see that Jesus is asking that my character change to God's character, and that is a lot of work for any individual and cannot be accomplished at all without first being saved. God never stops being fully Himself, so the consequence of that is we, the people of God, need to be full of Him.

There have been many churches that I have been a part of that have shown that to be true, and please, please do not think that I am gossiping about any family of God that I have been a part of. I am speaking of God's own, who have come to Him with a very willing heart, but when we endeavor to do good, especially in the Lord's name, then it should be what He wants achieved.

There was a church that I was a member of, but every couple of months, we had our business meeting. We would start with prayer and do a head count since individuals were rushing to the church after getting their children dinner or getting off work and so forth. Then we would discuss what our different groups had coming up for the year and at later meetings how those events were coming along. Sometimes we had deep discussions concerning the Lord or the miraculous on the event.

This church family loved the Lord and wanted to please Him. For me though, that initial prayer of Lord ("Your will be done") could have just continued. Our plans were for His will, but at the same time, we only had an hour or so before Bible study. We mostly spoke about where the monies were coming from, if we collected enough money for the men's retreat, and if not, if Pastor were going to get some donors. We were a poor church. Our plans were not bad, but we (I) did not stop and ask, "Lord, what is your plan this summer, this Easter, this Thanksgiving, our anniversary? What do you want instead of what do I think You want?"

That is being presumptuous with the living God, as if He could not get it right without me telling Him what He needs to do. I think that is enough of that. It feels like gossip, and I can spend about ten more chapters on the many things I have done wrong.

But if we, the church/body of Jesus, want it to be right, then all of us need to surrender ourselves to His will, out of love and respect for His choices. For me, since I do not like being told what I need to do, then I should be the first to respond and ask our Lord exactly that, "What do You want me to do, Lord?" His stuff is only for everyone's good.

B1 : The End is Here.

Ecclesiastes 12:13 reads, *"Now all has been heard; here is the conclusion of the matter."*

God the Father, God the Son, Jesus, our anointed One, and God the Holy Spirit. Amen.

Printed in the United States
By Bookmasters